ETERNAL

ALSO BY KRISTI COOK

Haven

Mirage

KRISTI COOK

Simon Pulse

NEW YORK LONDON TORONTO SYDNEY NEW DELHI

This book is a work of fiction. Any references to historical events, real people, or real places are used fictitiously. Other names, characters, places, and events are products of the author's imagination, and any resemblance to actual events or places or persons, living or dead, is entirely coincidental.

SIMON PULSE
An imprint of Simon & Schuster Children's Publishing Division
1230 Avenue of the Americas, New York, NY 10020
First Simon Pulse hardcover edition September 2013

Jacket design by Angela Goddard

For information about special discounts for bulk purchases, please contact
Simon & Schuster Special Sales at 1-866-506-1949
or business@simonandschuster.com.
The Simon & Schuster Speakers Bureau can bring authors to your live event.
For more information or to book an event contact the
Simon & Schuster Speakers Bureau at 1-866-248-3049 or
visit our website at www.simonspeakers.com.
Interior design by Mike Rosamilia and Regina Flath
The text of this book was set in Berling LT Std.
Manufactured in the United States of America
2 4 6 8 10 9 7 5 3 1
Library of Congress Cataloging-in-Publication Data
Cook, Kristi.
Eternal / Kristi Cook. — First Simon Pulse hardcover edition.
p. cm.
Sequel to: Mirage.
Summary: Back at Winterhaven, seventeen-year-old Violet must find a way
to save her vampire boyfriend, Aidan; balance the demands of her psychic visions;
and prepare for an upcoming vampire war.
[1. Psychic ability—Fiction. 2. Vampires—Fiction. 3. Love—Fiction. 4. Boarding
schools—Fiction. 5. Schools—Fiction. 6. Orphans—Fiction.] I. Title.
PZ7.C76984Et 2013 [Fic]—dc23 2013011430
ISBN 978-1-4424-8532-7
ISBN 978-1-4424-8533-4 (eBook)

For Dan,

my own eternal love . . .

1 ~ Feel the Burn

Aidan ~ Paris, France

Flames licked at the restraints, crackling noisily as the smell of singed flesh filled the small space. *My* flesh. Burning, then healing—then burning again. At intervals, spikes pierced my sides, the jagged barbs tearing through skin and muscle and then retracting until the wounds healed over.

The searing pain was endless, relentless. I had no idea how long I'd been there in the torch-lit chamber beneath the Tribunal's headquarters. Hours? Days? Weeks?

I swallowed hard, my elongated canines scraping my lower lip, drawing blood. *Blood.* I needed to feed. Denied my elixir, the thirst was driving me mad. I could smell it, somewhere up above, pulsing through veins and warming the skin of the living. The metallic tang made my mouth water, made me tremble with need. I closed my eyes, fighting the bloodlust, denying it.

When I opened my eyes again, she was there, standing before me.

Violet.

The orange flames flickered across her face, throwing shadows across her cheekbones. Her mouth curved into a smile as she reached a hand out to me, beckoning me.

My heart thudded against my ribs as my hungry gaze swept over her, devouring her. I tried to call out her name, to beg her forgiveness.

I'm sorry, Vi. So very sorry.

She shook her head, her brows drawn over the emerald eyes that had haunted my days and nights in this miserable, agony-filled existence that was my life since I left her.

"Come back to me," she begged, her voice a ragged whisper. "Please, Aidan. I need you."

I tried to reach for her, raging against the restraints that dug into my wrists, manacling me. A sob tore from my parched throat as I struggled ineffectually, the metal bruising and biting my skin, breaking my bones.

And then she began to fade away, her form dissolving like wisps of smoke that looped and curled toward the ceiling before fading into nothingness.

No.

Pure, undiluted rage filled me. Roaring like an animal, I redoubled my efforts, fighting against my restraints. It didn't take long before I began to weaken, no match for the chains that bound me.

At last spent, I sank to my knees. The flames lapped at my thighs now, reaching toward my hips. My bare chest was slick with sweat, with blood mixed with tears. I didn't even flinch when the spikes pierced my shoulders, tearing through muscle and bone.

My chin dropped toward my chest, my head bowed in defeat. I'd lost her. Lost *us*. Any humanity left inside this monstrous body was gone, ripped away like a useless limb.

I did not deserve her. I did not deserve to live. And yet I *would* live, trapped in this nightmare of pain and despair for an eternity.

Violet was nothing but a dream—the most beautiful dream imaginable—and I was just a broken, burning monster.

Violet ~ New York, New York

"It's been ten days, Cece!" I paced back and forth, wearing a path in the rug at the foot of my bed. The hand that held my cell against my ear shook, the plastic case digging into my palm as I tried to tamp down the panic that crept into my voice. "C'mon. You've got to help me out here."

Cece sighed. "I swear I'm trying. I've tried to project every single morning. I don't know what else I can do, Violet. There's got to be some sort of shield around Mrs. Girard or something—around all of them." I could hear the frustration in her voice. "You tried calling Winterhaven, right? Someone there has to have a cell number for her."

I shook my head. "No one at Winterhaven will tell me anything. I think she must be in Paris—Aidan says that's where the Tribunal meets. They must have taken him there." *To punish him. Torture him.* I inhaled sharply, trying to banish the horrible images from my mind.

"Well, they must have some sort of system to keep everything under wraps. I'm sorry, Violet. I'll try again later, but don't get your hopes up."

I let out my breath in a rush. "It's not your fault. It's just . . . I don't know what else to do."

"Well, what about Dr. Byrne?"

I shook my head. "What about him?"

"She's his boss. Doesn't he have any idea how to get in touch with her?"

"No, and it gets worse. He says she's left word that she's taken a temporary leave of absence. Dr. Ackerman is acting headmistress until she gets back."

"What? That's crazy. What the heck is going on?"

"I have no idea. I'm losing my mind here, Cee. This past week has been a total disaster."

That was putting it mildly. Understandably, it had taken a good three days to calm Whitney down. To say that she was completely freaked out would be the understatement of the century. I mean, c'mon—a vampire had attacked her, a vampire who happened to be her best friend's boyfriend. It doesn't get much more terrifying than that. Luckily, she'd managed to pull herself together enough to go to her audition at Juilliard.

Still, it had been a tense few days. After Aidan had left, intent on turning himself over to the Tribunal, I'd had all these grand plans to clear him by figuring out who'd tampered with his work. But I hadn't been able to focus on Aidan's situation, not until I'd put Whitney in a cab bound for Newark Airport.

But things weren't any better after she'd left. I hadn't been able to get in touch with Mrs. Girard—couldn't locate her, not even with Cece's help. And Trevors, the only one besides Mrs. Girard who might know where Aidan was, wasn't returning my calls. I'd gone to Aidan's town house several times and banged on the door till my knuckles bled. No response. If Trevors was there, he wasn't answering.

I was at a complete and total loss, no closer to solving the mystery of what had turned Aidan into the murderous "Vampire Stalker" than I'd been a week ago.

"You still there?" Cece asked. I could hear laughter in the background. Someone was singing—very loudly and off-key.

I let out a sigh. "Yeah, I'm here. Sorry. I got lost in my thoughts. But hey, it sounds like there's some family fun going on over there."

"Those are my cousins. I told you they were crazy. I swear, the minute I get on the phone, they start acting up. Hey, watch it!" she called out. "You guys are going to knock over the tree!"

I couldn't help but smile, imagining Cece there in New Orleans, surrounded by her extended family, everything all festive and cheery. Glancing around Patsy's apartment, I took in my lame excuse for a Christmas tree sitting in the middle of the dining room table—a little potted fir, about two feet high and topped with a red velvet bow. That was it, the only sign that a major holiday had come and gone. Which was fine by me, as I certainly hadn't felt like celebrating. Not this year. Not alone.

My phone beeped, and I glanced down at the screen. *Matthew.*

"Hey, my *Megvéd's* beeping in," I told Cece. "I better go see what he wants." He was taking his job as my "protector" very seriously. Not a day had passed that he hadn't either come by or called to check in. Which might be nice if it weren't so freaking weird.

"Ooh, Matthew," Cece said in the singsong voice she reserved for Dr. Byrne. "Yeah, you better go. Give him my love."

I rolled my eyes. "Shut *up*."

"Sorry. I couldn't help myself." Cece was laughing now. "Call me tomorrow, though, 'kay? I'll try to project to Mrs. G. again in the morning."

"Okay, thanks." I hit end, then connected the call with Matthew. "Hey, what's up?"

"Is Patsy back yet?" he asked without preamble. This had become typical Matthew over the past week. No "Hello, how are you" or anything mundane like that—he just cut right to the chase.

"No. I think she's flying in tomorrow night." Just as I'd seen in my vision, she'd gotten stung by a bee on a golf course the day before her scheduled flight home from Turks and Caicos. Thanks to my prodding, she'd been prepared with EpiPens. Still, her reaction had been bad—*really* bad. They'd kept her in the hospital for two nights, and she hadn't been feeling well enough to fly. I didn't care—didn't even mind that she'd left me to spend Christmas alone. She was alive, and that was all that mattered. My vision had saved her.

"I'm coming over. I mean, if that's okay," Matthew added, his voice softening.

I shrugged, tapping my fingers against my thigh. "Sure."

"Have you had dinner?"

"No." I wasn't hungry. I hadn't been hungry in days.

"Okay. I'll pick something up on my way over." I could hear him jangling his keys. "How 'bout Thai?"

"Sounds good."

"Thai it is, then. See you in a few."

I tossed down my phone and flopped onto my bed with a sigh. God, this was crazy. Aidan was off somewhere being tortured, and all I could do was sit around eating Thai food with one of my teachers. Okay, technically he wasn't *my* teacher—I didn't take any science classes—but he was Sophie's, and that was weird enough.

Closing my eyes, I took a deep, calming breath—in through

my nose, out through my mouth—but it didn't help. This was *wrong.* I hated this feeling of complete and utter helplessness. More than anything, I wanted to take the credit card Patsy had given me for emergencies, hop a cab to JFK, and catch the first flight to Paris. I needed to find Aidan. I missed him so badly, I could barely stand it. I physically felt his absence, like a big, fat hole in my heart that grew larger with each passing second.

Reaching a hand to my temple, I focused everything I had on him, conjuring an image in my mind's eye.

Come back to me, I called out telepathically. *Please, Aidan. I need you.*

I knew he couldn't hear me, not with thousands of miles and an ocean between us. Still, I swear I felt the faintest flicker of a buzz in my head. A rush of hope made my heart race, my breath come faster. Rising, I hurried to the window that looked out on Park Avenue and laid one palm flat against the cool glass.

Aidan? I tried again. *Can you hear me?*

Nothing. I shook my head, confused. I could have sworn I felt . . . something. I took another deep breath, renewing my focus. My eyes still closed, I rolled my shoulders, trying to relax.

And then the traffic noise receded—just like that. The glass seemed to warm beneath my palm. Inexplicably, there was heat warming my ankles, lapping at my calves. The heat intensified, making my legs feel as if . . . as if they were on fire. And then a sharp, tearing pain stabbed at my side, making my breath catch as I doubled over in agony.

My eyes flew open, my focus gone. I blinked several times as I straightened, trying to get my bearings. Below, a siren blared. I watched as an ambulance came barreling down the street, its lights flashing as cars scattered around it. Chilled, I pulled my hand away from the window, cradling it against my body.

Had I imagined those sensations—the heat, the sharp pain? I must have, I reasoned. Unless . . . unless there was a vampire close by and I'd somehow breached its mind. I shook my head. Not likely. It didn't work like that—at least, not unless the vampire was in the apartment next door. Nope. I'd imagined it. I was losing my mind. It was the only reasonable explanation.

Of course, since when were "reasonable explanations" a part of my life?

I glanced over at the clock by my bed, wondering how much time I had till Matthew showed up. Probably not much, I decided, thinking I should set out some plates and silverware. On my way out, I paused by my dresser, my gaze drawn to the clear plastic container tucked up against the framed picture of Aidan and me at the Halloween Fair dance, both of us decked out in attire circa 1905.

I popped open the case and reached inside for the silver circlet pin that had once held the fragrant orange blossoms Aidan had given me on that night. I inhaled deeply, almost sure I could smell a hint of the sweet citrus scent left behind. The overhead light glinted off the crystals as I ran a finger over them, the faceted stones forming a perfect, unbroken circle.

I flipped it over, examining the back side. It was perfect, as unblemished as the day I received it, the smooth, shiny surface reflecting the light. Silver would have tarnished by now, I realized with a start. Which meant it was probably white gold—maybe even platinum. Curious now, I tipped it this way and that, taking a closer look.

And then I noticed something that I hadn't before—words, etched into the metal beneath the clasp. My fingers shaking, I clumsily unhooked it, swinging away the metal pin. My heart began to race as I read the engraving: *Eternal love.*

Tears flooded my eyes, blurring my vision. One spilled over, tracing a path down my cheek. As I wiped it away, I tried to remember what he'd said to me on that crisp, cool October night as he'd pinned the circlet to my dress—something about how flowers had meaning back in his day, that orange blossoms meant eternal love. He'd never given them to anyone before he'd given them to me.

And now? He never would again. I had to choke back the sob that threatened to topple my sanity.

2 ~ The Chicken or the Egg?

I shoved away my half-eaten plate of pad thai with a scowl. "I'm really not hungry."

Matthew paused, a forkful of noodles halfway to his mouth. "Come on, Vi, you've got to eat."

"Please don't call me that." I swallowed hard, my throat suddenly tight. Aidan called me "Vi"—no one else did. No one else *could*. "I . . . it's just Violet, okay?"

He raised one brow, eyeing me sharply. "Okay. Sorry about that."

"No, I'm sorry." I exhaled sharply. "This really sucks, you know? And it's all my fault."

With a sigh, he pushed aside his own plate. "What's all your fault?"

"Everything." I swept one hand in a wide arc. "Aidan, off at the Tribunal getting punished. Us, sitting here eating and trying to act like nothing's wrong."

He folded his arms across his chest. Involuntarily, my gaze was drawn to the tattoo on his right biceps—his *Megvéd* mark, the tip of the inked dagger exposed beneath the edge of his T-shirt's sleeve.

"Look," he said, his voice settling into lecture mode, "you've got to come to grips with the fact that Aidan was out there hurting people. Five victims with puncture wounds and severe blood loss. They're lucky they're alive. All of them." He shook his head, his eyes narrowing a fraction. "He *killed* that woman in the woods near school, Violet—just left her there to bleed out. Don't you understand that?"

I swallowed back bile. The thought of Aidan, a cold-blooded murderer—it didn't compute. I mean, okay, I knew he was a vampire, and I knew he'd killed before. But those were murderers and rapists and really bad guys who'd hurt people that he'd loved, not random junkies who happened to find themselves in the wrong place at the wrong time.

I took a deep, calming breath before I spoke. "He didn't know what he was doing, Matthew. You saw him—you saw how totally out of it he was. It was that stupid serum. Someone messed with it. I should have known that the vision in the lab meant something. That it was trying to tell me something important."

He actually rolled his eyes. "How could you possibly have known that?"

I shrugged. "Because all my visions have meaning. None of them are just everyday, throwaway stuff."

"So that's what you're blaming yourself for? Not realizing what the vision meant? C'mon, Violet. It's not like the visions come with a voice-over. Cut yourself some slack, why don't you?"

"Anyway, there's more," I continued, wanting to get it all off my chest. "The other vision, the one with Whitney." I swallowed hard. "*I* sent her out of the apartment. It was *my* fault she was in the park."

"Okay, yeah," he said with a nod. "She was in the park because you sent her out of the apartment. I'll give you that. But if you'd somehow convinced her to stay *in* the apartment, he would have just attacked her here instead. And worse, neither of us would have been around to stop it, right?"

I just nodded.

"The only way you could have possibly thwarted it would have been to stop Aidan beforehand and somehow change *his* course. He was on his way here when whatever it was kicked in and set him off into attack mode. Where Whitney happened to be when he caught up with her—this apartment, the park, or somewhere else entirely—was irrelevant."

I shook my head, confused. "I don't get it."

He leaned toward me, his elbows resting on the table now. "Think of it this way: Remember that vision you told me about where your grandmother's housekeeper fell and broke her hip?"

"Lupe," I offered.

"Right, Lupe. You stopped her, because she was the one whose intent you interrupted. But let's say you had seen someone *with* her in that vision—a friend, or something. Convincing the friend not to be there when Lupe slipped and fell wouldn't have necessarily altered the outcome."

"So, following your logic, if I had somehow convinced my dad *not* to take that assignment in Afghanistan, the kidnappers would have come for him anyway? Is that what you're saying? Because that doesn't even make sense."

"No, that's not what I'm saying." He raked a hand through his hair, leaving it sticking up in all directions. "You're not taking intent into account. In that case, their intent wasn't to kidnap and murder your father, specifically. They meant to capture an American journalist, who just happened to be your father. I can only assume that if you had convinced him to stay, it would have been some other journalist who suffered his fate instead."

I threw my hands up in frustration. "Ugh. I can't wrap my head around this. It's like the whole chicken-or-the-egg argument, only worse."

"Well, that's what you've got me for. It's an honor to serve you," he said with a grin, obviously trying to be funny.

"Yeah, lucky me." Instantly, I regretted my words, my cheeks flushing hotly. "I'm sorry, Matthew. I don't mean to sound like an ungrateful brat. Seriously. I'm just so freaked out right now. I'm worried about Aidan, and I miss him like crazy." I stood so abruptly that I nearly knocked over my chair. I steadied it, gripping the back so hard that my knuckles turned white.

"I know it doesn't make sense," I continued. "Not with me being a *Sâbbat* and all. But I didn't ask for this. I'm not interested in playing Buffy and ridding the world of vampires. And besides, if you think this is some kind of . . . of *honor*," I sputtered, nearly choking on the word, "then I'm never going to be able to make you understand."

As calm as always, Matthew stood, holding a hand out to me. "Come here, Violet."

I took a deep breath, spent now. I took his hand, allowing him to pull me into an embrace. I choked back a sob, pressing my face against the soft fabric of his shirt. Beneath my cheek, I could feel his heart thumping against his ribs as my tears spilled over.

"Shh," he said, patting me on the back. "Go on and cry."

"I hate this," I blubbered, wiping my nose with the back of one hand. "I really, really hate it."

"I know you do."

I tried to force back the tears, but it took a good two or three minutes before I managed to pull myself together. It felt comfortable there in his arms, I realized. Safe. Which was pretty embarrassing, actually.

"Sorry about that," I mumbled, my voice muffled against his chest. I took a step back, my cheeks flaming.

"You okay?" he asked, peering down at me with drawn brows.

I nodded, reaching for a tissue. I blew my nose, then dabbed at my damp, swollen eyes. "Yeah, I'm fine. Tired, that's all." On shaky legs, I made my way to the sofa and sat down.

He followed me, settling onto the far side of the sofa. A nice, safe distance away.

Warily, I watched him.

He looked slightly discomposed, his eyes troubled. "For the record, this isn't all that much fun for me, either. I never understood it—the pressure I felt to excel at school, to graduate early, to do a PhD in record time. Now I know why, of course. I needed to be in the right place at the right time in order to find you—just a two-year window at Winterhaven—but I didn't know that at the time."

I shook my head in amazement. "How did you do it?"

"I rode myself ragged. I doubled up on courses and gave up any semblance of a social life in order to push myself as hard as possible academically. Do you have any idea what it's like to go off to college at sixteen? I didn't have my driver's license. I'd never even been on a date. Trust me, it sucked."

With a start, I realized that he was giving up his social life now, too. After all, he'd spent pretty much every spare moment of the break with *me*. "Sorry about that," I muttered.

He tipped up my chin so that my gaze met his steady brown one. "Don't be sorry, Violet. This is my purpose. I've made peace with it."

"How can you accept it like that?"

He shrugged. "Because it is what it is. I've known about the *Megvédio* since I was twelve. Say what you want, but I'm proud of my heritage. My father made sure I realized what a privilege it would be to find my *Sâbbat*, how rare and special. I never even imagined . . ." He swallowed hard, his Adam's apple bobbing in his throat.

"Never imagined what?" I prodded, an uncomfortable knot in the pit of my stomach.

Again, his gaze met mine, steady and intense. "It *is* special," he said softly. "I would do *anything* for you."

"Oh, man. You realize how weird this is, right? I mean, you shouldn't be saying this stuff. If people were to hear . . ." I bit my lower lip. "Do you have any idea how skeevy it sounds?"

"Just know that it's not like *that,* okay?" he said, his cheeks reddening. "It's more . . . I don't know"—he shook his head—"brotherly or something. I want to protect you; that's all. I *have* to protect you. Can you understand that?"

"Not really," I said with a grimace, even though deep down I felt it too—the bond. I'd never admit it, not in a million years. Not to him, not to anyone. My feelings for Matthew were . . . complicated. But somehow it felt right when he was by my side. I felt complete. At least, as complete as possible without Aidan in my life.

"I know it's crazy, this whole *Sâbbat-Megvéd* thing. I'm not saying it isn't. I mean, you're just a kid."

"I am *not* a kid," I argued. "I'm almost eighteen."

The corners of his mouth lifted with the hint of a smile. "You can't have it both ways. Either it's skeevy because you're a kid, or you're not a kid and therefore it's not all that skeevy. Choose one."

I decided to change the subject. "My birthday's in March, by the way. The twenty-seventh. Are you going to take me to get my tattoo? It seems like you should get the honors, right?"

"What tattoo?"

"You know, my 'mark.' A stake, on the inside of my right wrist," I explained, describing it just as I'd seen it in my mind. "With a butterfly resting on it."

"Why a butterfly?"

I let out my breath in a huff. "I have *no* idea. Maybe because my transformation will be complete?" It popped into my head, just like that. "I'm having to figure this out as I go along, you know. You're lucky you had your dad to explain it all to you. I have *one* page from some ancient book, and that's it."

A shadow flickered across his face. "What book? You never mentioned a book to me."

I hadn't, I realized. "Hold on and I'll go get it."

3 ~ Phantom Pains

I hurried to my room, digging out the book from where I'd stashed it in the dark recesses of my closet, away from prying eyes. A minute later, I was back in the living room, trying not to sneeze as I flipped through the dusty pages until I found the folded page with Luc's translation.

I unfolded it and handed it to Matthew. "There isn't much, really. You probably know it all already."

I chewed on my thumbnail while he read.

"Yeah, not much new here," he said at last, handing the page back to me.

"What about this?" I tapped my finger against a line that made me particularly uncomfortable.

If she fails in her quest and her blood runs through
a vampire's veins, the Megvéd*'s life is extinguished.*

"What do you make of that?" I asked, my breath catching. "It doesn't mean what I think it means, does it?"

"Yeah, I'm pretty sure it does." He rubbed his jaw with the palm of one hand. "Basically, if a vampire gets you instead of the other way around, then it's lights-out for me."

"B-but," I stammered, "does that mean the vampire has to kill me? Or just drink my blood?"

"Does it matter? Oh, wait. Right," he said sarcastically, his features hardening. "Your boyfriend's a vampire, which puts a whole new spin on it, doesn't it?"

My mouth was suddenly dry. "Because, uh, well . . . he kind of bit me just before break, remember?" I reached a hand up to my neck, rubbing the pads of my fingers across the spot where Aidan's teeth had pierced the fragile flesh. "It wasn't a big deal. I swear. Just, you know . . . a nip. And then he healed it right away." *Please, please don't say you're going to die because of it.*

Matthew's eyes widened. "Christ, I'd forgotten about that. He broke the skin?"

"Yeah, but I'm pretty sure he didn't drink my blood. It was more like a scratch, that's all." A scratch—okay, maybe a small puncture wound—and then his saliva doing that thing it did. I squirmed in my seat, remembering. Nope, I wasn't going to mention *that*.

"Well, your blood doesn't run through his veins, right? So I guess I'm safe. For now, at least," he added.

"For always," I said, my voice thick as a wave of hopelessness washed over me. "He's gone, remember? He's not coming back."

A sharp, fiery pain shot through my shoulders—both of them at once. With a cry, I pitched forward, doubling over in agony.

In an instant, Matthew was by my side, one hand on my back. "What happened?"

"I—I don't know," I sputtered, trying to catch my breath. "It's my shoulders." Hot, searing pain continued to radiate down toward my elbows.

"What can I do? Do you need ice or something?"

"No, I don't think so." I forced myself to sit up straight and unzip my hoodie, exposing the tank top I wore beneath. I examined one shoulder, then the other, not quite sure what I was looking for. Considering the magnitude of pain I was experiencing, I half expected to find torn, ragged flesh, broken bones. Instead, everything looked perfectly normal, my skin unblemished.

I shook my head as the pain receded, disappearing as quickly as it had appeared. "It's gone now."

"Something to do with that old fencing injury?"

"No. This was *both* shoulders. And the pain was totally different—like I was being stabbed or something. Like my skin was tearing."

"That's odd. They look fine." He was examining me now, his brow knitted with concern. "Maybe you should have it checked out."

"Maybe I'm losing my mind," I countered.

"What about Sophie? Can you call her, ask her to come over and check it out?"

I nodded. "That's a good idea. She just got back from Saint Bart's last night."

"Perfect," he said, pulling out his phone and glancing at the time. "I'm supposed to be somewhere in a little bit anyway."

"Let me text her and see what she says." Maybe I'd ask her to sleep over. I hurried to my room and grabbed my phone, quickly typing out the message and hitting send. She answered before I'd even made my way back to the living room.

"She's on her way," I called out.

"Great. I'll stay till she gets here, and then I've got to run."

"You really don't have to stick around," I said, wanting to

avoid the awkwardness of a Sophie/Dr. Byrne meet-and-greet. "Seriously, she'll be here in half an hour. I think I can survive on my own till then."

He just glared at me, unmoved.

I couldn't help but roll my eyes. "Wow, you really take this whole 'protector' thing seriously, don't you?"

His phone began to buzz, the name "Charlie" emblazoned across the screen. "Sorry," he said, rising and moving toward the window. "I've got to take this."

"No problem," I said with a shrug. Hurrying over to the dining table, I busied myself with the remains of our dinner, closing up the containers of food and moving everything into the kitchen.

He kept his voice low, but I couldn't help overhearing little bits and pieces of his conversation. "I know . . . didn't forget . . . I told you, it's complicated. Just give me a half hour, okay?"

"Sorry about that," he said at last, looking a little discomposed as he followed me into the kitchen.

"Everything okay with him?"

"With who?"

"Your friend," I clarified. "Charlie. Sorry. I saw the name on the screen."

"Oh, right." He shoved his phone back into his pocket. "Yeah, she's fine."

She's fine?

"Her apartment's around the corner," he continued. "I can wait for Sophie. I want to see what she has to say about your shoulders."

"Suit yourself," I muttered, my cheeks flushing hotly as I fought back unwelcome stirrings of jealousy. Who was this Charlie, and what did she mean to my *Megvéd*?

And more to the point, why did I care?

"Okay, that was kind of weird, right?" Sophie said as soon as the front door closed behind Matthew.

"Welcome to my world." I collapsed onto the sofa, frustrated. Matthew had made Sophie check my shoulders the minute she'd walked through the door, but she hadn't found anything that would explain the pain I'd experienced. Apparently, the joints were free of inflammation, the muscles and tendons perfectly normally.

Which meant it was all in my head. I really *was* losing my mind. "Thanks for coming over," I said, scooting over to make room for her beside me.

She kicked off her shoes and sat, folding her legs beneath her. "Hey, no problem. Trust me, I've had just about enough of my parents."

"How was Saint Bart's?"

"Nice. The weather was great. Anyway, where's Aidan? I thought you two were supposed to stick together over break?"

I took a deep breath, bracing myself. I hadn't called her to tell her what had happened. I couldn't. After all, I knew that she genuinely liked Aidan. They *all* did, my friends, but Sophie most of all.

And, okay, there was more—the more people I told, the more real it seemed. Besides, I had hoped to have some answers before I told them that Aidan was the Vampire Stalker. Instead I had nothing.

"What's going on, Violet?" Sophie asked, her brow knitted. "You just went ten shades of pale. Is Aidan okay?"

I shook my head, my windpipe constricting painfully. "I don't know. He's at the Tribunal right now. For all I know, they might have destroyed him." But they hadn't—couldn't have. I would have felt it. I was sure of that.

Sophie's eyes went wide, the color visibly draining from her face. "Destroyed him? What? Why?"

I swallowed hard. "Tyler was right. Aidan is . . . he was the Stalker."

"No way." Sophie shook her head. "Not Aidan."

"He had no idea what he was doing, Soph. It was the serum

he was working on, doing something awful to him. He was in a trance, completely disassociated. It was Aidan, but it wasn't."

She covered her mouth with the palm of one hand. When she let it fall, I saw that her fingers were trembling. "How do you know? I mean, are you sure?"

"I had a vision last fall. I thought it was a dream, since I wasn't able to replay it. But on the last day of school, it happened just like I saw it. He went after my friend Whitney in Central Park. Matthew and I got there just in time. I was able to stop him, but"—I shook my head—"but yeah, I'm sure. He left that night to turn himself in to the Tribunal. He's not coming back," I choked out, tears welling in my eyes. "Not in this lifetime."

Sophie scooted closer, wrapping an arm around my shoulders. "And you didn't call me? You've been here all by yourself?"

I wiped my eyes with the back of one hand. "Matthew's been around. A lot," I added.

Releasing me, she shot me a glare. "I still can't believe you didn't call me, even if you *did* have Dr. Hottie hanging around."

"There wasn't anything you could do. Anyway, I didn't want to ruin your vacation."

"Well, what about Cece? Does she know?"

I nodded. "She's been trying to project to Mrs. G. Cece thinks she must have some sort of shield around herself, around Aidan, too. I've got to find her, though. I need to tell her about my vision. I think I saw something that might clear Aidan."

"Okay, slow down." She held out a hand. "What vision?"

"One I had just before break. I saw something in the lab, but I didn't realize what it meant at the time. I think someone was tampering with Aidan's serum. Mrs. Girard needs to know that it wasn't Aidan's fault, that someone *did* this to him. Intentionally."

"Do you know who it was?"

"No. I couldn't see anything but hands. At the time, I thought they were Aidan's. I wasn't really paying much attention. It was just boring, everyday science stuff, as far as I could tell."

"So you can just replay the vision, right? Look for clues this time."

"Matthew's been trying to talk me through it, but so far, nothing. I don't know . . ." I shook my head. "What if *he*'s the one who tampered with the serum? I think that's why I'm having such a hard time with the replay."

"Do you need him to talk you through it? Or can you do it on your own?"

"It's easier with him, but sometimes I can do it on my own."

Sophie scooted to the edge of the sofa. "Okay, let's do this. What do you need?"

I sat up straight, looking around the apartment. "I wish we

had an old-fashioned clock here. You know, one that ticks really loud."

A slow smile spread across Sophie's face as she reached into her back pocket and pulled out her phone. "There's an app for that. Hold on a sec." She started tapping her screen. "It's got all kinds of sounds that are supposed to be relaxing. Okay, check this out." She tapped an icon that looked like an antique grandfather clock, and there it was—*ticktock, ticktock.*

"That's perfect!" I cried, closing my eyes and settling myself back against the cushions. *Ticktock, ticktock.* "Okay, just stay really quiet and let me focus. I can do this."

A deep breath, in through my nose, out through my mouth—once, twice. I emptied my mind of extraneous thoughts, hyperfocusing on the sound of the clock. Seconds passed, a minute, maybe two. And then the room fell away.

I was in the lab back at Winterhaven. Just like before, microscopes lined the far wall, a Bunsen burner on one of the black-topped tables. I saw the hands, holding a dropper, extracting a liquid from a small vial and dropping it into a test tube. One drop. Two. Three. Then the vial was capped and put into a little wooden rack. As the hands reached for a second vial, I forced myself to pull back, to look around the room. The clock on the wall read five forty-five; one long, rectangular fluorescent light was flickering, making a faint buzzing sound. I pulled back farther, mentally moving myself toward the door. Turning my head to the left, I found him—the owner of the hands. His back was to me, but I could tell he was tall. Blond. Familiar. He capped a second vial, placing it in the rack, turning slightly so that I could just make out his profile . . .

"Oh my God!" I cried, my eyes flying open as I was pulled from the vision. "I know who it was."

4 ~ Jack of Spades

As soon as we were all back at Winterhaven on Sunday afternoon, I gathered everyone in Cece's and my room and told them about the vision—and about my successful replay.

"It was Jack," I said.

"Seriously?" Kate chewed on her lower lip. "I mean, yeah, he turned into a total douchewaffle, but still. Why would he do something like that to Aidan? I thought they were friends."

"I have no idea," I said with a shrug. But it had been his face I'd seen in my vision—Jack's. I was one hundred percent sure. My visions didn't lie.

"Maybe I should start tailing him," Cece offered. "You know, astrally speaking. See what the boy's up to."

"No way. That's against the COPA. I don't want you getting in trouble." I shuddered, remembering the vision I'd had last fall—the one where Cece had been expelled. It had something to do with me sending her out snooping for clues. There was no way I was going to risk it. Nope, not a chance.

"So . . . what now?" Sophie asked. "What does Dr. Byrne think?"

"I haven't told him. Aidan's kind of a—a sore subject with him. I'm pretty sure he thinks it's better this way. That I'm better off without him." I glanced over at the window, where fat, soft snow fell silently against the glass, and sighed.

Where was Aidan, and what were they doing to him? I'd asked myself these questions a million times a day, and yet I was no closer to answering them now than I'd been two weeks ago. The moment I'd arrived back at Winterhaven, I'd gone straight to the headmistress's office, ready to confront Mrs. Girard. Only Mrs. Girard wasn't there. Just as Matthew had said, she'd taken a temporary leave of absence and Dr. Ackerman was acting headmistress. No one could tell me where Mrs. Girard was or when she was expected back.

What the hell is going on?

Anger shot through me, quickening my pulse. Jack had done

this to Aidan. *Jack*, whom I'd always considered a friend. He'd been on our side, one of our Scooby Gang. I was going to find him and kill him. Okay, maybe not literally, but—

"Hey! Earth to Violet!" Cece was gesturing toward my desk. "Isn't that your phone?"

It was Matthew's ringtone. *Great*.

I let it go to voice mail. I was pretty sure he was over at Charlie's, which is apparently where he went when he wasn't here at school. I knew it shouldn't bug me, that I had no right to care one way or the other. But it *did* bug me.

I mean, he took the *Megvéd* stuff so seriously. And according to the legend, that meant he was supposed to be my "mate" in every way. So what the heck did that make Charlie? Also, what kind of name was "Charlie" for a woman? It sounded silly and immature, like she was trying too hard to be cool or something.

Jealousy thrummed through me, and I forced myself to shake it off. I was *so* not going there. Matthew was a teacher—a *teacher*—and besides, I was in love with Aidan. I was going to find Aidan, even if it meant slaying the entire freaking Vampire Tribunal to get to him. If they doubted I was capable of it, then they were going to be in for a surprise when—

"God, Violet—snap out of it!" Cece peered up at me with drawn brows.

"I—I'm sorry," I stammered. "I'm just . . . really distracted right now. I need to find Jack."

Kate rose, her hands clenched into fists at her sides. "I'm going with you."

I shook my head. "I think I need to do this alone."

Kate's determined gaze met mine. "No way. He may need a little helpful persuasion to talk. I'll make sure you get your answers." For such a tiny thing, she looked fierce. I almost felt a little bit afraid of her.

Sophie glanced from Kate to me, a scowl on her face. "So, what do you want me to do? Just sit here twiddling my thumbs while the two of you go gangbusters on him?"

"Where's Marissa?" I asked her, stalling.

Sophie wrinkled her nose. "Where do you think? Somewhere with Max."

"Hey, speaking of, have you seen Tyler yet?" Kate's expression softened a measure.

For a moment there, Sophie looked confused. "What does Tyler have to do with—oh, right. Roommates. Didn't you see him over break?"

"No. He was in Texas. And unlike you, my astral self goes nowhere. We texted some and talked a couple of times. I dunno, though . . . He was acting kind of weird."

"That's because he *is* weird," Sophie shot back.

Kate waggled her brows. "If by weird you mean totally hot and freaking adorable. I'm telling you, that boy can do things with his tongue that—"

"Ugh, stop!" Sophie held up one hand. "Please. I don't even want to think about it."

"Um, Jack?" I reminded them.

Kate nodded. "Right. First things first. Let's go kick some ass."

My mouth widened into a smile. "Now, that's what I'm talking about.

We found him a half hour later inside one of the labs. The moment we stepped through the door, Kate had him in a telekinetic choke hold with the help of his shirt's collar.

"Why did you do it?" I asked, cutting right to the chase before Kate strangled him.

"Do what?" he managed to choke out.

In response, Kate slammed him back against a black-topped table. He struggled to right himself as test tubes skittered across the table and smashed onto the floor at his feet.

His eyes widened as he tugged at his collar, gasping for air.

"Let him talk," I said. "I want to hear what he has to say for himself."

She released him, and he took a big, gasping breath before answering. "I told you, Kate. You were a distraction. I needed to focus on . . . on the team," he stammered. "You know, football. And on my research. Anyway, what does it matter? I heard you and Tyler Bennett are already hooking—"

"We're not talking about *that*, you moron." Kate's cheeks were flushed a deep scarlet.

I launched myself at him, jabbing a finger at his chest. "He trusted you," I said, my voice thick with rage. "How could you do this to him? You—you—*destroyed* him."

"Look, I have no idea what you're talking about," Jack said, trying to back away. His eyes appeared hollow, almost blank. He was lying; I knew he was. "But why don't you call off your pit bull here"—he tipped his head in Kate's direction—"and maybe we can talk."

"Like hell she will." Kate slammed him back against the table for emphasis. "You're the one who's going to talk. And you better start—*now*."

Kate must have tightened her grip on his collar—his eyes were nearly bulging out of his head, his face turning purple. He made a frantic motion with one hand.

Glaring at him, I folded my arms across my chest. "Let him go, Kate. I think he's ready now."

He collapsed to the floor with a gasp. Kate and I stood over him, waiting for him to catch his breath.

He directed his cold, blue gaze at Kate. "I'm turning you in for violating the COPA," he finally managed to croak. "Crazy-ass bitch."

"Yeah, you go right ahead and do that, asshole," Kate shot back. "You make sure and tell Mrs. Girard why I did it, too. Tell her what you did to Aidan."

He scrambled to his feet, knocking over a chair in the process. "Who the hell do you think made me do it?" he said, his face a mottled red now. "I had no choice. No. Choice. Don't you get it?"

I shook my head, confused. *What is he saying?* "*Who* made you do it, Jack?"

He glanced around the room, then dropped his voice to a near whisper. "Mrs. Girard. Listen, if there'd been any other way, if I could have just . . ." He trailed off, shaking his head. "She threatened my brother, okay? She's a vampire, in case you forgot. A fucking vampire, and I thought—I thought—" He leaned back against the table for support, his eyes closed, his face pale and ashen now.

Finally, he opened his eyes. It took a moment for them to focus on me and Kate, standing there gaping at him in shock. "I couldn't risk it," he said. "I couldn't risk *him*. You've got to believe me. I never set out to destroy Aidan. I was just, you know, messing with stuff. I had no idea that my changes to the serum were making him go out and attack people."

I dropped my head into my hands. "I can't believe this. I can't freaking believe it. Why? Why would Mrs. Girard do this?"

"He doesn't know."

I glanced over at Kate, who was watching Jack intently, her eyes brimming with unshed tears. "He doesn't know," she repeated. "He's telling the truth. They're playing us—first Dr. Blackwell and now Mrs. Girard. Pitting us against each other."

"What are we supposed to do now?" I asked, looking from Kate to Jack and back to Kate again. Oh my God, the way he was looking at her, like his heart was breaking into a million pieces.

"Wait, that's why you broke up with her, isn't it?" I asked, realization dawning on me. "Because of this. Because of what you were doing to Aidan."

A muscle in his jaw flexed. "No shit. I couldn't face her—*touch* her—after what I'd done."

"Damn straight," Kate murmured, but I could see her resolve crumbling.

Jack reached a hand out to her. "I'm sorry, Kate. Really, really sorry."

"Do you have any idea what you . . . I mean . . . just . . . ugh! I can't do this right now." She turned and fled, pausing at the door. "I'll see you later, Violet. Come find me when you're done here, okay?"

"Okay," I assured her. "Go on. I'll catch up with you."

As soon as the door slammed shut, I turned back toward Jack, eyeing him with a mix of pity and disgust. "So, you sabotaged Aidan's work. You betrayed a friend. You dumped Kate, walked away from *all* of us. What are your big plans now?"

"I don't know what to say, Violet." He reached up to rub his temples. "I *am* sorry about Aidan. But this is my little brother we're talking about. Aidan's already had his chance—his life. Now my brother will get his."

I slumped into the nearest chair. "But why? *Why* would she do this?"

He shook his head. "I wish I knew. I did what she asked me to do, and there's no going back. I don't expect you to forgive me. I don't expect any of you to."

"Yeah, don't hold your breath," I muttered, then let out a sigh. "Okay, so Mrs. Girard was blackmailing you into doing something that landed Aidan in trouble with the Tribunal. *Big* trouble. Now he's gone for good, and she's disappeared." I drummed my fingers against the table, racking my brain for answers. "How could it possibly benefit *her* to have him locked away at the Tribunal's headquarters or prison, or whatever it is? And why am I asking *you*, the traitor?"

Jack just shrugged, ignoring that jab. "I don't know. Maybe something big is going down in the vampire world? Maybe she needs his help and he's not really locked up. Or maybe she just wants to keep him . . . I don't know, hidden away? Protected somehow?"

I rose on shaky legs, my heart suddenly racing. "Oh my God, Jack. That's it." The wheels in my brain were spinning now. That time I breached her mind in her office, she was thinking about a war—some sort of vampire war—and Aidan was somehow connected to that thought. Aidan, and the fact that he's the biological offspring of King Edward VII.

He can't know, not till war erupts.

Maybe war *had* erupted. Maybe Mrs. Girard was off fighting it. And maybe, just maybe, Aidan was fighting, too. Not destroyed. Not locked up and being tortured.

An unfamiliar feeling surged through my veins, quickening my pulse—*hope,* I realized. For the first time in weeks, I had hope.

"I've got to go," I said, my heart banging noisily against my ribs. "But hey, maybe you should talk to Kate. Give her a few hours to cool down and then, you know, talk."

"Talk to Kate about what?"

My head swiveled toward the voice coming from the doorway. There stood Tyler Bennett, leaning against the doorjamb.

Of course.

"Well, hey there, Violet," he said with his trademark cocky grin. "Miss me?"

5 ~ Frenemies

Speak of the devil," Jack said, glaring at Tyler.

"Y'all were talking about me? Wow. I'm flattered."

Still leaning casually against the doorframe, Tyler didn't seem to notice the hostility directed his way. In fact, he looked perfectly comfortable in his low-slung jeans and faded flannel shirt.

"Yeah, don't be," I launched back. "Trust me. It wasn't at *all* flattering."

"Man, that's harsh." His eyes danced with their usual mischief. "Anyway, I was looking for Aidan. I think it's time we have a little chat. You know, get some things straight. Mano a mano, as we say in Texas."

The now-familiar pain sliced through my heart at the mention of Aidan's name. I swallowed hard, struggling to rein in my emotions, to compose my features into something that resembled normal. "Yeah, well, you're too late for that," I said at last. "Right, Jack?"

Jack ignored that, instead busying himself with sweeping up the broken glass on the floor.

I just glared at him, waiting to see if he was going to own up to what he'd done in front of Tyler. But he didn't—of course not. He just kept on cleaning up the mess as if we weren't standing there watching him.

"Okay, what's going on here?" Tyler asked, breaking the uneasy silence.

As soon as Jack dumped the broken bits of glass in the trash and returned the surviving test tubes to their racks, he grabbed his backpack off the counter and made for the door. "Sorry to break up the party, guys, but I've got to go to football practice."

"Coward," I said under my breath.

"Let him go." Tyler reached for my arm. "Seriously, Violet, what's going on?"

Taking a moment to gather my courage, I dropped my gaze to my scuffed sneakers, noticing a rip in one seam. "Prepare your 'I told you so's," I said, resisting the urge to bend down and pull on the loose threads. "You're going to love this."

I looked up to find him studying my face carefully, his mouth drawn into a tight line. "Actually, I don't think I am," he said.

Best to just blurt it out, I decided. "You were right. Aidan was the Stalker. Thanks to our good friend Jack, that is, who was tampering with his serum."

"What the *hell*? You're saying that Aidan really *was* attacking those women?"

I nodded, chewing on my lower lip.

"When did you find out?"

"The last day of school. That night, in Manhattan," I clarified.

"And you're just now telling me because . . . ?"

"Because it was a lot to deal with, that's why. Besides, what was I supposed to do? Call you in the middle of Christmas dinner with the happy news?"

"Trust me. It's not like my Christmas could have gotten any worse than it already was," he said with a shrug. "So what the hell happened? I mean, if he's the World's Kindest Vampire like you say he is, why'd he do it?"

"Long story short, he had no idea what he was doing—he'd test the serum on himself and then basically black out while the Stalker took over. Like Jekyll and Hyde or something. As soon as he figured it out, he turned himself in to the Tribunal. That very night."

"The Tribunal?"

I nodded. "Yeah, it's like the vampire high court. The ruling body—something like that. Anyway, they're in charge of all vampire punishment, and after what he did . . ." I trailed off, unable to finish the thought. "Aidan's gone, and he's not coming back."

He reached for my hand, giving it a squeeze. "God, Violet, I'm so sorry. But Jack"—he shook his head—"I mean, are you sure? How do you know he was involved?"

"Because I *saw* him, that's how," I said. "In a vision last fall. Only, I just figured out what it meant. Anyway, he confessed. Kate managed to get it out of him—that's why he was so pissed off."

He dropped my hand. In an instant, he was at the door.

"Where are you going?" I hurried to catch up with him, reaching for his sleeve to stop him.

"To find Jack and kick his ass, that's where."

I shook my head. "Don't bother. He had his reasons, okay? I can't believe I'm saying this, but . . . well, it's not like he had a choice. Not really." God, I hated that I was excusing Jack. I wanted to blame him. To hate him. But Mrs. Girard had threatened his little brother. What was he supposed to do? What would any of us have done in his place?

"You're actually *defending* that asshole?"

"Well, there's more to it," I said, wondering just how much I should tell him. "But can we talk about it later? Right now I need to find Kate and make sure she's okay."

I could have sworn I saw a flicker of a smile at the corners of his mouth. "Why don't you let me deal with Kate?"

I shook my head. "I'm not sure that's such a good idea. I think she's pretty confused right now." Yeah, that was putting it mildly. I'd seen the way she was looking at Jack just before she ran out—she was *so* not over him; I was sure of it. And now that she knew why he'd broken up with her, well . . .

"What about you?" he asked, interrupting my train of thought. His brow furrowed as he peered down at me. "Are *you* okay?"

Tears burned behind my eyelids, but I managed to blink them back. I was *not* going to cry. "What do you think, Tyler? No. No, I'm not okay."

He pulled me into his arms. "No, course you're not. I really *am* sorry, Violet. Seriously, you just tell me what you need me to do."

I took a deep, steadying breath. "I just . . . I need you to be my friend, that's all."

Cupping my face with his hands, he tipped my head up till our gazes met. He nodded once, then pressed his lips against my forehead. His kiss was quick, entirely chaste.

"You got it," he said.

And this time, I believed him.

"And really, Tyler—mano a mano?" I was smiling now, hoping to break the heavy tension in the air. "Does anyone actually say that in Texas?"

He laughed, the familiar playful gleam back in his eyes. "Heck if I know. It sounded good, though, right?"

"What's for lunch?" I asked, tossing my bag to the empty chair beside Sophie.

"Chili," Marissa said, pointing to the steaming bowl on the tray in front of her. "And it's pretty good." Beside her, Max gave a thumbs-up with one hand while he shoveled a spoonful into his mouth with the other.

The spicy smell made my stomach roil. "Maybe I'll just get a sandwich."

"Yeah, me too." Sophie rose and fell into step beside me.

"Hey, wait up!" Cece hurried to catch up with us.

We were halfway across the dining hall when Joshua waylaid us, stepping into our path with a frown. "Hey, I just heard what happened to Aidan. You guys okay?"

As always, bad news traveled fast at Winterhaven. We hadn't even been back at school a full twenty-four hours yet. "Who told you?" I asked, curious.

"Tyler. We've got third period Spanish together." He glanced over one shoulder, toward the table where Jack sat surrounded by his football buddies. Shaking his head, Joshua turned back toward us. "He told me about Jack, too. Unbelievable."

"I know, right?" Cece shot Jack a deadly glare.

"Dirtbag," Sophie added.

"So," Joshua said, "what's the plan?"

I shifted on my feet, feeling vulnerable. I could have sworn that every pair of eyes in the dining hall was focused on us, watching us. "The plan?"

"Yeah, you must have some sort of plan. Right? Oh, and Bronwyn and I kinda broke up over break. It's a little awkward right now—do you mind if I sit with you guys?"

"What? No, of course not. We're just getting sandwiches." I shook my head, confused. I was getting mental whiplash from trying to follow the train of conversation.

"Thanks." His mouth widened into a smile, and I couldn't help but notice that his gaze shifted to Cece and lingered there a little longer than it should have. "Okay, I'll see you back at your table and we can talk about the plan."

I nodded mutely. He was going to be disappointed to learn that I had nothing. No plan.

When we finally made our way back to our table with our

sandwiches and drinks, Kate, Tyler, and Joshua had joined Max and Marissa. Even without Aidan, it was going to be a tight squeeze.

"Where's the rest of the band?" I directed at Max. He always sat with them at meals—at least, he always had before now.

Max just grunted, motioning toward the table behind us. Beside him, Marissa smiled sweetly. A battle hard fought, I supposed.

Sophie leaned toward me. "Marissa told him everything," she whispered into my ear. "Well, almost everything. Just so you know."

I didn't have time to ask her what she meant by "almost everything" before Joshua launched right into investigative mode. "Okay, so you think this Tribunal is somewhere in France?"

"Paris," I said. "At least, that's what I heard."

"And Cece tried to project to Mrs. G.?"

Cece nodded. "A bunch of times. No luck, though. I think the place is protected, wherever she is. I can't project to her or to Aidan."

"So presumably they're in the same place," Tyler reasoned.

Joshua drummed his fingers on the table. "And you talked to Ackerman?"

"Yep. No luck there, either," I answered. "Ackerman had some story about a family emergency. Which we all know is a bunch of crap."

"The woman's got to have a cell phone, right?" Tyler said. "There must be a faculty directory or something."

I shook my head. "Matthew says he's never seen her with a cell. He showed me the directory, and it only lists her Winterhaven office number."

"Matthew?" Max asked, his brows drawn.

"Dr. Byrne," I corrected, my cheeks flushing hotly. "Sorry."

Max still looked confused. "What has Dr. Byrne got to do with this?"

Marissa kicked me under the table. *I didn't tell him everything,* she mouthed. It occurred to me then that Tyler didn't know about the *Megvéd* stuff either—which meant neither did Joshua.

I swallowed hard. "He's . . . my psychic coach, that's all. I asked him if he could help me contact her."

Somehow, I was glad the guys didn't know. It just felt . . . I don't know, too personal to share with them. Of course, it also meant they were missing a big piece of the story.

I glanced over at Josh, who was now busy debating the wisdom of asking other teachers if they knew how to contact Mrs. G. His expression was earnest, his concern evident. I remembered the sight of him standing beside Jack on the edge of that blood-soaked field last spring, remembered how he'd created—or somehow became—the distracting fog that helped save us all. He'd risked so much by joining us in the fight and all because Aidan and I had stood up for him and his shifter friends.

Yep, I trusted Joshua. Completely.

My gaze slid over to Tyler. He was a friend, no doubt about it. And yet it had been so easy to imagine that he'd been the one tampering with Aidan's work. I didn't trust him, not fully. And it wasn't just that he'd hooked up with Kate when he was supposed to be at a dance with Cece. No, there was more to it than that. I couldn't quite figure him out, wasn't entirely sure what motivated him.

What had drawn him into our little group? Was it just our connection on the fencing team? Or was there something more? I shook my head, realizing there was a lot about Tyler that I didn't know.

Still, there was no doubt that he *was* a part of us now. Max too. And if they were going to help me find Mrs. Girard and get Aidan out of wherever they were keeping him, then they probably needed to know the whole story, skeevy bits and all.

They *deserved* to know. Which meant I needed to talk to Matthew and get his permission first. Because this was his secret as much as mine, and—

"Violet?" Cece nudged me in the ribs. "What do you think?"

"About what?" I shook my head, trying to clear it.

"You haven't been listening to a word Josh said, have you?" she asked.

I felt my cheeks flame. "Sorry."

"We were talking about this whole 'war' thing," Kate offered. She turned toward me. "Remember what Jack said yesterday, about how Mrs. G. might be trying to protect Aidan? It makes sense, really, when you think about it. If he's her 'greatest creation' and all that. I mean, maybe this is just part of some big plan."

Joshua nodded. "Yeah, maybe she needed him to get into trouble so that she had an excuse to lock him up somewhere safe."

Tyler looked unconvinced. "Well, why wouldn't he be safe here?"

"Julius and those two female vamps were able to track him here," Marissa said, suddenly looking pale. She combed a hand through her long dark hair, her fingers visibly trembling. "Wherever they've got him, it's with a bunch of powerful vampires, right? Probably the best place for him, if something big is going down. If they want to keep him safe, that is."

"Yeah, but safe from *what*?" Sophie asked.

"The war," Joshua answered with a shrug.

I sighed in frustration. "Which brings us right back where

we started. And no closer to getting Aidan out than we were before."

"But think about it, Violet," Kate said. "If we're right and she's got him somewhere to keep him safe or whatever, she's not going to just let him go. There's no more 'clearing' him—she set him up, remember?"

Kate was right, of course. Telling Mrs. G. that Aidan was set up was pointless if *she* was the one who had ordered the sabotage. It wouldn't matter, not one bit. *Unless Jack was lying.* "If I could just *talk* to him somehow. You know, make sure he's okay."

"We really should eat," Cece said, and I glanced down at my untouched sandwich. "Lunch is almost over, and I've got to get over to the gym for tennis."

Marissa pushed aside her bowl with a frown. "I thought you were quitting the tennis team."

Cece looked glum. "Apparently not."

"Parental pressure?" Max asked, reaching for his spoon and scraping out the remaining bits of chili from Marissa's bowl.

"Yeah, even though college apps are already in. What difference does it make now?" Cece took a bite of her sandwich.

I shrugged, reaching for my own sandwich. I'd just taken a bite when everyone's heads swiveled toward a spot just over my shoulder. I turned to find Matthew standing there.

"Sorry to interrupt, guys. Violet, can I see you after sixth period today in my office?"

"Sure," I mumbled around a mouthful of tuna salad.

With a dazzling smile, Matthew raked a hand through his dark hair, mussing it. The girls surrounding me seemed to be holding their breath, mesmerized as they watched. "Okay, great. I won't keep you long." He clapped a hand on Tyler's shoulder. "And I'll see *you* fourth period, right?"

"Right, you will," Tyler answered. "Biochemistry and Molecular Studies, here I come."

"Hey, me too," Sophie said, smiling broadly.

"Good to hear. I'll make it fun. I promise. Okay, later, guys." He gave a little salute before heading back through the crowded dining hall.

"A science elective?" I asked Sophie, whose fair, freckled cheeks were now scarlet. "You mean, in addition to your *regular* science class?"

"I like science," Sophie mumbled.

"*And* Dr. Hottie," Marissa added, poking her playfully in the ribs.

Max rolled his liner-smudged eyes as he piled empty dishes on his tray. "What is it with everyone and Dr. Byrne? Seriously, he's such a stiff."

"I am *so* not going to touch that one. Not with a ten-foot pole," Cece said with a laugh.

Marissa grinned mischievously, making me groan aloud—I knew what was coming. "No, we'll leave that to Violet, won't we? After sixth period."

The table erupted in laughter. Luckily, I was saved by the bell that indicated the end of lunch period. Three more periods to get through—two of which I normally shared with Aidan.

It was going to be a *long* day.

6 ~ Mischief Managed

I was still sweaty from fencing practice when I knocked on Matthew's office door later that day. I had no idea why he wanted to see me, but it was good timing, actually. I wanted to ask him about Tyler, Max, and Joshua—and how much I could tell them.

"Come on in," he called out.

When I stepped inside, I found him leaning against the bookshelf behind his desk, talking on his cell. "I'll be off in two seconds," he whispered as I slid into the seat across from his desk. He turned his back toward me, but I could still make out what he was saying. "Okay, no problem. I'll call you when I'm done. Yeah, you too."

Turning back toward me, he ended the call and put the phone in its charger, looking slightly embarrassed. As if I'd caught him doing something he shouldn't. Which could only mean . . . *Charlie*.

"How's Patsy doing?" he asked, coming around to the front of his desk and leaning against it.

"She's fine. Much better, actually. Believe it or not, she made a show of pretending like she wanted to drive me back to school herself. Said she could rent a car. Luckily, Paul talked her out of it." The last thing I wanted was Patsy here at Winterhaven. She would ask about Aidan, want to say "hi" or something. And what could I possibly tell her? "Anyway, how's Charlie?"

The sudden rise of color in his cheeks told me that I was right in assuming that he had been talking to her when I'd walked in.

He took a deep breath before responding. "Annoyed with me. As always."

"Hmm, that doesn't sound good. Care to elaborate?"

He cleared his throat. "Actually, it's probably not appropriate for us to talk about Charlie."

"You're kidding, right? I mean, we've spent the past couple of weeks talking about how I'm supposedly your predestined 'mate,' and now you're telling me that it's not *appropriate* for us to talk about your girlfriend?"

I saw him wince as my words hit their mark. "Well, we

probably should be a little more"—he shook his head—"I don't know . . . formal . . . now that we're back at school. And besides, Charlie's not my girlfriend."

"Really? That's your answer? That she's *not* your girlfriend? Because honestly, I'm not buying it."

He rubbed one cheek with the palm of his hand, watching me closely—studying me. "Would it matter to you if she was?" he said at last, catching me completely off guard. "Seriously, dig down inside your psyche. Find the powerful *Sâbbat* residing there. What does *she* think about it?"

For a moment, I just sat there goggling at him. And then I did what he asked. I turned off my mind and searched my instincts instead. It took only a moment to find the answer. There was a heavy, uncomfortable feeling in the pit of my stomach. I couldn't really explain it, but the very idea of Matthew with a girlfriend just seemed wrong. Really, really wrong.

"It matters," I blurted out before I thought about what I was saying. "I know it shouldn't. Ugh, can I take it back?"

"Nope," he said with a tight smile. "Sorry for pushing you like that, but I was just trying to show you what we're up against. Natural instincts are powerful things, Violet. And that's why Charlie *isn't* my girlfriend—not really—and why she never will be."

Catching his meaning, I exhaled sharply. "I'm sorry, Matthew. Seriously."

He shrugged. "Like I said before, it is what it is."

"But . . . wait. Your dad is part of the *Megvédio* too, right? Second son of a second son."

Matthew just nodded.

"But he's married to your mom. What if he'd found a *Sâbbat* after marrying her—his *Sâbbat*? What then?" I was picturing all kinds of messy scenarios.

"There's a very small window—just a decade. Sixteen to twenty-six. He married my mom when he was thirty-one."

"You never told me that! Wow, so we just barely made it."

"I'll be twenty-six next week," he said quietly.

"That sucks, doesn't it?" I shook my head. "If you'd just been *one* year older."

By the look on his face, I knew that we were headed toward the old argument again—the one where I went on about how awful and awkward our situation was, while he insisted it wasn't that bad, really.

"Well, I'm glad that I wasn't," he said, confirming my hunch. "You don't have to do this alone, Violet. You've got your stake, I've got my baselard, and we've got each other."

"Baselard?" I asked. "That's your dagger, right? You've never shown me. Did you have it that day in Central Park?"

He nodded. "Since I met you, I'm never without it."

"Show me," I demanded, but I wasn't expecting what came next.

Without a word, Matthew started unbuttoning his plaid shirt.

Uh-oh.

"Wait," I called out, half rising from my seat. I stopped myself when I saw the form-fitting heather-gray T-shirt he wore beneath the more conservative button-down.

"What?" he asked. "You didn't really think I was going to strip shirtless right here in my office, did you?" There was an unmistakable twinkle in his eyes, mocking me.

He shrugged out of the shirt, revealing a shoulder-harness sheath over his left pecs, worn over the T-shirt. From the sheath, he removed the most beautiful weapon I'd ever seen. The handle was dark gray, H-shaped, the narrow, silver double-edge blade sharpened to a deadly tip. My breath caught at the sight of it. I rose, inexplicably drawn to it.

He held it out to me, and I took it with trembling hands, tracing a finger down the length of the blade and back up again. I paused just above the hilt, where an intricately scripted *M* was engraved into the metal. I glanced over at his right biceps, where the dagger was depicted in ink, and then back to the weapon itself, amazed at the likeness.

"It looks so old," I said, my voice full of awe. "So fragile."

"This one *is* old. Probably late fifteenth century or so, forged in Switzerland specifically for the *Megvédio*. But don't be fooled by its age or fragility. I've been assured that it can still do its job as long as I hit my mark. And I promise you I can. I've been training with it since I was twelve."

I shook my head in confusion. "But I don't understand. I didn't think you could kill a vampire."

"I can't. That's *your* job. It's *my* job to strike the vampire's eye with the baselard. That disables it long enough for you to get a clean shot at the heart."

"But . . . but the blade's so short," I stammered. "Wouldn't you have to get awfully close to a vampire's fangs to reach its eyes?"

He cocked an eyebrow, looking somewhat amused. "Not if I throw it."

"Ah, I see." Goose bumps rippled across my skin as I imagined it, trying to picture a scene where Matthew and I worked in tandem to take out a vampire. Would it come to that?

Of course it would. There was no hiding from destiny.

"I've already killed three vampires," I said, my voice shaky now. "All by myself."

"I know," was all he said, but the pride in his voice spoke volumes more.

I swallowed hard. "You better put your shirt back on."

"That's what she said," he quipped, slipping the dagger back into its sheath. "It's a joke," he added, looking suddenly embarrassed as he reached for his shirt and slipped it back on.

"Yeah, I know. I've seen the show."

In seconds, he'd buttoned up. Only now . . . now I was hyperaware of what the plaid shirt concealed. I wondered briefly if it was as uncomfortable as the makeshift sheath I'd worn to carry my stake back when Julius had been threatening us.

Suddenly, it was as if my right side started to hum. Vibrations pulsed down my arm, concentrating in my palm. "Wow," I said as unfamiliar sensations washed over me. I extended my arm, flexing my hand several times in an attempt shake it off. "It's like I feel its absence now. My stake. It's like . . . like it *belongs* with your baselard."

I dropped my head into my hands, my cheeks flaming with mortification as I realized how dirty that sounded. "Please pretend I didn't just say that," I muttered.

"Hey, look at me," he said, his voice sharp. "It's just going to get stronger, these feelings, the closer we get to your eighteenth birthday. We've got to"—he shook his head—"I don't know, find a way to get comfortable with it, okay? I mean, obviously we have to respect the boundaries, but for safety's sake, we've got to learn to trust each other. I'm talking one hundred percent, absolute trust. And yeah, it's going to get awkward sometimes. But I've got your back. Always, every moment of every day."

I just nodded, unable to speak. Conflicting emotions overwhelmed me, warring against one another. A part of me wanted to pledge equal devotion to him, an 'every moment, every day' declaration to match his. But another part of me . . .

Aidan. Oh, Aidan. "Here's the thing, though," I said cautiously. "I still have to find him. Find him and get him out of there."

"Aidan, you mean?"

I just nodded.

He let out a sigh, looking frustrated—defeated, even. "I'm sure you're going to try."

"You've got to understand, I—"

"I get it, Violet." He held out a hand to silence me. "I do. And for the record, it's not your relationship with Aidan in theory that I disapprove of. If he were mortal . . ." He trailed off, shaking his head. "But he's not. He's the enemy, no matter how nice and decent and smart he might be. I'm not saying you should destroy him—or any of them, for that matter, if they're not a threat. I'm just saying that it's against your nature, and it's only going to lead to heartbreak. I mean, from the looks of it, it already has."

I digested that in silence, annoyed that he'd resort to such a low blow. Anyway, it didn't matter what Matthew thought. I was unwilling to accept the idea of failure. I *would* find him.

For a moment, neither of us spoke. We simply sat, watching each other warily. As the seconds passed, I became aware of the ticktock of the clock on his desk, the one we used for coaching. "Why did you want to see me, anyway?"

"To talk about our Saturday-morning sessions." He walked around his desk and took his seat opposite me, all official-like now. "I'd like to get back to them, but it's up to you."

"Is there anything more you can teach me about the visions?" Because I'd already perfected the replay. I'd gone over the three remaining unfulfilled visions—Cece getting expelled, a short-haired me in an antique-looking bed with a lustful and possibly bloodthirsty Aidan, and one that seemed to indicate I would attempt to slay Aidan again. I shuddered at the memory of that last one. "Any new tricks to learn?"

"Not really. I was thinking that we should take our sessions in a different direction. You know, talk about situations we might encounter, share what we know about vampires and what threats might be lurking out there. And then start on some combat training."

"Combat training?"

"Yeah, I think we need to get the mechanics down—learn how to work as a team. That kind of stuff."

"I guess," I agreed. I couldn't help but remember those training sessions with Aidan, where he'd taught me how to use my stake. I remembered the mental and physical exhaustion, the strain it had put on our relationship. I wondered if this would be easier, more natural. After all, there was nothing natural about learning how to kill a vampire . . . from a vampire. But this—at least *this* made sense.

"Maybe one of your friends could help us out now and then," he suggested. "You know, play the role of the vampire."

"Yeah, sure." That'd be easy. I had no doubt they'd be falling all over each other to volunteer. "And speaking of my friends, I wanted to ask about telling the guys—Joshua, Tyler, and Max—about our situation. I mean, they know so much already. It just feels sort of weird keeping it from them. Especially since all the girls know."

"Do you trust these guys?"

I nodded. "Yeah, I do. They're with us now—a part of our group." Besides, Winterhaven students by nature were good at keeping secrets. For most of us, it was just a part of who we were.

"Well, I'll let you make that call. Though with Tyler's fencing training, he'd probably be pretty handy for us, training-wise. I wish I could think of somewhere other than my office to meet, though." He glanced around the space, looking thoughtful. "There's really not enough room in here for what I want to do. I guess I could reserve one of the studios in the gym, but I'm afraid people will start to wonder—"

"I know a place," I interrupted. "The chapel. It'll be empty on Saturday mornings—it's pretty much always empty." Especially now, with Aidan gone.

"Good idea. Want to make it a little earlier, though? Say, ten, so we have a couple of hours to work before lunch?"

"Sure, why not?" Cece was up early for tennis practice anyway.

"Okay, then—Saturdays at ten. But if you have any sort of problem in the meantime—anything at all—don't wait till Saturday, okay? You've got my number. Call me, text me, whatever. *When*ever. Got it?"

"Got it," I replied, standing and reaching for my bag. "I guess I'll see you later, then."

He nodded, and my gaze was involuntarily drawn toward his left pecs, to the spot where I now knew his silver dagger—his *baselard*, I corrected myself—rested in its sheath. I reached for my right wrist, rubbing it with my thumb, picturing it inked with the tattoo that would mark me as a full-fledged *Sâbbat*.

Just a little more than two months from now.

I turned to leave, but suddenly remembered something he'd said earlier. "Wait," I said, turning back to face him. "What day next week?"

He already had his cell back in his hand. "What day what?"

"Your birthday," I clarified. "You said it was next week."

"Oh, right. Thursday. Why?"

"Just curious." With a wave, I sauntered out, already plotting a surprise as I left him to his phone call.

To *Charlie*, no doubt.

"Wow, student council went really late tonight," I said, glancing at the clock by my bed when Cece strolled in later that night.

Cece tossed her bag to the floor and collapsed onto her bed facing me. "Nah, we got done a couple hours ago. I ran into Joshua on the way back to the dorm, and we ended up going over to the café together. I have no idea how it got so late."

I scooted over to the edge of the bed. "Just you and Josh?"

Her face lit up with a smile. "Yeah. We got to talking, and next thing I knew, the café was closing."

"Um, okay." I wasn't quite sure what to say. I'd noticed the way Joshua was looking at Cece earlier in the dining hall, but I wasn't quite sure if I should mention it. I didn't want to jinx anything. *If* there was anything to jinx, that is.

"What?" Cece said, grinning now. "Why are you looking at me like that?"

"How am I looking at you?" I hedged.

She wrinkled her nose, making a face at me. "Okay, fine. So I'm kind of crushing on Josh. Just a little bit," she added, holding up a finger and thumb to indicate about an inch. "But ho-ly crap! When did he get so cute? Seriously, the boy must've shot up a foot and a half since last year, and he filled out nicely. Don't tell me you didn't notice."

I was grinning now too. "I noticed. I just wasn't sure that *you* did."

"It's just . . . you know, the whole shifter thing. I mean, I don't care what anyone else thinks." She waved one hand in dismissal. "But I dunno . . . it's kind of out there, right? As far as abilities go."

I shrugged. "My boyfriend is a vampire, remember?"

"He asked me to the early movie on Saturday." She was literally bouncing on the bed now. "I said yes, so we'll see."

"This is an interesting development," I said. "I like it."

"I somehow figured you would. Anyway, we were talking about the whole Aidan situation, and we had an idea. There's got to be something in Mrs. Girard's office—a note, a book, maybe an e-mail—some sort of clue to help us figure out where she is. Or where the Tribunal is, at least. I'm going to project there in the morning, before Ackerman gets in, and take a look around."

"I don't think it's a good idea. What if someone catches you?"

She looked almost insulted. "How's someone going to catch my astral bad-boy self? My body's going to be right here, in bed."

I wasn't convinced. "I don't know. What about other projectors? Couldn't they somehow see you?"

"Yeah, but there's not that many of us here. I mean, what are the chances? I won't take long—just do a little bit of snooping, and then I'll come right back."

I glanced over at the window. Outside, the ground was covered with the season's first snowfall. Not much, just a few inches, but enough to remind me of my vision, the one where Cece had been expelled. "No," I said resolutely. "You can't risk it. I'm serious, Cece. It's too much like the vision. You know how badly I want to find him, but there's got to be another way. If you get expelled, I'll never forgive myself. Just . . . promise me you won't."

"Okay, okay." She rolled her eyes. "Sheesh. You and your visions."

"My visions are going to save your butt," I said. "Look, I've already lost Aidan. I can't lose you, too."

She leaned over and reached for my hand. "You're right. I'm sorry."

"I appreciate the offer, though." I gave her hand a squeeze before releasing it. "Hold up. You've been at the café all this time and you didn't bring me back anything? Where's my decaf mocha?"

"Hey, don't blame me. I texted you three times asking if you wanted anything. Don't you ever check your phone?"

"Crap, I turned the sound off and forgot about it." I'd been talking to Whitney, and then I'd switched it off so I could read my English assignment—several poems by Wordsworth and Coleridge—in peace. Even though they should have been quick, painless reads, my brain had been stumbling over the words, and what should have taken an hour ended up taking two. "Are you going to bed now?"

"Nah, I've still got homework." Cece stood, stretching her arms toward the ceiling before hurrying across the room to retrieve her bag. She tossed it to the bed, pulled off her shoes, and then sat back down with a groan. "It's not fair—the first day back should be a homework-free zone."

"Yeah, I'm not going to bed anytime soon. I've still got some history to do." I was giving up on the poems. It was a losing battle—I wasn't in the right frame of mind for romantic poets and their jibber jabber about sunsets and moonlight and the delicate curve of their beloved's cheek.

Cece pulled a thick paperback from her bag. "Okay, I'll read my English assignment, and then you want to go over the French homework together?"

"Sounds good," I said, reaching for my history reader and turning to the first assignment. *The British Peerage System*, the title read. A quick scan of the first page made my heart sink. If it wasn't love poems, it was barons and dukes and viscounts, oh my.

Why did *everything* have to remind me of what I'd lost?

7 ~ Family Ties

What's this?" Matthew asked as we all filed into his office the following week bearing a cardboard tray of cupcakes purchased at the café. Max lit the candles—I wasn't asking where he got the lighter—while we all broke out into a rousing chorus of "Happy Birthday."

I set the tray in front of Matthew. "What, did you think I'd forget?"

He blew out the candles and then leaned back in his chair, his hands folded behind his head. "Actually, I was so sure you wouldn't that I skipped dessert and came back to my office early," he said with a grin. "I've just been sitting here, waiting."

I rolled my eyes. "Don't go getting all insufferable on us."

"Wow, 'insufferable.' I'm impressed," Matthew said. "Are you reading Jane Austen in English or something?"

"I wish," I said. "No, we're studying the romantic poets right now. Actually, Sophie and I have a test tomorrow, so we can't stay long."

"Well, thanks for coming, guys. C'mon, help yourselves—these look great." He reached for a cupcake topped with blue buttercream icing and pulled the wrapper off. "Hey, red velvet. My favorite."

Somehow I'd known it would be. It was my favorite too.

"Maybe to show your appreciation, you could excuse me and Soph from tonight's homework," Tyler suggested, draping an arm across Sophie's shoulder.

Casting an apologetic glance in Kate's direction, Sophie wriggled out from under Tyler's arm. "Speak for yourself," she said, shooting him a deadly glare. "Some of us already did our homework."

Tyler's eyes widened. "Seriously?"

"Yup." Sophie nodded solemnly. "There's this thing after dinner called study hour. You should try it sometime."

"Yeah, well, I was gearin' up for party mode. Didn't want to let Dr. Byrne down or anything."

"It was my fault," Max offered, licking the icing from his empty cupcake paper. "I was playing him my new song, wanting some feedback."

"And?" Matthew prodded.

"I liked it," Tyler answered. "Sounded great acoustic. I had no idea the dude could sing like that."

"I heard your set at the Halloween Fair dance," Matthew said, nodding approvingly. "I was impressed. You guys are really good. Do you ever book gigs in the city or anything like that?"

"Yeah, they played a few this summer," Marissa said. "They were awesome."

Max shrugged off the compliment. "It was just a couple of bar sets."

Matthew looked thoughtful. "Actually, I have a friend who's involved with the Mercury Lounge. Maybe I could talk to him, see if he could hook you guys up with a gig. You know, like a showcase night."

"Are you kidding me, man?" Max's eyes were nearly bugging out of his head. "There's, like, record label types at those things!"

"That's what I hear," Matthew said. "Can't hurt, right?"

"Mercury Lounge," Max muttered, looking suddenly pale beneath the shock of spiky black hair. "I mean . . . wow."

"Whoa, Dr. B." Joshua said, clapping Max on the back. "You're gonna give the guy a coronary or something."

"Quick, hand him another cupcake," Cece quipped.

Kate obliged, and soon we were all laughing and chattering away, excited about this possible opportunity for Max and his band. No one looked happier than Marissa, her cheeks flushed and her dark eyes shining with obvious pride.

I was glad we'd decided to surprise Matthew, pleased to see everyone getting along so well—like a family. This large, boisterous group *was* my family, I realized with a start, a slow smile spreading across my face. Sure, we didn't always get along, and we'd had our problems, but I felt a kinship with them all, even Tyler. And Matthew . . . Matthew was like the big brother I never had. I felt better when I was with him—with all of them together. Better and whole.

Immediately, my smile disappeared. Guilt washed over me, making my stomach lurch uncomfortably. How could I possibly consider myself whole when Aidan was gone, either being tortured or used as a pawn in a dangerous vampire war? Did he really mean so little to me that I could forget him as easily as that?

I *hadn't* forgotten, I assured myself. And I wasn't giving up. For a brief moment, I closed my eyes and searched for that connection to Aidan, for that thread that somehow bound us. I called out to him telepathically, something I hadn't allowed myself to do in a while, knowing it would only lead to disappointment. But now . . . I wanted to feel like he was still a part of us, if only in my head. I had to at least try.

Aidan? I tried, forcing aside the celebratory sounds there in Matthew's office, making them recede to an indistinguishable hum.

Nothing. No reply. Had I truly expected otherwise? I tamped down the disappointment, refusing to acknowledge it.

And then I gasped as red-hot heat seared my legs from my hips down. It felt as if the skin were melting from my bones. I could smell it—singed flesh—sickening me, making me gag. Flames lapped at me, the heat unbearable now, like I was being burned alive.

I screamed, falling to my hands and knees on the hard tile floor.

"Violet!" Matthew shouted. Everyone scattered, and he was by my side, kneeling on the floor with one hand on my back.

I was aware of his presence, aware of the words he was saying in my ear. And then . . . I wasn't.

His office fell away and I was in some sort of dark, shadowy place—a dungeon, maybe. The walls were made of stone, dark brown and gray and dingy. Acrid smoke lingered in the air, mixed with the metallic scent of blood. I tried to lift my head, but I couldn't. I was weak, exhausted, paralyzed with the most overwhelming sensation of despair I had ever felt.

I wanted to die. *Please, let me die. End this. End it now.*

The thoughts were not my own, I realized. And yet . . . and yet the feeling of despair didn't lessen, didn't release me from its iron grip.

A tear slipped down my cheek and onto my lip, tasting salty and bitter. *Enough. Please, enough.*

"Violet! C'mon, pull out of it!" someone was shouting into my ear.

I whimpered, wanting to get away, to never see this awful place again.

"Violet? C'mon, kiddo. Come back. Damn it, come back!" There it was again, that voice. Angry and scared. I recognized it. Matthew. My *Megvéd*. My protector.

"Matthew!" I cried out, my voice hoarse.

I felt cool fingers against my wrist, pressing against my pulse point. "I'm right here, Violet. You've got to pull yourself out of it, okay?"

I swallowed hard, forcing my heavy eyelids to open. Matthew's face swam into focus. My friends gathered around him in a protective circle. Cece was crying. So was Sophie, her face pressed into Tyler's shoulder. Tyler's other arm was wrapped protectively around Kate, who was chewing on her lower lip.

"Hey," I whispered.

"Hey, back," Matthew said, brushing the damp hair from my cheeks. "You want to tell me what that was all about?"

"Yeah, what the *hell* just happened?" Tyler asked.

"A vision, you moron!" Kate snapped, extricating herself and kneeling down beside me. "You need some water?"

"No. I mean, yes. Water. But it wasn't a vision. It was . . ." I shook my head. "God, I don't know. First it was just pain—heat, like my legs were on fire. And then . . . then I was somewhere else. A dungeon, maybe. But I wasn't me. Not like in my visions."

"Has anything like this ever happened before?" Matthew asked, his face paling.

"Yeah . . . once before," I said. "At Patsy's, before school started. The heat and then later that thing with my shoulders, remember? You made Sophie check it out." And then, just like that, the most likely explanation dawned on me, stealing away my breath entirely. *Oh my God!* "I think . . . I'm feeling . . . whatever they're doing to Aidan," I choked out.

"No. I can't imagine—I mean, I've never heard of anything like that before," Matthew said. "Here, can you sit up?"

I did, and took the paper cup of water that Kate handed me.

I knocked it back in one long gulp. "Wow, this was some birthday celebration, huh?"

"Definitely memorable," Joshua agreed. "You look better. You know, more color." He made a sweeping motion with one hand, indicating my face, I suppose.

With a wince, I ran a hand down my right leg, testing it. I was surprised to find that it felt completely normal. "I swear it felt so real. I really *am* losing my mind."

Matthew shook his head. "There's got to be a logical explanation. I just don't know what it is yet, that's all. Unfortunately, none of this stuff is an exact science. It's all legend and lore, entirely imprecise and unpredictable."

"Spoken like a true science teacher," Joshua said.

"Speaking of which, why didn't you study anthropology or ancient history or something like that?" Cece asked. "Considering . . . I mean . . ." She trailed off, looking embarrassed.

Matthew reached for my hand and helped me to my feet. "Considering I knew I was a *Megvéd,* you mean? Part of vampire lore? Yeah, that's a good question. I guess because I like science—the thrill of discovery. But hey, science might very well help us out in the end. At least, Aidan thought it could. I'm still working on his project. His serum," he clarified.

"What do you mean?" Tyler asked.

"Just that I'm still playing around with the formula. We'd gotten really close; I was sure of it. Aidan was sure of it too. This is the most exciting work I've ever done—far beyond my malaria research, and that was considered groundbreaking. Think about what it would mean, the cure. And not just for Aidan."

Still feeling dizzy and slightly disoriented, I slid into the chair opposite Matthew's desk. I tried to wrap my head around what Matthew was saying—tried to imagine what a cure might mean for us as *Sâbbat* and *Megvéd*. "But who are you going to test it on?"

"Aidan left me plenty of tissue and DNA samples to work with. It's not exactly the same—not a hundred percent accurate—but I should have a good enough idea if I'm getting closer or not."

"I'll help," Tyler offered. "Just tell me when."

Matthew nodded in his direction. "Thanks, Tyler. I appreciate it."

Sophie stepped up behind me, one hand resting on my shoulder. "I'll help, too."

"That's makes two of my best advanced sci students," Matthew said. "We'll make a great research team."

I was glad that they were going to try—glad that Aidan's work would continue, even in his absence. Somehow it felt like a tribute of sorts. And maybe if I found him—*when* I found him—he'd be that much closer to a cure.

"Here. Have a cupcake," Matthew said, handing me a purple-frosted one. "You look like you need it."

"Thanks." I took it, suddenly craving the sugar. I ripped off the paper and took a bite, savoring the gooey sweetness. Okay, so it wasn't a Magnolia Bakery cupcake—my favorite—but it was pretty darn close.

Tyler sidled up beside me. "You've got icing on your nose. Here, I'll lick it off." He bent toward me, a cartoonish leer on his face.

I swatted him away. "Ugh, you're disgusting," I said, but I was laughing now. I could always count on Tyler to lighten the mood, to try and make me smile.

"Hey, I just offered to help cure the boyfriend, remember?"

I wiped the icing from nose. "Yeah, I remember. Thank you."

Everyone was trying to help, each in their own way. Hope surged through me, despite my efforts to quell it. Was it possible, or had we lost him forever? Had *I* lost him forever?

I let out a sigh, forcing back the memory of the horrible sensations I'd experienced—the excruciating pain, the overwhelming despair. Somehow, I'd been inside Aidan's head. I was sure of it. Whatever they were doing to him was bad enough that he wanted to die, hoped to die. And if that was true, well . . .

Just what would Aidan be like if I *did* find him?

8 ~ Exes and *Ohh*s

How many weeks had passed since we'd returned to school? Five? Six? I'd lost count. I glanced up at the calendar pinned to the wall above my desk, surprised to see that it was February already. Mid-February, I corrected myself. Almost Valentine's Day.

Memories of last year's Valentine's Day came flooding back, and I shuddered. That stupid miniature—the one with Aidan's ex, who happened to look just like me. *Isabel.* Aidan and I had fought about it, and then I'd skipped the dance that night. Months had passed before I'd been able to forgive him, time that I could never get back.

"You okay?" Cece asked me, looking up from her laptop with a frown on her face.

"Yeah, it's just . . . I'm not looking forward to the weekend, that's all." I hated to be such a downer, especially with Cece all excited about going to the dance with Joshua.

Cece set aside her laptop and hurried over to wrap her arms around me. "Aww, I'm sorry. I know it's going to be hard for you."

I inhaled her familiar scent—coconut shampoo—and felt a little better. "When was the last time you tried?" I asked, unable to stanch my curiosity. "To project to either of them, I mean. Aidan or Mrs. Girard."

"Yesterday morning." Cece released me and perched on the end of my bed facing me. "No luck, but I think I've combed just about every square inch of Paris by now. There are a lot of projectors roaming that place, by the way. It's kind of crazy."

I shook my head. "That is so weird. Cool, but weird."

"Tell me about it. I wish there was a way to go private. You know, flip some internal switch and go incognito. That way, I could search the headmistress's office without having to worry."

I stiffened in my seat, fear making my heart race as I glanced out the window. Last week's storm had dumped nearly a foot of fresh snow on the ground. We were still in the danger zone, as far as my vision went. "You promised me you wouldn't, Cee. The vision. Remember?"

"I know." She waved a hand in dismissal. "But c'mon, you really think they'd expel me?"

"Yes! How could you possibly explain what you were doing there? It's not like you could tell Dr. Ackerman the truth. She'd have to expel you."

"Yeah, I know." She sighed resignedly. "Hey, I have an idea. Why don't you request a weekend pass, just to get away? I mean, it's not that I don't want you here, but you were just talking about that new temporary exhibit at the museum—you know, that one about vampires and werewolves and zombies. You should go."

"That's not a bad idea," I said, glancing up at the calendar again. "I think it opened last week. They've got a bunch of artifacts and old texts on display—you never know what I might come across."

"Exactly. And hey, Sophie was just complaining about all the Valentine's Day hoopla and saying how she was dreading it too. You should see if she wants to go with you."

"You're a genius," I said, reaching for my cell. All it took was a quick text conversation, and the plan was set. Sophie's parents were going out of town for the weekend, so she'd stay with me at Patsy's. We'd check out the museum exhibit, eat a lot of takeout, and escape the pink hearts and cupid cutouts that would take over campus for a few days. All we needed was Dr. Ackerman's permission.

I rose, plugging my phone back into its charger. "Okay, Sophie's meeting me in the lounge and then we're walking over to Ackerman's office together. Want me to get you something from the vending machines?"

"Yes! Skittles, please. Two bags and I'll be your friend for life."

"Wow, if I'd known you were *that* easy, I could have saved myself a lot of trouble."

She wrinkled her nose at me. "Ha-ha. Now go," she said, making a shooing gesture in my direction. "You'll feel much better when this is all settled."

"Okay, wish us luck." We were going to need it, since the administration frowned on last-minute weekend pass requests. Somehow we'd have to couch this as an educational opportunity, highlighting our plan to visit the museum.

"You got it, girlfriend," Cece said with a grin.

I beat Sophie to the lounge. I'd already bought three bags of Skittles—two for Cece, one for me—when she arrived, out of breath and sporting a thin sheen of perspiration on her forehead.

"What'd you do, run? Where were you?"

"Over at the chem lab," she huffed and puffed. "With Tyler and Dr. Byrne."

"So, you really *are* doing it? Working on Aidan's serum?"

She nodded. "We really are. It's pretty cool too."

I swallowed a lump in my throat. "Have I told you lately how much I love you?"

"Right back at you," she said with a smile, then pointed to the colorful bags I was clutching in one hand. "What's with all the Skittles?"

"Cece has a sweet tooth. So, how is it working out with Tyler? I can yell at him if he's being obnoxious."

Oddly enough, Sophie's cheeks reddened. She bent down, fiddling with her shoelaces. "No, it's . . . he's fine."

"Um, okay." I refused to allow myself to read anything into her reaction.

"Just let me check my mail, and then let's go," Sophie said, smoothly changing the subject. "I think Ackerman's office hours end in fifteen minutes and we don't want to miss her."

I nodded, following Sophie over to the mail cubbies. I almost never checked mine, since I rarely got anything. Except . . . there was a small padded envelope sitting there in my box. Maybe something from Lupe? She'd sent me the delicate silver crucifix necklace last year, which I still wore tucked under my shirt every day—a link to home and to the people I loved there.

I reached for the envelope, turning it over in my hands. It was addressed to me in an unfamiliar hand, with no return address.

"What's that?" Sophie asked, peering over my shoulder.

"I have no idea. I'm almost afraid to open it." My hands were shaking, I realized. Something about this felt . . . *off.*

The postmark was dated January sixth. Had it really been that long since I'd checked my mailbox?

Ignoring the feeling of unease, I ripped open the seal and reached inside, pulling out the packet's contents with a frown. It was a small, cream-colored square card with a key taped to it. Beneath the key, there were four numbers—a security code, maybe?—and a single word scrawled in script. *Trevors.*

Aidan's butler, Trevors, had sent me a key. A key to *what*?

"Okay, that's weird." Sophie examined it, then lifted her gaze to meet mine. "It looks like a house key, right?"

"Maybe," I said, my heart accelerating as I considered the possibilities. A key . . . to a house. Aidan's house? If so, what did that mean? Was it some sort of sign from Trevors, a hint that maybe Aidan was somehow back in Manhattan? My stomach did a little flip-flop, my mind racing dangerously fast as I processed the thought. Was it possible, or just wishful thinking?

Only one way to find out, and that meant obtaining the necessary weekend pass.

"We've got to get to Dr. Ackerman's office," I said, glancing down at my watch. "Now!"

* * *

"You're sure you don't want me to go with you?" Sophie asked, her hazel eyes troubled. She was leaning against the kitchen counter, a soda in one hand. Our weekend pass had been successfully acquired, and we'd taken the afternoon train into Manhattan and stopped for takeout burgers and fries before heading over to Patsy's. Now that we were done eating, I was eager to get over to Aidan's and test the key.

"I really think I need to do this alone. Whatever I find"—I swallowed hard, imagining the possibilities—"or don't find, I can handle it."

"You've got your stake?"

I pointed to my black messenger bag. "Got it."

"Maybe you should call Dr. Byrne." Sophie was wringing her hands now.

"I'll be fine," I assured her. "Clearly Trevors wants me to go over there, and I trust him. Patsy's staying over at Paul's, so you've got the place to yourself. I won't be gone long. I promise. I'm just going to go check things out."

"Okay," she conceded. "Just . . . text me when you get there. And when you're on your way back."

"Deal," I said.

It was a quick, easy walk from Patsy's to Aidan's town house, but I took a cab anyway, tipping the driver generously. My heart was banging around in my chest as I stepped out of the cab and made my way up the stairs to the black-lacquered door.

The snow had mostly melted in the city by now—still, it was obvious that someone had recently shoveled Aidan's walkway. It was clean and dry, without a trace of the dirty, melting slush that remained on the edges of the sidewalk. That was a good sign, I decided. It hinted at recent occupation.

I tried the brass lion's-head knocker first with no response and then paused to search my instincts. Was he here? He had to be, I decided. Why else would Trevors have sent me the key? And yet . . . I didn't sense his presence. I didn't sense Trevors's, either.

Please let him be here. Please, please, please.

I repeated the words in my head like a prayer, over and over again as I took the key from my bag and attempted to fit it into the lock. My hands were shaking so badly that it took several tries, but eventually it slid into place.

Holding my breath, I turned the key and pushed open the door. I was greeted by the high-pitched beeping of a security alarm. I reached blindly for the switch and flipped on the foyer light and stepped inside, quickly punching in the code on the alarm's keypad, silencing it. Before I forgot, I retrieved my cell phone from my bag and texted Sophie—*I'm here!*—then stuffed my cell into my back pocket. My sneakers squeaked noisily against the marble-tiled floor as I took off my coat and hung it on the umbrella stand by the door with my bag, then turned to survey my surroundings.

The house was eerily silent, the air slightly musty and stale. Drapes were drawn shut, furniture covered by canvas cloths. It was immediately obvious that no one was home. Disappointment washing over me, I moved farther inside, past the staircase into the living room, then the dining room, flipping on lights as I went. I continued my trek through the kitchen, the TV room, down the hallway that led back to the foyer and the curving marble stairs illuminated by an enormous crystal chandelier.

One hand trailing along the mahogany banister, I made my way up the stairs, my footfalls echoing loudly in the heavy silence. There were only two bedrooms on the second floor—the enormous master suite and the "rose room," aptly named for its decor. I entered the rose room first, allowing the memories to rush back. I'd stayed here once, slept in the big antique bed hung with pale pink drapes. It seemed like forever ago—a different lifetime. That night, I'd thought that learning Aidan was a vampire was the craziest, most outlandish truth I'd ever encounter. How wrong I'd been.

I scanned the room—it looked pristine, untouched. Bed,

dresser, washstand, all exactly as I'd remembered it, all accented with rosebuds and cream-colored lace. The door on the far side of the room led to the attached bath; the door on my right opened directly into Aidan's bedroom. I walked toward it hesitantly, heart pounding and palms dampening.

The rational part of my mind warned me that, just like the rest of the house, the room was empty, that Aidan wasn't here. If he were, I would have felt his presence by now, heard his voice in my head. And yet . . . I couldn't help but hope, couldn't help but imagine him there on the other side of door, waiting for me.

I approached the arched door and paused, wiping my hands on my jeans. Taking a deep breath, I tried to calm my nerves, but it was no use. When I reached for the cut-glass doorknob, my hand was trembling wildly. Twice, my fingers slipped off. On the third try, I managed to grasp the knob and turn it.

Pushing the door open, I stepped inside and flipped on the light. Immediately, my breath caught in my throat. I had to reach for the doorjamb with both hands to steady myself as I took in the sight—and scent—that greeted me.

9 ~ Eternally Yours

There were orange blossoms everywhere—floating in a round crystal dish by the bed, in a vase on the table in the center of the room, scattered across the deep blue velvet duvet. The scent filled the air, sweet and citrusy and achingly familiar.

Eternal love.

I took a few steps forward, my legs feeling wooden and stiff. Slowly, I made my way toward the table—what Gran called a pie-crust table—and the arrangement there. The vase was tall, nearly a foot high and rectangular in shape. The milky white blossoms were still attached to their stems, nestled between the sturdy green leaves. They were fresh, not yet wilted and still full of scent.

They could only be hothouse flowers this time of year. But how did they get here?

Mystified, I glanced over at the flower-strewn bed, noticing now that what I'd originally thought was a white throw pillow amidst the pile of blue and gold tasseled ones was actually paper—a sheaf of papers with an envelope on top. My heart was in my throat as I hurried over to the side of the bed and reached across the duvet, sliding the papers closer. My name was scrawled on the envelope in a familiar hand—Aidan's. I ripped open the seal and took out the slip of heavy, cream-colored paper. Unfolding it with shaking hands, I began to read.

Violet,

I haven't much time, so this will be regrettably brief. I've deeded this house and all of its contents to you, held in trust for you until your eighteenth birthday. Additionally, I've made provisions for taxes and upkeep. Trevors will have taken care of the paperwork, which you will find accompanying this letter. As soon as you receive this, contact my attorney here in New York—you'll find his contact information with the paperwork—and he'll go over the specifics with you regarding the housekeeping schedule, gardener, security, etc.

I wish I had more time to tell you what you've meant to

me, what joy and light and happiness you've brought into my life. Suffice it to say that I will never forget you, not as long as I walk this earth.

Eternally yours,

Aidan

Tears burned behind my eyelids as I refolded the page and returned it to the envelope. I took a deep breath, digesting his words in silence, trying to make sense of it all. He'd deeded the house to me? The house and all of its contents? I glanced around the room in wonderment. What was I supposed to do with it all?

I took the sheaf of papers and removed the clip, leafing through them without understanding much of what I was reading. It was paragraph after paragraph of legalese, occasionally interrupted by lines with signatures, Aidan's and someone else's—the attorney's, I supposed.

I swallowed hard, completely overwhelmed. The town house itself was worth millions—a plum piece of Manhattan real estate. Add in the antique furnishings, the artwork . . .

Thanks to my art history class, I now recognized several of the gilt-framed paintings throughout the house as originals, some by masters. I was pretty sure that the pretty landscape above the fireplace was a Seurat, the portrait by the staircase a Gainsborough.

But I didn't want any of it, Aidan's possessions. I wanted *him*. Here with me. Now.

I dropped the sheaf of papers to the bed and rose, hurrying over to the chest of drawers in the room's corner. I opened one drawer, then another. There were jeans, T-shirts, all familiar and folded neatly inside, abandoned. I picked up a shirt—a worn, black tee—and lifted it to my nose. It smelled clean, like fabric softener, not a trace of Aidan's scent remaining. There must be something, some hint of him somewhere.

I tried the dressing room next, peering inside the heavy armoire. Several button-down shirts hung there, all in shades of blue, a color that Aidan seemed to favor. There were also several hoodies stacked on a shelf. I lifted one sleeve to my nose, again inhaling deeply, searching for his scent. Once more, I was disappointed. The soft cotton smelled freshly laundered, entirely sanitized. It might have belonged to anyone.

There was a hamper in the corner opposite the fireplace, but upon inspection, I found it empty. Obviously, the entire room had been cleaned and put in order after he'd left. But then . . . I saw something, a hint of color wedged between the wall and the hamper. My heart racing, I bent down and reached into the space, my fingers closing around something soft.

It was a T-shirt, I realized. A dark gray one, one of Aidan's vintage punk-rock shirts. Somehow, whoever had cleaned the room and done the laundry had missed it. It still smelled like him—just barely, but still . . . I would recognize it anywhere. Nearly weeping with relief, I clutched it to my chest as I hurried out.

Back in the bedroom again, there was one more piece of furniture to inspect, a beautiful desk with a large, roll-top compartment on one side. Glancing wistfully at the framed picture that sat atop the desk—me and Aidan at last fall's Halloween Fair dance, the same photo I kept on my dresser at Patsy's—I pushed open the rolling lid and peered inside.

There were several small boxes, one with an engraved pocket watch and another with several pairs of cufflinks. A third held a small signet ring with a crest. I flipped through a brown leather address book, mostly filled with foreign addresses that meant nothing to me. In the back was a larger wooden box—a jewelry box, I guessed. I opened the lid.

Nestled inside was a treasure trove of jewels—his mother's and sisters', I supposed. I lifted the top tray to reveal a second layer, which held nothing but a small blue velvet pouch along with another envelope with my name on it, again in Aidan's script.

The rush of blood through my veins was near deafening as I removed the card inside and read the words scrawled on it.

This was my great-grandmother's wedding ring, passed down to my father from his mother. Someday, it would have been yours. I hope you will take it and wear it—something to remember me by.

There was no signature, just the letter *A* in the bottom right corner. I just sat there staring at the card, reading it over and over again, the words blurred now by my tears. One rolled down my cheek and fell onto the card with an audible *plop*, leaving a wet splotch.

Finally, I set the card aside and reached for the pouch, almost afraid to open it. I took a deep breath before loosening the strings and dumping the contents into my palm. For a moment, I closed my fingers around the treasure, holding it there with the metal biting into my hand as I waited for my breathing to slow. Finally, I opened my hand and stared down at the ring, my eyes widening in appreciation.

It was a delicate piece, set in pink-tinted gold. The center stone was a rectangular-shaped diamond, set sideways. Flanking it on either side were smaller oval diamonds, also set sideways. It was simple but beautiful, and clearly very, very old.

I slipped it on my finger, surprised to find it a perfect fit. But how could I ever wear something like this? And yet . . . it felt so right there on my finger, a link to Aidan and his past, his history. I reached down to remove it, but stopped myself, not wanting to break that link. Instead, I tucked the velvet pouch and the card into my pocket.

And then I broke down. A sob tore from my throat, and I hurried over to the bed, still clutching the gray T-shirt. Tugging down the heavy duvet, I climbed between the covers, scattering the orange blossoms as I did so. Curling up into a ball, I buried my face in the downy pillow and cried, my tears soaking the soft cotton linens.

I have no idea how long I lay there crying—fifteen minutes, maybe a half hour. Eventually, my sobs gave way to sniffles and I forced myself to get up and head to the master bathroom, where I washed my face with cold water, avoiding my reflection in the mirror as I did so. I didn't need to look to know that my face would be red, my eyes puffy and swollen.

I needed to get back to Sophie. I was sure she was worried about me. Besides, we could come back tomorrow, after the museum. Maybe she could help me go through his stuff, decide if there was anything else I wanted to take back to school with me. I also had to figure out what I was going to tell Patsy.

Quickly, I remade the bed and tossed the throw pillows back where they belonged. Operating on autopilot now, I gathered up the legal documents with Aidan's note and his T-shirt, flipped off the light, and headed back downstairs. I made a quick circuit around the ground floor, shutting off all the lights before retrieving my coat and bag from the front hall. I stuffed the T-shirt and papers into my bag and then reset the alarm.

I stepped outside, pausing to pull on my coat and lock the door. I just needed to send a quick text to Sophie and then I'd walk back to Patsy's. I needed the extra time to cool off, to get my emotions under control before I had to face anyone.

But as soon as I turned toward the street, I froze, a scream stuck in my throat. There was someone there, sitting on the top step. I stumbled back against the door, reaching into my bag for my stake when the figure turned to face me. "Hey, you okay?"

"Matthew!" I gasped. "What the hell? You scared the crap out of me!"

"Did you really think I was going to let you come here by yourself?"

I shook my head. "How did you even know where I was?"

"A vision. Come on. Sit down for a second and catch your breath. I didn't mean to scare you." He took my hand and drew me down beside him.

I sat, the stone step cold and hard beneath me. "A vision? I don't understand—nothing bad happened to me in there."

"I know, but I knew you'd be upset afterward. I can't explain it, Violet, but this is the way it works for me now. My visions, I mean. They're linked to you. Apparently, any sort of strong emotion on your part is enough to trigger one now."

I just nodded, unable to speak. I was suddenly glad for his company, happy that I wasn't alone. I leaned my head against his shoulder, allowing him to wrap a comforting arm around me.

We sat like that for several minutes in silence, listening to the sounds of the city. A car horn honked, brakes squealed. A couple walked by hand in hand, laughing. In the distance, a siren blared. I took a deep, cleansing breath, filling my lungs with the brisk winter air.

"You going to be okay?" Matthew asked.

I swallowed hard before replying. "I think so. This was just . . . not what I was expecting." I had no idea what I *had* been expecting, but certainly home ownership hadn't made the list of possibilities. I glanced down at the ring on my finger, the diamonds glinting in the dull yellow lamplight from the street.

"It'd be easier if you just tell me where you're going," Matthew said, drawing me out of my reverie. "You know, rather than making me rely on my visions. They're pretty damn inconvenient, to tell you the truth."

"I know," I murmured. "Sorry about that. I was afraid you'd tell me not to come."

"As if that would stop you," he said with an easy laugh. "You want to talk about it? What you found in there, I mean."

"Not right now," I said. "Later, okay? I'm assuming you're here for the weekend, too."

"If you are, then so am I."

"Then I guess you might as well come with us tomorrow to the museum—you know, that new exhibit on vampires, werewolves, and zombies at the Museum of Natural History?"

"Sounds right up my alley. It's a date." He made a quiet sputtering noise. "Not a *date* date. I didn't mean—"

"Yeah, I knew what you meant," I said, bumping him with my shoulder. "Sheesh."

He cleared his throat, obviously uncomfortable now. "You ready to head back to Patsy's?" He rose, holding out a hand to help me up. I took it and stood unsteadily, dropping his hand as I reached for my cell.

"Just let me text Sophie and tell her I'm on my way," I said. My fingers numb from the cold, I clumsily typed out a message—*on my way home now*—and then glanced over at my *Megvéd*. His cheeks were reddened, a knit cap pulled low over his dark hair. He wore a thick fleece jacket zipped up to his chin and warm-looking boots, but his hands were bare, like mine.

It occurred to me that he'd probably been sitting out in the frigid cold this whole time, waiting for me, giving me the space to do what I needed to do without complaint. My heart swelled, and I reached for his hands, rubbing them between mine to warm them.

"I'm glad you found me," I said, surprised to realize that I meant it. "Let's go. I think I owe you a cup of hot chocolate, at least."

10 ~ Invisible

As soon as Sophie and I returned to campus on Sunday, we headed over to the café to meet up with everyone else. Our group had grown so large that we actually had to push two tables together. I found myself at one end with Cece and Joshua on one side of me and Tyler and Sophie on the other.

Kate, I noticed, was sitting at the far end of the table with Marissa and Max, as far away from Tyler as possible. Which, of course, made me wonder what I'd missed over the weekend.

When Jack came in, my curiosity was ratcheted up a notch. He sat a couple of tables away with his football buddies, but I noticed him sneaking glances in Kate's direction every few minutes, causing her to blush.

"I still think Violet should let Cece try," Joshua said, drawing my attention away from Kate. "Just a quick astral sweep of Mrs. Girard's office. In and out, and I can cover her."

I rolled my eyes. "How are you going to cover her? You can't even *see* her when she's . . . you know. Astral."

"I can sense her," he insisted.

"Really?"

"Yeah, we've"—he cleared his throat loudly, his cheeks reddening—"you know, tested it out."

Cece giggled, then tried to cover it by reaching for her mug and taking a long, noisy gulp of whatever she was drinking.

"I don't think I even want to know what you mean by that," I said, shaking my head. "Anyway, what were you planning to do? Turn into fog? How's that going to help?"

Joshua fixed me with a level stare. "I can do *way* more than turn into fog."

"What exactly *can* you do?" Tyler asked. "No disrespect, dude. I'm just curious. No one's ever explained it to me before. The shifters at Summerhaven kept to themselves."

"And they don't here?" Sophie asked.

Tyler leaned back in his chair, folding his arms across his

chest. "Uh, last time I checked, Joshua was sitting right *there*."

"Because he's got good taste," Cece said, smiling coyly. "Anyway, Josh, tell them what you told me. About the shifting."

Joshua nodded. "Basically, a shifter has two options, distortion or camouflage. Distortion is what you call the fog. It's not all that different from what micro-telekinetics can do—manipulating matter. Body cells, in our case. And then with camouflage, it's just an issue of manipulating the cells to blend into your surroundings. Simple, really," he added with a shrug. "Like a chameleon."

"I wish you could show them," Cece said. "You know, just something really quick."

Joshua glanced around furtively and then nodded. "Blink and you'll miss it. Camouflage, okay?"

We all nodded. And then . . . for a split second, Joshua was gone, blending into the background, as if his chair were suddenly empty. And then, just as quickly, he was back again.

"Did you all catch that?" Joshua asked, grinning now. "If I'd stayed shifted longer, you probably would have noticed that something wasn't right. But from ten, fifteen feet away? The illusion is seamless."

"Okay, that was so cool!" Sophie said.

"I know, right?" Cece was beaming now.

Even Tyler looked impressed. "Way cool, dude."

"Thank you, thank you very much," Joshua quipped.

"Hey, what'd we miss?" Marissa shouted down the length of the table.

"We'll tell you later!" I shouted back, but she wasn't listening now—Max was nuzzling her neck, making her giggle softly as she made a halfhearted attempt to push him away. My gaze slid over to Kate, who was turned sideways in her seat, still making googly eyes at Jack. Then there were Cece and Joshua, obviously a couple now. I wasn't sure, but I thought they might be holding hands under the table.

And Sophie and Tyler . . . I didn't know what the heck was going on with those two. They were both acting really weird around each other, and Sophie had been very careful not to mention him once over the weekend, which was odd in and of itself. Bitching about Tyler was part of our repertoire now. At least, it always *had* been.

Somehow, I felt suddenly *alone*. I tried to push aside the thought, telling myself that I was crazy—that I was just feeling sorry for myself. Still, I couldn't shake the feeling, even with—

That thought cut off abruptly as I gripped the edge of the table, my vision tunneling, the familiar hum in my ears drowning out the café's din.

I was in a ballet studio. There were floor-to-ceiling mirrors along one wall, a long wooden barre on the opposite one. In the room's corner, a gray-haired woman sat behind an enormous grand piano, playing what sounded like a slow waltz.

I looked around, trying to orient myself, to figure out why I was there. And then I saw Whitney, third from the end. She was wearing a black sleeveless leotard and pink tights, her blond hair pulled back severely in a bun. The sunlight streaming in through the long, rectangular windows told me that it was daytime, but there were no clues to mark the season. No holiday decorations, I noted. No calendar on the wall.

I turned my attention back to Whitney, who looked markedly pale and thin as she slowly lifted one leg up toward her ear. I could sense her struggle, her jaw clenched tightly as sweat poured down the sides of her face. And then her standing leg buckled. She collapsed to the floor, the back of her head striking it with a sickening thud.

Chaos ensued as girls in leotards surrounded her, looking terrified. An older woman—the dance teacher, maybe—knelt by her side, checking her pulse. "Is she breathing?" someone asked.

"Yes, but it's shallow. Someone call 911!"

One girl nodded and ran toward the door.

"Does anyone know if she's eaten anything today?" the older woman asked.

"I . . . I don't think so," a tall, dark-haired girl answered. "She just had some coffee at lunch."

And then, just like that, I was back in the café. Tyler was standing beside me, a steadying hand on my shoulder. "Hey, that's one way to get my attention," he said. "You okay? I thought you were going to fall out of your chair."

I shook my head, trying to clear it. "Yeah, I'm . . . I just had vision, that's all."

"How bad?" Cece asked.

"Pretty bad," I muttered.

Cece stood up, pushing aside her empty mug. "Let's get you back to the dorm, then. You look really pale."

I started to protest, but decided against it. I really did feel queasy. Instead, I nodded, reaching for my bag as Tyler helped me to my feet.

"Who's walking back with us?" Cece asked, glancing around the table.

Every single one of my friends clambered to their feet, pushing aside plates and mugs and gathering their belongings. Suddenly, I didn't feel alone at all. I wasn't, and I never would be.

Not at Winterhaven.

"Want to try this one more time?" Matthew asked.

I nodded, wiping the sweat from my brow with the hem of my T-shirt. "Yeah, once more. Tyler, you okay?"

"Couldn't be better," he said, rising from the chapel's pew.

I had to admit he was being a good sport, allowing me to wale on him repeatedly as he played the role of vampire in today's training session. "You sure?" I asked, noticing that he was moving much more slowly now.

He raised his shirt, exposing the broad expanse of his chest—which now sported a faint purplish blue bruise over his heart. "Hey, I look hot in purple, right?"

"Sorry about that," I said with a wince. I wasn't using my stake—just my closed fist, and a little too much brute force by the looks of it. "I'll take it easy on you this time."

"Nah, you gotta stake 'em hard, remember?"

"I remember." Did I ever.

"Okay, back to our starting positions," Matthew ordered. He had precisely choreographed our every move, and it was Tyler's job to respond differently each time, changing up the variables. Of course, considering the fact that Matthew couldn't really throw his dagger into Tyler's eye any more than I could stake him, we just had to hope that our practiced movements would create the desired effect—namely, a destroyed vampire.

Once Matthew gave the signal, we went through the motions again—Tyler turned, ducked this time, and then wheeled around, coming up behind us. Matthew made a quick half turn on the balls of his feet, lifted one arm, and mimed throwing the baselard at its target. As soon as Tyler reacted, Matthew caught him in a headlock, holding him upright and immobilized while I executed the deathblow to his heart.

It was over in a matter of seconds, effectively illustrating that, in a real-life situation, there'd be no time to think, only to react. I would have to rely on my ability to breach a vampire's mind, to know his intentions—and then make a snap judgment.

Over the past several Saturdays, we'd pretty much come to an agreement on what would earn a vampire's death sentence. Any intent to kill or inflict serious harm—any malicious intent whatsoever—and they were toast, as was any vampire who posed a threat to us, both real or imagined. We couldn't afford to take any chances. But beyond that? It was going to be my call.

Matthew and I had also worked on devising a series of hand signals so that we could communicate nonverbally. It all seemed so surreal—I hoped we'd never have to put any of this training to use. But if we did, well . . . at least I was starting to feel prepared.

I glanced down at Tyler, who was lying on the ground clutching his chest. "Sorry about that. I tried to take it easy on you this time."

"Yeah, sure you did." He groaned as he dragged himself to a sitting position. "Oh, man. How did I let y'all talk me into this?"

I just shrugged and lowered myself to the ground beside him.

"Feel free to kiss it and make it better," he offered, smiling wickedly now. "You know, if it'll help ease your conscience and all."

I rolled my eyes. "In your dreams, Bennett. Are we done?" I asked Matthew.

"Yeah, that's it for today." He was already reaching for his jacket. "I've got to run to a dorm masters' meeting. I'll see you both later, okay?"

"Have fun," I called out, then collapsed onto my back, staring up at the chapel's ceiling.

Tyler flopped onto his back beside me. "Later, Dr. B."

Matthew's footsteps receded, and then the heavy door slammed shut.

"You should probably ice that," I said to Tyler. "You know, to keep the bruising down."

"Nah. I'll wear it as a badge of honor. If anyone asks me what happened, I'll just say that you got a little rough with me. Make 'em wonder."

I turned my head to glare at him, but he just grinned back at me. "You wouldn't dare," I said.

"You know me better than that, Vi. Course I would."

"You want to get Kate mad at me?"

"Aw, you don't have to worry about Kate. I'm pretty sure she's moved on to greener pastures. Of the ex-boyfriend kind."

"Speaking of that, what happened last weekend at the dance? With you and Kate, I mean. I thought you two were going together."

"Nah. She needs time to sort stuff out. You know how it goes."

"I guess," I said with a shrug.

"Anyway, Max's band was playing a set, so I helped them out with equipment and stuff."

"Oh, yeah? You're one of his roadies now?" I teased.

"Hey, I'm his best roadie. His *only* roadie." He reached for my ponytail and gave it tug. "How are you holding up? Seriously, I'm worried about you."

I sighed heavily. "I'm okay. I feel better since I talked to Whitney. Did I tell you that she's agreed to enter some sort of program?"

"An eating disorder thing?"

"Yeah. It's just an outpatient program, but it's better than nothing. I think she's taking it pretty seriously."

"It's a good thing you can tell her about your visions."

"Yeah. I think this one really freaked her out. I had to tell her, though. I'm glad I did."

For a moment, neither of us said anything.

"Just so you know," he said at last, "I actually miss the boyfriend."

"Yeah?" I asked, my voice catching in my throat.

"Yeah. Art history just isn't the same without him sitting there glowering at me, you know?"

I laughed, careful that it didn't turn into a sob. "Yeah, I know."

"Sophie tells me you got kind of a shock over the weekend."

I sat up sharply. "What did she tell you?"

"Just that, and nothing else, the secretive little wench." With a groan, he rose to a sitting position. "I assume it has something to do with that new ring I've seen you sporting?"

I glanced down at my finger, bare now. I kept the ring tucked safely away in my room during my training sessions, but otherwise I wore it everywhere I went. But I didn't want to talk about the ring—not now, and not with Tyler.

"He left me his house," I said instead. "And everything in it. It's all held in trust for me till my birthday next month."

Tyler's eyes widened with genuine surprise—meaning that Sophie hadn't spilled the beans. "Seriously? That's gotta be worth millions."

"Yeah," I said with a nod. "But what am I supposed to do with it? I mean, if he doesn't come back?"

He took a deep breath, looking as if he were carefully considering his words. "Byrne thinks he will."

"What do you mean?" I asked, my heart pounding furiously now.

"He's never come out and said it, not in so many words. But I can tell he thinks it. And he wants to have the cure ready for him when he does."

God, I hoped he was right. Was it possible that Matthew had seen something in a vision—something that he wasn't telling me about? But if that were true, why would he keep it from me?

Supposedly we shared some sort of psychic bond, which, for now, seemed limited to Matthew's visions. Maybe there was more to it, something still untapped. Maybe there was a way I could get inside his head. I vowed to work on it, to test it out.

"You ready to bust this joint?" Tyler asked, rising and reaching a hand down to help me up.

"I'm ready." I took his proffered hand and hopped to my feet.

He released me, readjusting his colorful string bracelets. "So . . . early movie tonight—whaddya say? I'll buy the popcorn and Coke."

I somehow had a feeling I was going to regret what I was about to say. "Sure, but I'm buying. I owe it to you after all the abuse you took today."

He raked a hand through his damp, shaggy hair, leaving it sticking up in all directions. "Did I ever tell you that I like a girl who can kick ass?"

"Yeah, like a million times. Now shut up and go take a shower."

"Deal. It's a date." With that, he turned and jogged toward the door.

"It's not a date, Tyler," I called out after him. "It's *not* a date. Seriously, I'm asking Sophie to come too!"

He paused briefly by the door, turning to smile innocently at me. "Hey, the more the merrier."

With that, he took off without me.

11 ~ Seeing Ghosts

"Okay, folks, don't forget we've got our field trip to MoMA on Friday." Dr. Andrulis was passing back our graded quizzes, his hands sheathed in tan gloves, as always. "We'll meet by the bus at ten a.m. sharp. Make sure you have all your teachers sign the slip so they'll know where you are. Nice job, Miss McKenna." He handed me a paper with a ninety-eight written in red and circled at the top.

"Thanks," I said, taking it with a smile.

Teacher's pet, Tyler mouthed beside me.

I stuck my tongue out at him. Truth be told, art history had quickly become my favorite class. It turns out I really enjoyed learning about art and artists, particularly the history behind the different movements. I was even considering majoring in art history now, especially if I managed to get accepted at the American University of Paris. And AUP was now my top-choice school, since I assumed that Aidan was in Paris somewhere. Maybe our telepathy would work better at close range.

It wouldn't be long before I found out if I got in or not—acceptance letters would start going out in mid-March, less than a month away. I made a mental note to check Aidan's mail at his town house at some point in April, before the decision deadline. If we both got in, I'd send in his acceptance along with my own. I wasn't giving up hope, not yet.

"Thanks for killing the curve," Tyler grumbled, holding up his paper with an eighty-six scrawled at the top.

"How'd you do?" I asked Joshua, who sat on my other side in what had been Aidan's seat.

"Ninety-two," he answered, looking pleased with himself.

We mimed a high five.

"This will be similar to the Met trip," Dr. Andrulis continued, back at the front of the classroom now. "You'll break up into groups of three or four, and each group will take a checklist of pieces I want you see. At the end of the visit, you'll narrow down your focus to two pieces—a painting, plus something from another medium—and prepare a full report on both, including information about the artist, materials, context, and history."

Dr. Andrulis kept talking, but I was distracted by a weird tickle in my brain. I sat up straight, shaking my head to clear away the cobwebs, but there it was again.

Please don't let me have a vision right now, I silently pleaded. I fidgeted in my seat, waiting for the telltale humming in my ears to begin, for the vertigo that followed.

Tyler prodded me with his pen. "Hey, you okay?" he whispered.

I just dropped my head into my hands, my elbows resting on my desk as I willed away the sensation.

"Dr. Andrulis!" Tyler called out beside me, his voice laced with alarm. "Something's wrong with Violet. I think she needs to go to the nurse."

No. No, I was fine, just—

Violet?

Oh my God. It was Aidan's voice, there in my head. Faint and muffled, but undoubtedly his. My heart began to race and I half rose from my seat.

"Aidan?" I didn't even realize I'd said it aloud until a half dozen heads swiveled in my direction, eyes wide with surprise. "I'm . . . uh, sorry," I mumbled, sitting back down again, my cheeks flushing hotly.

Aidan? I tried again, silently this time.

Here. That was it, a single syllable, nearly indistinguishable.

Just then, the phone on the wall behind Dr. Andrulis's desk rang shrilly, startling me so badly that I knocked my notebook to the floor.

While Dr. Andrulis took the call, Tyler slipped out of his seat, kneeling to retrieve my notebook. "What the hell's going on?" he asked me. "You look like you just saw a ghost."

Joshua leaned toward me. "Did you have a vision or something?"

I shook my head, sure now that I had imagined hearing Aidan's voice. I must have. Wishful thinking. Otherwise—

"Miss McKenna?" Dr. Andrulis had hung up the phone and was moving down the aisle toward me now. "You're wanted in the headmistress's office."

The headmistress's office? "Now?" I managed to croak.

"I'm afraid so," he said, his expression unreadable.

"She's not feeling well," Tyler said, laying a steady hand on my shoulder. "I think I should walk her over there."

Dr. Andrulis nodded, his brow knit with concern. "Yes, she does look rather pale. Go on. I'll give you a late pass for sixth period."

I gathered my things with shaking hands. Why the heck

was I being summoned, and more important, by whom? Dr. Ackerman? Or did this mean that Mrs. Girard was back? I had no clue what was going on, and I hated walking into a situation blindly.

I needed to talk to Matthew, I realized. He was probably right in the middle of teaching a class, but what choice did I have? Besides, I was pretty sure that he'd want me to check in with him before gallivanting off to face who knows what.

"You ready?" Tyler asked, reaching for my bag. He slung it over one shoulder with his own, a late pass clutched in his hand.

"We've got a stop to make first." I grabbed my coat and followed him out into the corridor.

"Dr. Byrne?" he asked as soon as the classroom door swung shut.

I nodded. "Yup."

"You going to tell me what's going on?"

"I would if I knew, Ty. I was just sitting there listening to Dr. Andrulis and . . . and then I felt a buzz in my head and I could have sworn I heard Aidan's voice. You know . . . there." I tapped one temple.

"Seriously?" He pushed open the door at the end of the hallway, and we stepped out into the courtyard, making our way around the fountain toward the science wing.

"Yeah, and that's right when the phone rang. I have no idea if the two are somehow related." Shivering now, I zipped up my fleece.

"Well, what did he say? In your head, I mean."

"Nothing much. Just my name and then . . . *here*."

"Here? Like, here at Winterhaven?"

"I have no idea, Tyler!" Was it possible? I didn't dare allow myself to hope.

I followed Tyler into the science wing and up the stairs toward Matthew's office. We passed it, and Tyler stopped two doors down, in front of a classroom. Through the pane of glass in the door, I could see Matthew standing at the front of the room wearing goggles, surrounded by equipment. I waved, trying to catch his eye, but it was no use.

"You stay here," Tyler said before opening the door and slipping inside.

I watched as he approached Matthew, pulling him aside and gesturing with his hands as he spoke to him. Matthew removed his goggles and said something to the class before following him out into the hallway.

"What's going on?" he asked, his brow creased with worry.

Quickly, I told him what had happened.

"I'm going with you," Matthew said, reaching for the door.

"Wait." I grabbed his sleeve. "You can't go with me. I mean, does Mrs. Girard know about the *Megvéd* stuff?"

He shook his head. "No, but she knows I'm your psychic coach."

"Well, that doesn't really explain why you'd abandon your class to come with me, does it?"

"She's right," Tyler said.

"I'm still coming. I'll stay outside the office, pretend that I'm there to talk to Ackerman or something."

"In the middle of fifth period?"

He glanced down at his watch. "The bell's in ten minutes, and I don't teach sixth period. Let me go dismiss my class, and you go to the dorm to get your stake. I'll meet you in the East Hall lounge."

"My stake?" My voice rose in alarm. "This might just be a coincidence, right? Maybe Dr. Ackerman just needs to talk to me about something. She *is* the senior adviser."

Matthew looked unmoved. "If that were the case, couldn't it wait till after sixth period, Violet? C'mon, what do your instincts tell you?"

I took a deep, calming breath. For a moment, I closed my eyes, still breathing deeply. I explored my senses, searching for anything out of the ordinary, any hint of something not right. And there it was, a slight tingling sensation on my right wrist. Almost like a vibration running from my wrist to my fingertips. I recognized the signs now, knew what the sensation meant.

Vampire.

With an audible gasp, I opened my eyes. "Yeah, something's up. I don't know who it is exactly, but there's a vampire back on campus."

Matthew tapped his left shoulder. "I've got my baselard."

Tyler looked confused. "Your *what*?"

"Just get her to the dorm, okay?" Matthew turned back toward the classroom door. "I'll meet you there in just a few minutes."

With a nod, Tyler reached for my arm.

"Let's get this straight," I said, shrugging off his touch. "I don't need you to *get* me anywhere. I can get myself there just fine, okay?"

He raised two hands in surrender. "Hey, I got it. Just trying to help out here."

I let out a frustrated breath. "I know you are. I'm sorry. I'm a little on edge right now."

"Yeah, no kidding. Look, I told Dr. Andrulis I was walking you there. He thinks you're sick or something. Let's not give him any reason to think otherwise."

"I know. You're right. But let's hurry, okay?" Because what if it *was* Aidan I was sensing and he was somehow back at Winterhaven? I fought the sudden urge to take off at a sprint, abandoning Tyler and Matthew and all of their careful caution.

I needed to get to the headmistress's office. *Now.*

"Oh, no, you don't," Tyler said. "I know exactly what you're thinking, but we're not doing it that way. We're doing just what Dr. Byrne said. First we're going to the dorm and getting your stake, and then we're meeting him in the lounge. If the boyfriend's really here at Winterhaven, there'll be plenty of time for the happy reunion later. Okay?"

"Okay." I nodded, swallowing hard as my mind latched on to the phrase "happy reunion."

Was this it, finally? After two months of frustration, of worry and heartbreak? My stomach did a nervous little flip, my heart fluttering wildly in my chest.

"Isn't that your stake hand?" Tyler asked, and I glanced down at my right hand, surprised to find that I had been standing there, flexing it.

As if I were gearing up for a fight.

I pushed aside the thought, refusing to examine it further. Instead, I reached for Tyler's hand, clasping it tightly in mine. I was glad for the contact, relieved that the pressure on my fingers was dulling the strange sensations as I tugged him along beside me. "Just don't let go of me, okay?"

"Whatever you say," he quipped, grinning his cocky grin as he glanced down at our joined hands.

"I'm serious, Tyler. Forget what I said earlier—I really need you right now."

He paused by the door that led out to the courtyard. "Hey, whatever happens in the headmistress's office"—he took a deep breath, his steady gaze meeting mine—"I'm here for you. I know I act like an asshole sometimes, but friendship means a lot to me. Friends are all I've got, you know?"

"I know," I whispered, tears stinging my eyes. Because I did—I was an orphan, after all, with no living blood relatives save my Gran. Rising up on tiptoe, I pressed a kiss to Tyler's cheek. "I really do. Now, c'mon, let's go."

12 ~ Royal Blood

For several seconds, I paused outside the office's medieval-looking door, gathering my courage to face whatever—and whomever—was on the other side of it.

Please, please let Aidan be there.

"You've got this," Tyler said softly, laying a hand on my shoulder.

I nodded and then glanced over at Matthew, who sat on one of the benches against the wall. He was trying to look disinterested, but not quite pulling it off. Maybe I just knew him too well—I recognized that, despite his casual pose, the hard set of his jaw and the shadowed look in his eyes meant that he was worried. *Really* worried. I could sense the waves of anxiety rolling off him as I reached down and patted my stake, which was strapped safely against the inside of my left calf, tucked into the new sheath Matthew had made for me.

Silently, Matthew tipped his head toward the door.

Okay. I took a deep breath and let it out slowly, wiping my damp palms on my jeans before rapping sharply on the door three times.

"Come in!" a feminine voice trilled out.

Mrs. Girard!

I was nearly hyperventilating when I pushed open the door and stepped inside, pulling up short at the sight of the person standing there beside Mrs. Girard. I froze, unable to move a single muscle. I blinked several times, sure that my eyes were playing tricks on me.

"Shut the door, *chérie*," Mrs. Girard said, smiling broadly.

I did as she asked, and then launched myself across the room—right into Aidan's arms.

Without a word, he gathered me into his embrace, his face buried in my hair. I could feel his entire body trembling as my tears dampened his shirt.

"It's really you," I managed to whisper, my windpipe so tight I could barely breathe.

His only response was a strangled, choking sound, and I realized then that he was reining in his own tears. My hair was damp with them now. He lowered his head, pressing his lips against my shoulder.

All I could hear was the sound of my own heart thumping noisily against his chest as we stood there silently, clutching at each other like we'd never let go. The room seemed to fall away, and I didn't care who was there watching us.

And then Mrs. Girard cleared her throat, breaking the spell. "I know this has come as a bit of a shock, Miss McKenna, but if you'll take a seat, I'll explain it all to you."

Aidan released me, his gaze never straying from mine as I blindly reached for the chair that Mrs. Girard indicated and lowered myself into it. It was only then that I got a good look at him, and my breath hitched.

He was pale. Thin. Gaunt. His eyes were faintly rimmed in red, and there were deep, purplish blue shadows beneath them, looking almost bruise-like against his fair skin. I'd never seen him look so frail, so haunted.

Just what had they done to him?

"Don't worry, *chérie*. His physical form will heal soon enough, and he'll be just as he was before."

I wondered if I'd somehow let the barrier around my mind slip, or if she'd simply read my expression. Whichever the case, I made sure my mind was safely guarded now.

Mrs. Girard moved around her desk and sat in the enormous leather chair facing me. It was only then that I noticed the tall, dark-haired man standing beside the fireplace, one hand resting on the mantel. He was enormous, broad and muscular, with slicked-back hair that fell to his shoulders and piercing, pale blue eyes.

Mrs. Girard noticed that I was staring and turned to gesture at the man. "I'm sorry. Wherever are my manners? Miss McKenna, this is Luc Mihailov, one of my closest associates."

So *this* was Luc—one of the two male Tribunal members who'd been turned by Vlad the Impaler. Aidan had called him a friend, but right now I was willing to bet that Luc was acting as Aidan's guard. He seemed somehow . . . menacing. I couldn't help but notice that my right hand tingled, itching for my stake, whenever I looked at him.

I considered breaching his mind, but decided against it. At least, not yet. I didn't sense an immediate threat.

I turned my attention back to Mrs. Girard. "Okay, so what's going on?" I asked her.

"It's time for me to lay my cards on the table," she said. "We need your help."

"My help?" I chanced a glance at Aidan, who sat slumped in his chair, staring at the floor with empty eyes. Fear settled in the pit of my stomach.

What the hell is going on?

Mrs. Girard nodded. "Yours and Aidan's. War has erupted, you see. Isa, the Eldest, has been destroyed, the Tribunal disbanded."

"Okay, you've got to back up," I said, shaking my head. "Who, exactly, is at war?"

She narrowed her eyes. "I thought Aidan had explained it to you. The factions."

"Only a little bit. I mean, I know about the Propagators." I shuddered at the memory of Julius and his little harem.

"Yes, and they make up the largest portion of the opposition, along with the Wampiri—they hunt from noon to midnight—and a few feral, ancient tribes. Let me put it this way—our kind can basically be divided into two groups. One believes that vampires are the higher race, superior beings to mere mortals. Ultimately, they'd like to grow their numbers to the point that they can subjugate humanity. Do you understand what I'm saying?"

A shiver raced down my spine. "Yeah, I think I get it."

"The others," she continued, "feel far more connected to our humanity. Our aim is to coexist with mortals, to remain cloaked by the screen of myth and legend. We fear that the discovery of our existence would lead to panic and panic to mass destruction of our kind. Up till now, the two sides have managed to agree to disagree. Some of the dissenters choose to live under Tribunal law and therefore are afforded our protection, and some choose not to."

"What's changed, then?"

"The Propagators' numbers have swelled recently, and they've launched several mass attacks on the populace in Eastern Europe. We've contained the situation, but just barely. The Tribunal decided to send out an army, which basically amounts to a declaration of war.

"But then there was a coup from within. While the battle for the Eldest rages among the ancients, the Propagators are taking full advantage of our state of disarray. Worse, we've learned that a traitor—a member of the Tribunal—has given valuable information to our enemy. Information about our greatest weapon." She paused, glancing over at Aidan, who sat now with his head cradled in his hands.

This had something to do with him, obviously. I couldn't help but remember the time I had breached her mind, right here in her office. She'd thought of Aidan as her "crown jewel."

"Go on," I prodded.

"There's a legend—a prophecy, if you will—that the Tribunal has carefully guarded for centuries. The legend speaks of a leader—the *Dauphin*, we call him in my native tongue—who is a male vampire of royal blood, turned before his eighteenth birthday.

"There are several elements to the legend, including the fact that the *Dauphin*'s maker cannot know of her victim's royal blood at the time of his making. You see, so that no one sets out to intentionally fulfill the prophecy."

The full effect of her words finally sank into my muddled brain. Aidan was the *Dauphin*. At least, she thought he was.

"Other parts of the legend specify the *Dauphin*'s exceptional abilities. One, he cannot be destroyed—not by a vampire. Two, he will possess the ability to command the *Sâbbat* and the *Krsnik*, giving him power over both breed of vampire slayer."

I must have looked surprised by this, because she smiled, arching an auburn brow. "Yes, there's another kind, *chérie*. Perhaps Luc can answer your questions about the *Krsnik* later. Luc is, after all, the most knowledgeable of our kind where slayer legend is concerned."

I remembered the ancient, dusty book tucked away in my dorm room. It had been Luc who'd given the book to Aidan, who'd translated the page about *Sâbbats* and the *Megvédio*. Did they know the truth about Matthew? Or did I still have one secret left to keep?

"Anyway"—she waved one hand—"there's much, much more, but I won't bore you with the details. The most important thing is that the *Dauphin*'s power usurps all others, even that of the Eldest. He will take control of the Tribunal, and all will bow to him. He can bring peace, you see. Safety to the human race. With the *Sâbbat* and the *Krsnik* under his control, he can ensure that those who refuse to follow the law will be summarily destroyed."

"And you think Aidan is the *Dauphin*," I said, stating the obvious.

She nodded. "There's no doubt in my mind that he is. It would appear that Blackwell figured it out before I did. He was a clever one, that Augustus Blackwell—clever and ambitious. I should have known that, with his vast knowledge of legend and lore, he might eventually stumble upon something, a hint of some sort.

"But it was Goran Petrović who ultimately betrayed us all, giving Blackwell the specific information he needed about the prophecy, information that no one save the Tribunal was privy to. The Propagators made him promises he couldn't refuse—he would eventually rule all, they bargained, both vampire and subjugated mortal alike. All he had to do was destroy the *Dauphin*. Or have *you* destroy him, Miss McKenna, since a vampire cannot."

I looked over at Aidan, waiting for him to speak, to say something about that awful day last spring. But he didn't—he just sat there, as silent and still as a statue. "Bu-but Blackwell sent Jenna in to save us," I stammered, completely unnerved by Aidan's haggard, haunted expression.

Mrs. Girard shrugged. "That I cannot explain. A last-minute change of heart, perhaps? I suppose we'll never know."

I digested that in silence.

"So, you must see my dilemma. We need a leader. We need someone to restore the peace, to end the war and ensure the safety of both mortals and vampires alike. I couldn't very well have Aidan cure himself, no matter how sympathetic I might be to that cause. I didn't mean for the tampered serum to affect him the way it did—those attacks were an entirely unexpected consequence. But once they were discovered . . . well, I couldn't tip my hand and show him preferential treatment. He had to be punished. The outbreak of war and ensuing chaos provided the necessary opportunity to release him, and so here we are."

My heart was thudding in my chest now, anger racing through my veins. I still couldn't believe she'd done that to Aidan—turned him into a killer. I struggled to rein it in, to keep my voice calm and controlled. "So . . . why do you need *my* help?"

"Simply to help me persuade Aidan to do what he was created to do—to assume the role of the *Dauphin* and take his rightful place by my side on the newly formed Tribunal."

I sucked in a sharp breath. "And if I don't?"

Her smile turned my blood to ice. "Well, then I suppose I'll just have to make you destroy him, won't I?"

13 ~ Dead Man Walking

Instinctively, I reached for my stake. I stopped myself just short of pulling it from its sheath.

"I assure you there's no need for that, Miss McKenna," Mrs. Girard said quickly, rising from her seat, both palms pressed against the desk. "We're all friends here, on the side of right."

Straightening, I glanced over at Luc, expecting him to look as if he were ready to pounce. Instead, his attention was focused on Aidan. For a moment, I studied Luc closely, prodding the invisible barrier that protected his mind. Immediately, I felt the wall crumble, the thoughts tumbling out.

He must agree. We need him too badly—he's our only hope.

Other thoughts, mostly jumbled, took over my consciousness. I barely had time to make heads or tails of them, but the message was clear. I could sense Luc's desperation, his panic. I had to press my fingers against my temples to break the connection, hoping that I looked as if I were massaging away a headache or something.

"I think you two need some time alone." Mrs. Girard walked briskly around her desk, stopping at Aidan's side. She laid a hand on his shoulder, her touch surprisingly gentle. "Is there somewhere you can go, *mon chou*? Somewhere you can talk without fear of interruption?"

He nodded, a muscle in his jaw flexing.

"But . . . but what about sixth period?" I stammered nonsensically.

Mrs. Girard returned to her desk and reached for the phone. "Fencing, correct?" When I nodded, she continued on. "I'll call Coach Gibson and let him know that you're excused. Luc, can you escort them?"

"Of course, madam," he answered. His voice was deep, heavily accented.

He strode over to Aidan and looped an arm under his right shoulder, offering himself as a crutch as Aidan struggled awkwardly to his feet. If not for Luc, I'm pretty sure Aidan would have collapsed to the floor.

Oh my God. My stomach plummeted. Whatever they'd done to him, it'd been bad. Really, really bad.

I hurried to Aidan's side, wrapping an arm around his waist. Together we moved toward the door, Luc and me supporting Aidan as he shuffled toward it.

"Where are we going?" Luc asked, and I looked to Aidan for the answer, realizing I had no idea.

My room, he answered inside my head.

"I'll show you," I said to Luc.

As soon as we stepped out into the hallway, Matthew's head snapped up, his eyes wide with surprise. "What the hell?" he whispered harshly as we passed. "Is he okay?"

"I have no idea," I answered without turning around. There was no way I could stop and explain what was going on, not with Mrs. Girard there on the other side of the door. He would just have to trust that I was safe, that I could take care of myself for the time being.

We set off at a lumbering pace. Luckily, it was still sixth period, so the halls were empty. I was moving on autopilot, trying to wrap my brain around everything I'd just learned—and wondering what exactly I was up against in convincing Aidan to go along with Mrs. Girard's plan.

"This way," I said, tipping my head toward the stairwell on our right. "Down the stairs and to the right."

In Aidan's absence, I had memorized the route to his underground room. It had taken me several tries to find it without him. But still, I found some comfort in retracing my steps there and back. Now I felt only fear.

As if sensing it, Luc turned toward me, meeting my gaze over Aidan's bowed head. "She's not likely to force you to destroy him," he said. "A bluff, I think. Despite what she says, I don't think she could bear it. She'll simply lock him back in the dungeon, hoping that he'll eventually change his mind."

I just nodded, swallowing hard. I hoped he was right, though it didn't matter, not really. As far as I was concerned, neither was acceptable.

We walked on in silence. Another flight of stairs and two turns later, we finally reached the nondescript door, locked tight.

"Can you . . . ?" I tilted my head toward the door.

"Of course," Luc said. There was an audible click, and the door swung open.

Moving in tandem, we led Aidan to the daybed against the wall and helped him to sit on the edge of the mattress.

"I'll be just outside," Luc said, hooking a thumb toward the hallway. "Take all the time you need."

And then he was gone. Even though I knew it was pointless, I turned the lock anyway.

"Violet," Aidan whispered, his voice a gravelly rasp. It was the first word he'd spoken aloud, I realized with a start.

"Oh my God, Aidan." I rushed back to his side and knelt on the ground before him. "What did they do to you?" I gathered his cold hands in mine as I peered up at him, trying not to wince at the sight of his red-rimmed eyes, his hollow, gaunt cheeks. "Have they . . . did you feed before you came here?"

He nodded, bowing his head and pressing his lips against my knuckles. "This isn't real—it can't be. It's an illusion, like all the others."

I slipped one hand from his grasp and reached up to run it through his hair. "It's real, Aidan. I'm here. See? And I'm not leaving—not till they drag me out."

He reached for my hand and drew it down against his cheek. We sat like that for several minutes, the room entirely silent but for the beating of our hearts. "It's really you," he said at last. "Not a trick."

I shook my head. "Nope, not a trick."

"Can you . . . will you just . . . hold me?"

I sat beside him, drawing him down till we lay side by side. "God, I've missed you," I said, breathing in his familiar scent as he wrapped one arm around me, my head resting on his shoulder now.

"I've thought of you every minute of every day," he answered. As we lay there, he combed his fingers through my hair, our hearts beating in perfect unison. Fifteen minutes passed. A half hour, maybe more. Eventually his fingers stilled in my hair, and I wondered if he'd fallen asleep. But then he shifted, drawing me closer.

I scooted down, moving my cheek to his chest. "Please tell me you're going to be okay."

"I'm not the same, Vi," he said, his voice catching. "I'll never be the same. Not after what I did."

"It wasn't your fault. You know that. You heard what Mrs. Girard said. It was Jack—she made him tamper with the serum. She threatened his brother," I added, hoping to lessen the sting of betrayal.

"That doesn't mean I didn't do it. That I'm not capable of doing it again."

I took a deep breath. "What did they do to you, Aidan? I felt . . . heat. Burning heat. And my shoulders—there was this awful, tearing pain. Like my skin was being ripped open."

Absently, I rubbed a hand over my shoulder, remembering the horrific sensations.

"You felt that?" he asked, his voice laced with incredulity. "But . . . how?"

"I don't know. It's like I somehow got inside your head. At least, I assume it was your head. And that I was feeling some of what you were feeling."

He closed his eyes, his chest rising and falling with a ragged breath. "I am so very sorry, Violet."

I rose up on one elbow, gazing down at him with a scowl. "Why are you apologizing to me? You're the one they were torturing. God, how could Mrs. Girard allow them to do that to you? When she knew what happened—knew it was *her* fault!"

"She never should have let me out."

"What are you talking about? You didn't deserve to be in there in the first place!"

"—and now to drag you into this, into her plot. It's unconscionable."

I sat up sharply. "You've got to snap out of this, Aidan. I mean it. You've got to get yourself together and do what she's asking. Become her *Dauphin*, or however the hell you say it. It's the only way she's going to let you go free. Besides, it sounds like it's the right thing to do."

"I'd rather be destroyed."

My face blanched. "How can you say that?"

"You don't realize what you're asking of me. To join them, to lead their war . . ." He shook his head. "It's not what I want, Violet. I'm done. Finished. I've made peace with that."

"Done? What do you mean, done? You've got a second chance now. *We've* got a second chance." Now that I had him back, there was no way I was letting him go, not like this.

"I've brought enough trouble into your life already, don't you think? Besides, what chance do *we* have if I agree to their plan? I won't have my cure. If I accept this role, it's a lifetime sentence. In my case, that's an eternity. I can't be destroyed, remember? Except by you."

"I'm not destroying you."

"We're at a stalemate, then, aren't we?"

"If you just do what they're asking, you'll stay alive. Don't you get that?" My voice rose a pitch, my breath coming faster now. "Whatever the cost, it's worth it."

"Not to me. Don't *you* get that? I'd come so close—so very close—to finding the cure. To having it all, everything I'd ever hoped and dreamed and wished for. The darkness lifted. My humanity restored. And you, Violet." He brushed the back of one hand down the side of my face, eliciting a shiver that racked my entire body.

"Especially you," he continued. "It was within my grasp, and now it's gone, all of it. I can't go back, not now. Don't you see? All I had, all I lived for, was that hope. And now—now I have nothing. Nothing to live for, to hope for. Would you really wish that existence on me?"

The pain in his voice ripped my heart in two, and yet . . . call me selfish, but yes. Yes, I'd wish that on him. I couldn't bear the thought of the alternative.

"There's got to be some other way," I said in desperation. "We just . . . go along with it for now. Do whatever they need you to do to win the war and secure peace, and then we can renegotiate."

"The Vampire Tribunal doesn't negotiate, Vi. Surely you must know that by now."

"Bu-but you'll be their leader," I stammered. "They'll have to do whatever you say."

"My guess is that I'll be their leader in the same fashion that the Eldest is now—in name only. A puppet, nothing more. You heard what Mrs. Girard said—she wants me to take my place *by her side*. By putting me there, *she* becomes the most powerful vampire alive, not me."

I digested that in silence. He was probably right, I realized. It made sense, especially with what I knew about female vampires.

They were far more powerful, more aggressive than males. Still, it was our only hope. And I wasn't ready to give up, even if he was.

"I'm not letting you go back to that prison, Aidan. They can't destroy you—she said so herself. So you just leave. You go."

His lips curved with the trace of a smile. "Go where?"

"I don't know," I said with a shrug. "Somewhere. Anywhere. I'll go with you."

He let out a heavy sigh. "They'll find us, Violet. They'll hunt us down, to the far corners of the earth. It's no use."

"How do you know they will?"

"Because they think they need me. Nicole can't access the kind of absolute power she wants without me. They're not going to give up, not without a fight."

"But if they can't destroy you—"

"Even if they can't, they can overpower me, hold me captive. They can do whatever else the hell they want to me. Trust me, *Dauphin* or no, they had the best of me these past two months. Look at me—I'm weak. I'm young and inexperienced, as far as vampires go. They think I'm some mythical creature, a prophesized savior. Well, you know what *I* think? I think they're wrong. I can't save anyone, least of all myself. I'm just a dead man walking."

14 ~ Metamorphosis

Aidan struggled to sit up, wincing as he did so. He looked entirely drained after that last outburst.

I offered a hand, tugging him forward as I pushed the bed's single pillow behind his back. "You okay?"

"Just . . . exhausted."

I gave his hand a squeeze. "I am *not* letting you go, Aidan. Seriously. We've got to figure something out. We can talk to Matthew, see if he has any ideas."

"Matthew? Oh, right. Dr. Byrne. How is that . . . relationship . . . working out?"

"It's good. He's been like a brother to me—an overprotective big brother. And he's been working on your cure. Actually Matthew, Tyler, and Sophie are all working on it together."

"Tyler? Now, that's a surprise. I thought your little friend was the one who was ready to hand me over to the authorities from the get-go. I should think he'd be gloating."

"Nope. Believe it or not, he's going to be glad that you're back. Crazy, right?"

He dropped his gaze, refusing to meet my eyes.

"Don't," I said, shaking my head. "I'm serious. You're not going anywhere." I tightened my grip on his hand for emphasis.

"I like that you're wearing my ring," he said, changing the subject. "My grandmother's ring. It looks perfect there, doesn't it?" He lifted my hand, turning it so he could examine it from all angles. "I noticed it the moment you stepped into Mrs. Girard's office, you know."

"I can't keep it. Any of it, now that you're back."

"Of course you can. All the paperwork is in order. I assume you found it all?"

I just nodded.

"And the flowers? I left *very* specific instructions."

"The flowers were there." I could still remember their sweet, citrusy scent. "If you were trying to break my heart, you did an excellent job. Just so you know."

"I never, ever meant to hurt you." The pain, the undisguised despair in his eyes nearly stole away my breath.

I wanted to erase that pain. To heal his broken body, his broken spirit. Leaning in to him, I pressed my lips tenderly against his forehead. His eyes fluttered shut, a low moan escaping his lips as I feathered a kiss over one eyelid, then the other. His arms stole around me, drawing me against him till there was no space between our bodies.

"I can't believe you're here," I murmured, my lips trailing lower, toward the corner of his mouth before moving on to his jaw, his chin. "You're really and truly here."

One of my hands slid under his shirt, across the hard planes of his chest, while the other tangled in the hair at the nape of his neck, as silky and soft as ever.

"Dear God, Violet," he said, his voice a hoarse whisper.

"Dear God, Violet, what? Keep going?" I paused, my mouth hovering just above his parted lips. "Or dear God, Violet, stop now before you kill me?"

In response, his head bent toward me, his lips brushing softly against mine. I froze, temporarily paralyzed now, terrified that if I opened my eyes I'd find myself alone, awakened from a hazy dream. He'd be gone, a figment of my overactive imagination.

Please be real, I silently pleaded. *Please.*

When his lips found mine again, they were more persistent—less tentative, more demanding. I let out a whimper, overcome with a sudden sense of familiarity. His taste, his scent—the memories flooded back, overwhelming me. It seemed like both a lifetime ago and just yesterday that he'd last held me in his arms. An eternity and a split second, all at once.

Desire exploded inside me. Somehow, I ended up straddling him, my knees on either side of his waist as I kissed him back with a hunger I hadn't even known I'd possessed. There was a fire in my belly now, urgent and hot. I was not letting him go. I was *never* letting him go.

His hands were fisted into the bed's covers now, the air between us electric. Every moan, every shift of his body beneath mine made the fire inside me burn brighter, hotter. We kissed until we were breathless, and then I dragged my mouth away.

Our gazes met, his eyes as glassy and unfocused as mine, but still rimmed in red. Dangerously red, I realized. Still, the heat in his stare made it impossible for me to stop, to move off him and seek safety before things went too far. Instead, I slid lower, pressing my lips against the side of his neck, down to his collarbone. Pushing aside the soft cotton of his T-shirt, my mouth trailed lower.

Aidan made a sound deep in his throat and then released his death grip on the covers to grab the hem of his shirt and tug it over his head. I leaned back, my hands resting on the spot where the waistband of his jeans met his bare skin, just below the jutting curve of his hipbones. My breath hitched in my chest, my fingers itching to slip under that waistband, to brush across his silky skin. He wanted it, too—the evidence was pretty hard to ignore. He wouldn't stop me, not now, no matter how far I decided to push it.

And it was *my* decision; that was clear. He was leaving it up to me, patiently waiting while I worked it out in my head.

Oh, man. This was just *so* dangerous, in so many ways. But . . . maybe just a little . . . *more*. The word reverberated around my head, tempting me. *More*. I would stop when the fangs came out, I resolved. Yes, I could do that. That made sense, would keep things safe.

At least, as safe as I could be from a vampire who'd clearly been tortured and starved, who hadn't had access to his elixir since mid-December, who was looking at me now with a burning hunger for who knows what.

I took a deep, gulping breath and tugged off my own shirt.

At first his face registered shock, then appreciation. I could feel the weight of his gaze sweep over me, his eyes seeming to darken a hue. With a sigh, I slid down his body, fitting myself against him. The sensation of skin against skin—mine flushed hot, his cold—

made butterflies flutter wildly in my stomach. Somehow, we were kissing again, hot, hungry kisses. When I pulled away this time, we were both gasping for air.

Struggling to catch my breath, I laid my cheek against the taut muscles of his chest. For several minutes we just lay there in silence, my hands idly exploring every curve of his stomach, his shoulders. I listened to the raucous *thump, thump* of his heart as it pumped the infected, vampire blood throughout his body. His *royal* vampire blood.

At the reminder of our predicament, hot tears gathered at the corners of my eyes, threatening to spill over. "Please stay, Aidan. *Please*," I begged, the tears slipping from my eyes and dampening his chest now. "Let's just agree to Mrs. Girard's plan for now. Give her what she wants. You know it's the right thing to do. And then we'll . . . I don't know, figure out the rest later."

The cure. Matthew and the rest of them could keep working on it in secret. Mrs. Girard had only said that *Aidan* couldn't—she had no idea that her most scientifically gifted faculty member had taken up the project's reins. She had no idea why he'd want to. I was having a hard enough time understanding it myself.

For me. The thought popped into my head just like that. Matthew was doing it for me, because it's what I wanted most of all. Because he'd do *anything* for me. He'd said so himself. And that just made me cry harder.

"Shhh," Aidan said, his hands stroking my hair. Despite his weakened physical state, his hands were strong and firm. Comforting. "It's going to be okay, I promise you, Vi."

"Then promise you'll stay," I said, choking on the words.

He reached for my chin, tipping it up, forcing my gaze to meet his tortured one. "Do you really think I could leave you now? After today?" He shook his head determinedly, his jaw set in a hard line. "Never again."

But no matter what he said—and how convincing he sounded—I knew it was ripping him up inside. I was sure that, without me factoring into the equation, he'd simply disappear. Off the grid, away from everyone who cared about him. Hunted by his enemies forever.

But I couldn't let him live like that. I wouldn't. Maybe that made me selfish, but I would *not* extinguish that tiny flame of hope that still burned inside me. I glanced down at the delicate ring on my finger—*his* ring—knowing that it could never be enough. Just memories and tokens and photographs . . .

I wanted more. I wanted him—all of him.

Somehow, we could solve this. Mrs. Girard could have her *Dauphin*, and eventually Aidan could have his cure. Right now, he wasn't in any shape to deal with it, to take action or make decisions. I was the strong one now. It was up to *me* to figure it out, to make it happen. And if I had to move heaven and earth, to slay a thousand vicious vampires—hell, if I had to personally take out Mrs. Girard herself—I would.

There was not a doubt in my mind that I would.

15 ~ Wheeling and Dealing

The deal was struck. For now, Aidan was staying at Winterhaven. Obviously Mrs. Girard needed him badly—or at least she thought she did—because she was willing to give in to pretty much all of our demands.

She wasn't quite ready to use him yet, to reveal that she had the *Dauphin*, so he would remain hidden away at Winterhaven, under Luc's protection, until needed. Until after graduation, if at all possible. He was allowed his elixir but forbidden to work on his cure. He could travel with me to Atlanta for spring break, but only with Luc accompanying us.

That particular concession was hard won, but I was unyielding. There was no way of knowing what the future would hold, but I wanted these next few months to be as normal as possible. Maybe "normal" would help bring him back. It was worth a shot. Besides, I needed to see my Gran, and I couldn't leave Aidan, not when I'd just gotten him back.

I'd seen him safely to the infirmary—he was in Nurse Campbell's capable hands now. After dinner, I'd return to check on him, but right now I needed to find Matthew and tell him what was going on. I hoped he was in his office; otherwise, I'd have to go back to my dorm room and get my cell to track him down.

I was just reaching up to knock on his door when it swung open, nearly knocking me off my feet. "Thank God!" Matthew said, looking strangely pale. Reaching for my elbow, he dragged me inside, kicking shut the door as he did so. "I've been going crazy here. What's going on?"

I filled him in as best I could. When I finished, Matthew raked one visibly trembling hand through his hair. "That's completely insane" was all he said.

I nodded, my stomach in knots. "Yeah, tell me about it."

"Okay, tell me again exactly what you agreed to. You personally, I mean."

"Honestly, I'm not exactly sure. Just that I'd somehow help their cause. You know, as a *Sâbbat*."

"She knew that you'd agree to just about anything to gain his release." He drummed his fingers on his desk. "But Aidan . . . honestly, I'm surprised that *he* agreed."

I dropped my gaze to the floor, my cheeks flaming hotly as I remembered exactly what had preceded Aidan's acquiescence. The kissing. The touching. The lack of clothing . . .

"Ah, I see." Matthew sighed resignedly. "Of course."

"It wasn't like that," I said, feeling defensive now. "I wasn't . . . It's not like . . ." I shook my head, unable to find the words to explain myself. "I wasn't manipulating him, if that's what you're thinking," I managed at last.

"I'm sure you wouldn't. At least, not intentionally."

"Okay, can we drop this? Does it really matter, anyway?"

"I guess not. So . . . we're going to Atlanta for spring break, huh? I wish you'd given me a little more notice."

"What do you mean?"

"You don't honestly think I'm letting you go alone, do you? Even with Aidan. Who, I might add, doesn't exactly look like he's in any condition to travel."

"He'll be okay by then. I hope," I added. "But you can't be serious. About coming, I mean. What am I supposed to tell my family?"

He shrugged. "Just that it's a total coincidence that I'm there—

that I have family in Atlanta too. I'll get a hotel room nearby. Aidan can stay with me." He watched me closely, gauging my reaction. "You weren't really planning on having Aidan stay at your grandmother's, were you? What with everything you've told me about Lupe?"

He had a point there. I could totally imagine Lupe barring the front door, wielding garlic and a crucifix. "I hadn't really thought about it, but you're right. It's a good idea, the two of you staying together." At least, I hoped it was.

Matthew glanced down at his watch. "It's time for dinner. You going?"

"Yeah, I need to get back. Everyone's going to be wondering what happened to me." Especially Tyler.

"Okay." He nodded. "I think I'll go check on Aidan now, before I head down to the dining hall."

"Thanks, I'd appreciate that. Tell him I'll be back after dinner, okay?"

"Sure, no problem." Just then his cell began to ring, Charlie's name flashing across the screen until he hit the decline call button.

I couldn't help but wonder what he was going to tell *her* about spring break. Not that it was any of my business. Still, I was curious.

"I'll see you later," I said, making my way to the door.

When I let myself out, he was staring at his silent cell, an entirely unreadable look on his face.

I figured the noisy dining hall was as good a place as any to tell them. I kept my voice low as I recounted what had happened—again, sans mention of the intense make-out session.

"So, what are you supposed to do?" Joshua asked. "For now, I mean?"

"Nothing—just wait. Hopefully they won't need him till after graduation. There are pieces of her plan that have to fall into place first, I guess." I shrugged. "She really didn't go into specifics."

"When can we see him?" Sophie asked.

Cece nodded. "Yeah, is he up for visitors?"

"Let's all go together, as soon as we're done eating," I offered, pushing aside my tray of mostly uneaten lasagna.

Tyler raised one brow. "Even me?"

"Even you. I told him you were helping with the cure. Consider yourself redeemed."

"Well, thank God for that. Wouldn't want the boyfriend mad at me."

Sophie rolled her eyes. "You are such a dork, Tyler."

I turned and glanced over one shoulder, toward the cluster of tables where Jack and the football team usually ate. "Hey, where's Kate?"

"No idea," Sophie answered. "I think she's off somewhere with Jack. She didn't come back to the room after sixth period."

I glanced over at Tyler, watching for a reaction. Nothing.

"I still can't believe she and Jack are back together," Cece said, shaking her head. "I mean, after what he did?"

Marissa tossed her long, dark hair over one shoulder. "Well, they have a history together. You know how that goes."

It was so weird to hear Marissa defending their relationship. Just last year, she could barely contain her disapproval. It was a complete about-face on her part. I wondered if Max had something to do with it, if he'd somehow softened her hard edges. Likely so, I reasoned, watching as they rose together and took their trays to the trash. They moved in perfect sync, like two halves of a whole.

Cece pushed aside her tray. "Well, I'm ready to go see Aidan whenever you guys are."

Sophie nodded. "Me too."

"Yeah, let's bust this joint," Tyler said, rising.

Everyone was standing, looking eager. I joined them, grinning now. "Let's go, then."

Ten minutes later, everyone paused in the infirmary's antiseptic-smelling hallway while I slipped into Aidan's tiny room.

"Hey," he said, his eyes lighting up as he set aside a thick, leather-bound book.

My gaze skimmed over him, my heart soaring at the sight. He was wearing a gray T-shirt and a pair of plaid pajama pants—I had no idea where they'd come from, but he looked comfortable. In fact, he looked healthier already, more vital. Whatever Nurse Campbell had done for him, it was clearly working. Bless that woman.

"Hey," I said, smiling giddily now. "You've got some guests out there"—I tipped my head toward the door—"if you're up for it."

His mouth curved into an easy smile. "Sure. Of course."

With a nod, I reached for the door and threw it open. "Come on in, everyone."

I leaned back against the wall, watching happily as they streamed in—Sophie and Cece, Marissa and Max, Joshua and Tyler. Sophie reached his bedside first, wrapping her arms around him in a big hug. Cece followed suit, wiping tears from her eyes.

"Hey, man." Joshua executed a one-armed hug/fist bump combo. "Good to see you."

"Well, if it isn't the boyfriend," Tyler drawled, winking in my direction as he approached the narrow bed.

"Aw, Vi, you brought your little friend," Aidan shot back with a grin.

Next thing I knew, the two of them were doing that same little half hug, fist bump thing.

"Good to see you in one piece, man," Tyler said, sounding—was it possible?—a little choked up. "Though just barely. Shit, what'd they do to you?"

I couldn't stop the shudder that snaked down my spine, remembering those shared sensations.

"This is nothing," Aidan answered with a shrug. "You should have seen me last night."

I was suddenly glad I hadn't.

Joshua pulled up a chair beside the bed and sat, pulling Cece into his lap. "You think you'll be back in class soon?" he asked. "We've got an art history field trip on Friday—MoMA this time. Won't be the same without you."

Aidan nodded. "I'll be there. Hmm, it appears that I've missed some interesting developments," he said, raising one brow quizzically as Joshua absently stroked Cece's shoulder. "Anything else I should know about?"

There was a knock on the door, and everyone turned to look as Kate stuck her head inside. "Hey! Okay if we come in?"

We?

"I texted her where we were," Sophie whispered. "Hope that's okay."

"Of course," Aidan called out.

I could only stare in shocked silence as Kate walked in, a sheepish-looking Jack trailing behind her.

Tyler was on his feet in an instant, his face a mask of fury. "You've got a lot of nerve coming here, asshole," he said, stepping directly into Jack's path.

"It's okay," Aidan said sharply. "Violet told me why he did it. He didn't have a choice."

Tyler didn't back down. "You sure? Because I'd really like to kick his sorry ass."

Aidan closed his eyes and took a deep, shuddering breath, looking as if he were suddenly in pain. "Yeah, I'm sure," he said at last.

I hurried over to his side, perching on the bed beside him. I ran my hand over his forehead, not quite sure what I was feeling for. "You okay?"

He nodded. "I'm . . . fine. Just tired."

Cece rose off Joshua's lap. "Yeah, we should go and let you get some rest. I'm so happy to see you, though. You gave us all *such* a scare." Still clutching Josh's hand, she leaned down and kissed Aidan on the forehead. "Get better, okay?"

"I'll try my best," he said with a smile that looked forced.

I wasn't sure what was going on—didn't understand vampire physiology enough to know exactly how they'd damaged him—but he obviously wasn't well. At least, not as well as he'd like us to believe.

I remained there by his side, clutching his cold hand in mine while everyone said their good-byes. The feeling that we were family, my Winterhaven friends and me, comforted me. The deeply rooted friendship, the camaraderie there in the room was palpable. I couldn't help but wonder what was going to happen to us all when we went off to college, scattered about the globe. I couldn't think about it, not now. Not when we were finally back together again, all of us.

Finally, only Jack and Kate remained in the tiny, cramped space. I kept my gaze down, locked on Aidan's and my intertwined fingers. I couldn't look at Jack—didn't want to remember how he'd betrayed us all.

"I was hoping I could talk to you," Jack directed at Aidan. "I have . . . I mean, there's something I'd like to say to you. Alone."

Aidan shook his head. "It's not necessary. Trust me. I understand."

"It *is* necessary," Jack argued.

I rose, fiddling with the bedcovers. Clearly, Jack needed to say his piece. "I'll be just outside, okay?"

"I'll go with you," Kate said, then turned toward Aidan, patting his shoulder awkwardly. "It's really great to see you, Aidan. I'm glad you're back."

"Thanks," he murmured.

With one last glance back in his direction, I followed Kate out, leaving Jack to his apology. Perhaps then we'd all be right again. The Winterhaven Warriors—plus two, if you added in Tyler and Max—back together at last.

I only hoped that this time we wouldn't be called to a fight.

16 ~ Girl in the Mirror

"What about this one?" I stood in front of a colorful painting, tipping my head to one side as I considered it.

Aidan stepped up behind me, laying a hand on my shoulder. "You like this one?"

I nodded. I couldn't explain it, not exactly, but something about the image—a girl gazing into a mirror—captured my interest. Her weird, disjointed reflection was discordant with her equally odd figure. Still, I got it. I often felt that way myself. "Yeah, I do. What about y'all? And don't make fun of me," I added, seeing Joshua's mouth widen into a grin. For some unknown reason, he loved to tease me about my Southern accent. "Y'all is a very useful word, you know."

"Amen to that," Tyler said. "Yeah, this one's as good as any. Picasso, right?"

"Wow, you *have* learned something in class," I teased. "Go figure."

"Okay, I'm writing it down." Joshua took out the checklist Dr. Andrulis had given us when we'd gotten off the bus. "What's the title?"

Tyler stepped up to the card bearing the painting's information. "*Girl Before a Mirror*. From 1932."

"Ah, a fine year," Aidan said.

Both Joshua and Tyler turned to face him, looking puzzled.

"What? Young men's fashions were quite enjoyable then," Aidan deadpanned. "Way better than the 1950s, trust me."

I just shook my head, amazed as always at the reminder of Aidan's extraordinarily long youth.

"Dude, you are *so* freaking weird," Tyler said.

"Haters gonna hate," I said under my breath.

"I heard that." Tyler's eyes danced mischievously.

Joshua tapped the paper he was holding with his pen. "Okay, so that's our painting. Now we have to pick our second project. Want to try the sculpture garden? Or check out some photographs?"

"You think they've got a naked picture of Violet's twin at this museum, too?" Tyler asked with a leer.

"Yeah, what was the deal with that?" Joshua asked.

I just stared at him, caught completely off guard. Truthfully, I hadn't given Isabel a thought in months. I'd been way too terrified about the future to dwell on the past.

"What?" Joshua asked with a shrug. "I figured it was okay to ask now that Tyler knows the truth. I mean, that *was* Aidan in the photograph, wasn't it? At the Met?"

Beside me, Aidan reached for my hand. He looked suddenly pale, his eyes hollow.

"Hey, you okay?" I asked, giving his hand a squeeze. When he didn't reply, I squeezed harder. "Aidan? What's going on?"

"She didn't deserve it, what they did to her," he said, his voice barely above a whisper. His eyes had a distant, faraway look. "All because of me. And now . . . I've put you in danger too."

"Shh. I'm not . . . It's fine. C'mon, do you need to get some air?" I was flustered, surprised that he'd gone from his usual self—laughing and making jokes—to this shell of himself in such a short time.

"Yeah, you look like shit," Tyler said. "Maybe you just need something to eat." He must have immediately realized his error, because he visibly recoiled as soon as the words were out of his mouth. "Oh yeah. Right. Never mind."

"Guys, do you mind going on and picking out our second piece? I'm going to take him outside for a few minutes."

Joshua nodded. "Sure, no problem. Text me when you're back inside, and we'll meet up. Take your time, okay?"

I let out a sigh. "Thanks." Aidan didn't say a word as I led him outside into the bracing March chill. I found a stone bench, and we sat in silence for several minutes.

"You've got to tell me what's going on, Aidan," I said at last, unable to bear it for another moment. "Seriously. I'll just breach your mind if you don't. You're starting to scare me."

When his eyes met mine, they were slightly unfocused. His jaw was clenched, a muscle working furiously. *What the hell?*

"This is madness," he said, shaking his head. "I shouldn't be here. I should never have allowed you to agree—"

"You don't get to make those decisions for me," I snapped. "Okay? I *need* you here. Don't you get that?"

He was wringing his hands now. "You don't need me. Isabel certainly didn't need me. Neither of you deserved the fate to which I've sentenced you."

I reached for his hands, stilling them. "Look, I'm not some helpless little opera dancer, okay? Forget about Isabel—that was a hundred years ago. I'm here now, and I can take care of myself."

He closed his eyes, looking defeated. "You wouldn't be in any danger if it weren't for me."

I let out an exasperated huff. "I'm a *Sâbbat*, remember? Which means I'm going to be in danger pretty much my entire life, whether you're here or not. So what's your point?"

"And as a *Sâbbat*, you belong with your *Megvéd*. Not me. Never me. He can protect you in ways that I cannot."

"I *am* with my *Megvéd*. We've been training, you know. We're prepared to face whatever's coming our way."

He shook his head. "You have no idea what you're going to be up against."

"And you do?"

"They killed her, Violet." His voice broke on my name. "And there was nothing I could do, no way I could save her."

"But that's not going to happen to *me*. Okay? You've got to believe that."

I was that girl gazing into the mirror, I realized with a start. When Aidan looked at me, he saw Isabel—or, at least, someone who reminded him of his long-lost love. But the reflection that *I* saw staring back at me was someone entirely different. Stronger. More powerful.

Would Aidan ever see that girl?

"C'mon, you've got to give me some credit here," I said, taking his hand and laying his palm against my cheek. "Have some faith in me. In Matthew."

He sucked in a breath and let it out slowly. "I can't . . . This is ripping me apart. I shouldn't be here."

"This is exactly where you should be, Aidan. Here, with me."

Several seconds passed in silence, Aidan's ragged breaths beginning to slow.

Finally, he nodded. "You're right."

I turned my face into his palm and kissed it. "Thank you," I murmured. "You know, you probably shouldn't have come on this trip. You should still be in the infirmary, resting."

The light was back in his eyes now. "And send you off alone with Joshua and Tyler? Not a chance."

I leveled a stare at him. "Seriously? In case you didn't notice, Joshua and Cece have a thing going now."

"Oh, I noticed."

"And Tyler . . ." How could I explain Tyler?

"Yes?" he prodded. "Go on."

"Well, you know how he is. All talk. And you know what? He's been a good friend to me these past couple of months."

"I'm sure he has been."

I shook my head. "Not like that. He needs us, Aidan. I'd really like you to get to know him better. He *is* working on your cure."

"Indeed he is. I can't for the life of me figure out his ulterior motive. I'm certain he has one, though."

I decided to ignore that. "Are you ready to go back in?" I asked instead. "In case you didn't notice, I'm freezing my butt off out here."

He rose, offering me a hand. "God, Violet, I'm so sorry."

"It's okay." I stood, wrapping my arms around him. "Warm me up?"

"Always," he said, lowering his lips to mine.

"I heard Aidan went back to class yesterday," Matthew said, leaning against his desk. "How'd that go?"

Early for our usual Saturday-morning coaching session, I slumped into the chair across from him. "It was too soon. We took a field trip to MoMA, and I think it was too much for him. I mean, he mostly seems fine. But then someone will say something that just . . . I don't know . . . affects him weirdly. It's almost like PTSD or something. He gets this distant look in his eyes, and then he just withdraws. And when I try to drag him back . . ." I trailed off, shaking my head. "He's suddenly all broody and depressed. You know, like I'm going to die and it's all his fault. That kind of stuff."

"Well, there's no telling what they did to him. You've got to expect that he'll be somehow damaged. For a while, at least."

I reached up to rub my temples, fighting off a headache. "Yeah, I know. It's just that we don't have that much time. Together," I clarified. "You know, before they send him off to do his *Dauphin* thing, or whatever."

"Well, spring break starts next week. Maybe the time away will do him some good."

"I hope so," I said on a sigh. Truthfully, I was worried about the trip now. Worried that seeing Whitney would somehow set him back, sending him into a spiraling depression; that Lupe would react badly to his presence; that Aidan and Matthew staying together was a really, really bad idea. There were at least a half dozen things I was worried about, and yet I was excited, too. Talk about crazy.

"You look a little pale," Matthew said, pushing off his desk and circling around to his chair. "Headache?"

"Yeah. I took something when I got up, but it isn't helping much."

"We don't have to do any training today," he offered.

"Thanks. I'm feeling a little run-down."

His dark eyes flooded with concern. "Yeah? Have you seen the nurse? Maybe she can give you some vitamins or something."

I fought back a smile. "I don't think vitamins are going to help. But thanks. For the suggestion, I mean."

He folded his arms across his chest. "Are you up for trying something new today?"

"Depends." I sat up straight, eyeing him curiously. "What did you have in mind?"

"Just testing out our psychic connection. Your birthday's coming up, after all."

"Nine more days," I said with a nod.

"So maybe the bond is strengthening? For starters, I can feel your headache."

"You can?"

"Yeah, I can. Right here"—he rubbed the same spot on his temples that I'd been rubbing just a few minutes ago—"but worse on the left side. Kind of a pulsing throb."

He was right. Gooseflesh rose on my skin. "Okay, that's weird."

"Right? And I think I'm more in tune with your emotional state, too. Take yesterday, for example. I'm standing there teaching a class, and suddenly for no reason, I feel . . . frustration. For no reason whatsoever."

"What time? Do you remember?"

"It was the beginning of fourth period. Maybe one-ish?" One fifteen?"

"I was at MoMA then, sitting outside with Aidan. Frustrated that he was all doom and gloom, when fifteen minutes earlier he'd been laughing and joking."

"Well, I guess that explains it. It was fleeting, though."

"Yeah, I got over it pretty fast." We'd stood there in the cold kissing for a good ten minutes before we'd gone back inside and found our group. I hoped Matthew hadn't felt *that*.

"So it seems pretty one-sided, doesn't it? I'm seeing your visions, feeling your pain, and experiencing some of your emotions. But on your end . . . nothing?"

I closed my eyes, searching my instincts, looking for something—a feeling, a sensation—that wasn't entirely mine. I came up blank. "Not that I've noticed. But I don't know. I've been a little preoccupied lately. Maybe I'm just missing it?"

"Well, we can test it. You turn around and close your eyes, okay? Tell me if you feel anything."

With a nod, I started to turn my chair around before stopping and turning back to face him. "Wait, what are you going to do?"

"If I told you, it would defeat the purpose of the exercise."

"Yeah, right. Just . . . you know, don't do anything crazy, okay?" I was feeling suddenly unsettled.

"Hey, you've got to trust me, remember? Besides, do I look like I'd do something crazy?"

Before I had a chance to respond, my vision began to tunnel. I gripped the chair beneath me as the room fell away, Matthew's voice drowned out by the deafening buzz in my ears. Oh no . . .

I was outside, in the woods—a small clearing in the woods. I was disoriented, unsure if I was there at Winterhaven, down by the river, or somewhere else entirely. The sun was just beginning to set between the treetops, cutting wide orange swaths between the shadows.

"Someone call 911!" a voice shouted. "C'mon, we're losing him!"

It was Matthew shouting, I realized. I took several steps forward and glanced down, saw my friends surrounding a prone form on the ground. Cece was leaning on Sophie's shoulder, sobbing.

I moved around the crowd, straining my eyes in the fading light, trying desperately to make out the identity of the body lying on the ground, unmoving. Covered in blood. I could smell it, I realized, gagging now.

But whose blood? Panic rose in my breast, cutting off my airway as I struggled to see, watching as Matthew ripped a T-shirt into long strips and tried to stanch the bleeding, cursing as he did so.

Tyler was on his cell, screaming into it, but I couldn't make out his words. And Kate . . . Kate was kneeling beside the prone body, sobbing.

"C'mon," she cried. "Stay with us, Jack! You've got to stay with us. Don't leave me, damn it. Don't—"

And just like that, I was back in Matthew's office. "Oh my God!" I cried. "Jack. That was Jack."

"I know," Matthew said, his eyes slightly wild. "I saw. We won't let it happen, Violet. We'll do everything we can to stop it, okay?"

I just nodded, unable to utter a single word.

This couldn't be happening. Not now, not ever.

Not to one of us.

17 ~ Marked

Rubbing sleep from my eyes, I reached for my cell there on my bedside table. There was a text from Aidan, which meant I hadn't imagined the buzzing noise that had awakened me just as the first silvery light of dawn streamed across my bed.

Happy birthday, love. See you later?

I sat up with a smile, quickly tapping out a reply.

Of course! And thank you. Gran loves you, BTW.

Dinner the night before—our first night in Atlanta for break—had been absolutely perfect. Whitney had come over, and Lupe had made her favorite—country fried steak with rice and gravy. Gran had welcomed Aidan warmly, and if Lupe had sensed anything unusual about him, she hadn't shown it.

When I'd told them that Matthew was in town, coincidentally staying at the same Buckhead hotel as Aidan, they'd invited him over too. Between the two of them, they'd managed to charm everyone—Lupe, Gran, and even Melanie, Gran's private nurse. And best of all, Whitney's presence hadn't seemed to adversely affect Aidan.

So far, so good.

And now . . . I was eighteen. I closed my eyes and took a deep breath, trying to determine if anything felt different. It didn't. At least, I didn't feel an overwhelming urge to run out and slay a bunch of vampires, so I took that as a good sign.

Full-fledged *Sâbbat* or not, I was looking forward to the day ahead. I was meeting Matthew at ten, and he was going with me to get my tattoo.

My mark.

I hadn't told Aidan about it—I'm not sure why, but for now this was something between me and my *Megvéd*. After my appointment with the tattoo artist, I was meeting Whitney for lunch at the mall, and then Aidan had hinted that he had a surprise me for tonight. I assumed he'd planned a nice dinner out, something fancy. He *did* tell me to wear a dress, after all.

Somehow, I had the feeling that Whitney was in on it too.

Maybe even Gran. The anticipation was killing me—which was why I planned on staying busy all day.

There was a sharp knock on my bedroom door. "Are you up, *m'ija*? Your gran wants to see the birthday girl."

"Tell her I'll be right there!" I called out, scrambling from the bed and reaching for my robe.

A few minutes later, I hurried down the stairs toward Gran's room, my slippers thumping noisily against the carpet. After her stroke, we'd had to move everything from the enormous master bedroom down to one of the smaller rooms on the ground floor. Unless we put in a chair lift, she'd never be able to go upstairs again, which made me sad. But Gran had refused, claiming it would destroy the beautiful staircase, and besides, it wasn't worth the expense.

When I reached her room, I found her sitting in the overstuffed chair by the window, an afghan tucked around her waist. "There you are," she called out. "Why don't you shut the door and come sit by me. I've got something for the birthday girl."

I closed the door and hurried to her side. "You didn't have to, Gran."

She opened one gnarled hand and revealed a small velvet pouch. "This," she said, "is special. I gave it to your mother on her eighteenth birthday, you know. And my mother gave it to me on mine. It's been passed down for generations, from firstborn daughter to firstborn daughter. And now . . . since your mother isn't here, it's left to me to present it to you."

Tears stung my eyes as she carefully opened the pouch and tipped its contents into her palm.

"It has a name," she explained. "The 'daughter's eye.' I have no idea what that means, but there you have it." She held it up between her thumb and forefinger—a beautiful bracelet set in silver with dark, reddish-black oval stones separated by smaller, milky white ones. Each stone was surrounded by silverwork that looked like beads. The largest, the central stone—one of the reddish black ones—had more elaborate silver beading surrounding it, forming a triangular point on the top and bottom.

"It's beautiful," I breathed.

Gran looked pleased, her eyes twinkling. "Isn't it? The bigger stones are bloodstones and the smaller ones moonstones. Nothing fancy, really, and yet it's exquisite. You don't see workmanship like this today."

She placed it in my hand. "You'll have to ask Melanie to help you put it on. I'm afraid my arthritic fingers are useless these days."

I ran the pad of my forefinger over the largest stone, amazed by its unusual color. "I don't think I've ever seen anything like this. Did my mother wear it often?"

Gran shook her head. "Julia didn't think it suited her. Nor did I, to tell you the truth. But . . . it looks right for you, doesn't it?"

I just nodded, swallowing the painful lump in my throat.

"There's a bit of a legend that goes with the piece," she continued on. "Just a saying, really, but it's part of the tradition of handing it down. 'If the eye needs you, my daughter, you will know it.' Odd, isn't it? I have no idea what it means."

But I did. I understood completely. This bracelet had something to do with my *Sâbbat* lineage. It hadn't needed Gran or my mother. But it needed *me*—I was sure of that.

"I love it," I said, closing my hand around it, testing its weight.

Gran patted my wrist, smiling broadly. "I'm glad, dear. You can wear it tonight. I have a feeling that young man of yours has something special planned."

"I think so too. Do you like him, Gran? Aidan, I mean."

"I like him very much. It's obvious that he cares for you deeply, and I can tell that you feel the same way. There's something . . . I don't know." She shook her head. "Old-fashioned and gentlemanly about him. He's not quite like other boys his age, is he?"

I bit back a smile. If only she knew *just* how different he was. "Nope, he's not."

"There's something magical about first love, I always say. Hold on to it if you can."

"I will." As long as I could, at least.

Her eyes were damp now. "Okay, run along and have your breakfast now. Lupe's made your favorite—biscuits and sausage gravy."

I rose, wrapping my arms around her as I inhaled her familiar scent—Shalimar and rosewater. "Thanks, Gran. I love you like crazy."

"I love you too, sweetheart." She patted my cheek. "Now go; enjoy your special day."

I planned to do exactly that.

"Ouch," I cried, tightening my grip on Matthew's hand. "Is it almost over?"

"She's not even halfway done," he said with a laugh. "Seriously, I think you're crushing my bones."

I opened my eyes just enough to see the whirring needle press against my skin as the tattoo artist—Joni—worked. "Is it bleeding?" I asked, my voice rising shrilly.

She stopped long enough to shake her head. "No. That's just the ink. It'll be fine—I'll be done soon, I promise."

"Okay, okay." I squeezed my eyes shut again, bracing myself against the pain. "You've got to do a better job distracting me, Matthew. I had no idea it was going to hurt this bad."

He laughed softly. "I can't believe you're such a wimp, Violet. Where's your bravado now?"

"Screw bravado. Ouch!"

"You've got to hold still," Joni chastised.

"Sorry," I muttered. "C'mon. Distract, distract!"

"What do you want me to talk about? Faculty gossip, maybe? Or—"

"Charlie," I bit out. "Talk to me about Charlie. What did you tell her about coming here for break? With me?"

"I didn't tell her. Well, not exactly," he hedged.

My eyes flew open. "You lied to her? Seriously?"

I glanced over at Joni and saw her smirk knowingly.

Matthew's cheeks flooded with color. "Um, can we talk about this later?"

"Hey, don't stop on my account," Joni said. "You wouldn't believe the things I hear. This is nothing."

"Yeah, go on," I prodded. "This is *really* distracting."

"Fine. I told her I was going to Atlanta," he said stiffly. "For a conference. And I didn't mention that you'd be here."

Joni snorted.

"A conference?" I asked. "That's the best you could do? Ouch!"

"Apparently so. And hold still. She's almost done with the stake."

I could only wonder what Joni thought about my choice of artwork. I mean, who got a stake tattooed on their wrist? I knew it seemed weird—maybe a little goth or emo. Which contrasted sharply with the image I presented in my Lilly Pulitzer sundress and sandals.

She must think I'm nuts.

"Okay," Joni said. "The stake's done. You wanted a butterfly, too? Resting on the stake?"

"Forget the butterfly," I said, unable to bear the pain a minute longer. Anyway, the butterfly suddenly seemed all wrong. If I changed my mind, I could always have it added later.

"You're sure?" Matthew asked, his brow knitted.

I nodded. "I'm sure."

"Okay. Feel free to let go of my hand, then."

I did so, watching as he flexed it with a wince. "Yeah, sorry about that," I said.

"Hey, just consider it part of my services," he quipped.

"I'd sure like to get in on that," Joni said with a wink. "Whatever it means."

I shot her a glare. *My Megvéd*, my inner voice screamed.

"Okay," Joni said, setting aside her tools, her tone all businesslike now. "Keep it dry and out of the sun for a couple of weeks. Bandage stays on for two hours, that's it. When you take it off, wash it with soap and water and pat dry. Then apply unscented skin lotion as often as it takes to keep it moist while it heals, okay? About five days. Looks like you know the drill." She hooked her thumb toward Matthew's tattoo. "Make sure she takes care of it, lover boy."

Lover boy? I choked back a laugh, enjoying the stricken look on Matthew's face.

"I can't wait to show my boyfriend," I chirped.

"Let me guess," Joni said, a smile dancing on her purple-lipsticked mouth. "He doesn't know you're here, either?"

"Oh, he knows. Right, Matthew? In fact, they're sharing a suite at the hotel."

"Kinky," Joni said with an approving wink.

I was still busting a gut laughing as a glaring Matthew led me out of the shop and into the bright, midday Georgia sun.

So far, this was the best birthday ever.

18 ~ Surprise!

"Wow," Aidan said, his eyes widening as they swept over me. "You look"—he swallowed hard, his Adam's apple bobbing in his throat—"unbelievably beautiful."

I fidgeted with the straps of my pale green shantung silk dress, bought just hours before while power shopping with Whitney at the mall. She'd claimed the dress made my eyes sparkle like gems. I was just happy that it fit perfectly, because nothing else I'd tried on had. Apparently, I'd lost some weight since Christmas break.

"You don't look so bad yourself," I said, eyeing him appreciatively as he stood there in Gran's foyer, his hands thrust into his pockets. Leave it to Aidan to make a simple dark blue suit—worn sans tie, of course—look like something straight off the pages of GQ. "So, where are we going?"

"It's a surprise, remember?"

"Well, what are you planning on doing, then? Blindfolding me in the car?"

"Yes," he said with a grin. "Precisely that." He pulled a black silk blindfold from his pocket, dangling it from his fingers.

Okay, that was *hot*. "Oh," I managed to say, my heart suddenly racing. "Umm, wow."

He laid one hand against my back. "You ready?"

"Wait, can you help me with this first?" I reached into my little clutch and retrieved my bracelet.

"Sure," he said, his eyes narrowing a fraction. "What's that on your wrist?"

"Oh, right." I cleared my throat awkwardly. "I . . . um . . . got a tattoo today. Matthew took me," I added lamely.

"You did . . . *what*?"

"Yeah, it's a *Sâbbat* thing, actually. Remember that stuff in the book you gave me? The one Luc translated? I've officially taken my mark." I held out my arm, wrist up. "See?"

He moved closer, taking my hand in his as he examined the tattoo. "It's nice," he said at last. "Pretty, actually. And kind of badass."

"I know, right?" I admired it for perhaps the, oh, hundredth time that day, then pulled my hand from his. "Just be careful with it when you put on the bracelet, okay? It's still a little tender." That was putting it mildly, but I hated to sound like the wimp that I was.

"Why don't you wear the bracelet on your other wrist, then?" he suggested.

"No, it has to be this one." I had no idea why, but I knew with one hundred percent certainty that it belonged there on my right wrist, tender or not.

"If you say so." He looped the jeweled links around my wrist and secured the clasp. "There you are. It's beautiful—a gift?"

"Yeah, from Gran. Wait, whoa!" My wrist felt suddenly warm. It was almost as if heat were emanating directly from my tattoo and warming the stones on the bracelet.

And then I watched in amazement as the white stones—moonstones, Gran called them—began to . . . to . . . *glow*. "What. The. Hell."

"What?" Aidan asked, his brow knit with confusion.

"Look!" I held up my wrist, the stones glowing brighter now. "It's somehow working with my mark!" Full realization dawned on me, and I dropped my voice to a whisper. "I think . . . I think it's telling me there's a vampire present. White, because you're not a threat."

I wasn't sure how I knew, but I did. Just like that.

Wow.

"Well, I suppose that's useful," Aidan quipped, looking somewhat amused.

"Wait, what about Luc? Is he around somewhere?" Mrs. Girard agreed to let Aidan come with me to Atlanta only if Luc accompanied him, and yet I hadn't seen the man, not once.

Aidan leaned back against the doorframe. "He's around somewhere, now that the sun's set. Lurking in the shadows, I suppose."

"How's he supposed to guard you, if you can go out in daylight and he can't? I'm surprised he's not taking the elixir."

"Luc would never compromise his abilities like that. We've an agreement, though—he knows I'm not going anywhere. Anyway, you ready?"

I nodded. "I'm ready. I'll see y'all later," I yelled out toward the back of house. I was pretty sure everyone was gathered in the kitchen, trying to be discreet.

I heard a muffled reply that might have been "Have fun," as we stepped outside. The night was beautiful—balmy and unseasonably warm, the sky clear and starry, illuminated by a nearly full moon.

"It's a perfect night, isn't it?" Aidan asked, glancing up beyond the curving branches of weeping willow that hung over Gran's driveway.

I paused on the walk, allowing him to wrap one arm around my shoulders. "It is. So far, this whole day has been perfect."

"I'm glad," he murmured, pressing a kiss to the top of my head. Taking my hand, he led me to his rental car—a sleek, silver convertible—and opened the passenger door for me, helping me inside.

I'm not sure why it surprised me that he knew how to drive—after all, he'd had plenty of time to learn. Still, it was weird watching him climb in behind the wheel. This wasn't part of our normal routine, at least not in New York, where driving was pretty much unnecessary.

"Okay, blindfold on," he said, tossing the scrap of black silk into my lap. "Here, turn around and I'll tie it."

"You were actually serious about that?"

His mouth curved into a smile. "Completely. You trust me, don't you?"

"Why, were you planning on abducting me or something? I thought we were just going to dinner."

He leveled a stare in my direction. "Put it on, and perhaps you'll find out."

"Okay, okay." I lifted it up to cover my eyes, surprised to find that the silk smelled pleasantly of lavender and vanilla. Turning in my seat, I held up the ties and waited for Aidan to secure it.

As soon as he finished, he reached over me to grab the seat belt and pull it across my lap. I heard the buckle click into place, and then we were moving, backing down the driveway.

"I hope this doesn't make me queasy," I said, only half joking. "The day won't be so perfect if I puke all over the car, you know."

"Oh, I know. Just sit tight, Vi," came his disembodied voice.

Fifteen or so minutes later, I was convinced we were driving in circles. "Are you sure you know where you're going?" I asked, clutching my little purse with sweaty palms.

"Hey, are you questioning my super Spidey senses?"

"I'm pretty sure Spider-Man isn't a vampire," I said with a laugh.

"But wouldn't it be cool if he was? And just using the whole spider thing as a cover?"

"Hmm, I get the feeling you've actually thought this through."

"Oh, you've no idea the extent of it." He laid a hand on top of mine, gently stroking it. "We're just about there, by the way."

"Good, because I'm seriously feeling like I'm about to heave."

We began to slow, eventually making a sharp turn to the left. Seconds later, we made another turn—into a parking spot, maybe? Finally, he shifted into park and cut the engine.

"Okay, hold tight," he said. "Just let me come around and help you out."

"Wait, I still have to keep the blindfold on?"

He pressed a kiss to my temple. "Just a minute or two longer, love."

"Ugh, fine." My carefully applied mascara was probably all smudged by now, anyway. What was a few more minutes?

Still, even though I knew I was safe with Aidan, I felt vulnerable. And . . . oh, my God, I hadn't brought a stake. Not that I had any plans to use one, but still. Matthew would kill me if he knew I was traipsing around who knows where completely unarmed. But when I'd switched from my usual bag to the green silk clutch, I'd had to leave it behind. It's not like I could wear it strapped to my calf, not in this dress.

Beside me, the door opened. The balmy air slipped over my skin, caressing it as Aidan's hands reached for mine. "Careful, now," he said, helping me out. "Okay, just hold my arm. That's it, just a dozen steps or so, and then we've got some stairs to navigate. Don't worry. I've got you."

I nodded, stumbling along blindly beside him as best I could. "Couldn't you just do that thing you do? You know, where I close my eyes and hold on, and we go from here to there in an instant?"

He laughed softly. "I *could*. But where would be the fun in that? Here's the stairs I mentioned. Hmm, let's try this."

In an instant, he'd scooped me up into arms. "Hold on, love."

I wrapped my arms around his neck, holding on for dear life as he sprinted effortlessly up the stairs. I suppose it *was* effortless to someone who possessed superhuman strength and agility.

"Okay, down you go." He set me gently on my feet, steadying me with one arm wrapped around my middle. "Ready to take off the blindfold?"

I let out a sigh. "I thought you'd never ask."

I felt his fingers working the ties at the back of my head, and then the silk fell away from my eyes. I blinked several times, trying to get my bearings as my eyes adjusted to the sudden brightness. We were standing on a familiar white-columned porch lit by hanging brass lamps.

"The club?" I asked, surprised. "We're having dinner here?"

"Your gran said it was nice," Aidan answered with a shrug.

"It's *very* nice." Probably the most exclusive country club in the South—one of them, at least—and my family had been members for generations. I loved coming to the club, loved its formal elegance. I was suddenly glad Gran had suggested it. "But it's only five minutes from Gran's house. We were driving around for almost a half hour!"

He dipped his head closer to my ear. "Perhaps I wanted to keep you in that blindfold for as long as possible," he whispered, his British accent more evident now. "I was enjoying imagining the possibilities. For later, perhaps?"

Heat flooded my cheeks, my pulse rocketing up to an alarming rate. I had the sudden urge to get this boy alone, and fast.

"Miss McKenna!" one of the tuxedo-clad hosts called out, interrupting my enjoyable train of thought. The man hurried over to us with a solicitous smile while I struggled to force my expression back to neutral. "Your grandmother told us to expect you. I'm afraid your table isn't quite ready yet. If you'll just follow me, I'll find you a quiet place to wait."

"That'd be great, thanks." It was a little weird, actually, as my family had had a reserved table for as long as I could remember, but whatever. I glanced up at Aidan, who grinned at me with a wicked twinkle in his eyes.

I can hear your heart, he said inside my head. *Beating awfully fast now, isn't it?*

Shut up. I nudged him in the ribs as we followed the host down the long hallway, past the main dining room on the right, and turned left instead. He opened a door and motioned for us to enter.

Only, something wasn't right. Instinctively, I reached for my bag, wanting my stake. But then I remembered that I'd left it at home, that I had only my silly little clutch.

Crap.

Reluctantly, I took a step though the doorway and then froze, one hand gripping Aidan's sleeve. My heart thrummed against my ribs, my breath coming faster as I noticed that the room—the ballroom, if I remembered correctly—was completely dark.

Dark room. No stake. I didn't like this, not one bit. My panic ratcheted up a notch, and I struggled to tamp it down, to calm my breathing.

Aidan reached for my hand and gave it a reassuring squeeze. "Everything's fine," he said, dragging me forward now.

What the—

"Surprise!"

The crystal chandeliers flickered to life, the ballroom suddenly full of light—and people. *Tons* of people.

I let out my breath in a rush, relief washing over me as I glanced around the room, ticking off the familiar faces as they launched into an enthusiastic chorus of "Happy Birthday."

Whitney, Sophie, Tyler. Cece and Joshua. Marissa and Max. Kate and Jack. A dozen or so of my old friends from Windsor Day, including a couple of guys from the fencing team. A few of

Whitney's ballet buddies whom I'd gotten friendly with over the years.

And there in the back, standing beside a cut-glass punch bowl, was Matthew, one hand resting on the back of Gran's wheelchair. Beside them, Lupe and Melanie. Whitney's parents, even.

Tears sprang to my eyes as I took it all in—the colorful decorations, a table piled high with presents, a DJ set up in the back, an enormous cake beside the punch bowl. Round tables were set with lavender and cream-colored linens; china place settings gleamed beside heavy silverware and crystal glasses. In the center of each table sat a floral arrangement. I could smell them, even from where I stood just inside the door—orange blossoms.

Aidan bent his head toward mine, his breath warm against my ear. "Happy birthday, love."

19 ~ Dance of the Devil

"I still can't believe he pulled this off," I said, my gaze fixed on Aidan as he stood by the punch bowl, deep in conversation with Matthew, Tyler, and Sophie. About science stuff, I supposed.

Cece licked the remaining frosting off her fork and set it back on her plate. "Let's just say he was driven. He started planning it the day he got back."

"And you!" I said, turning toward Whitney, who sat on my other side. "Clearly his partner in crime. I can't believe you didn't give me some kind of heads-up."

"No way. I was sworn to silence," Whitney said with a smile. Surprisingly enough, she seemed perfectly at ease in Aidan's company, despite what had happened over Christmas break. I could only assume that the Aidan Effect had something to do with it, but whatever the case, I was grateful. And I was happy to see that her cheeks were more rounded now than the last time I'd seen her. She hadn't touched the cake, of course, but she had eaten a few bites of dinner—steak and lobster tails with garlic mashed potatoes and French carrots.

As soon as we'd finished dinner and cut the cake, Gran and the other adults had left—well, except Matthew. The DJ was just starting to crank up the music. And I was ready, my feet tapping to the beat beneath the table as one of my favorite songs started playing.

"Who gave the DJ the playlist?" I asked.

"Aidan put you in charge of music, didn't he, Cece?" Whitney asked.

Cece nodded, looking gorgeous in a pale pink sheath. "Marissa and Max helped too. A group effort, really."

"I still can't believe it." I shook my head in amazement. "I mean, you all flew to Atlanta just for this?"

Cece widened her eyes in mock surprise. "What do you mean, just for this? This is huge. Epic. Your eighteenth birthday!"

"You didn't have a big birthday blowout," I pointed out.

We'd quietly celebrated Cece's eighteenth just last month with cupcakes at the café. She'd refused to make a big deal out of it.

"Yeah, but you know"—she sighed heavily—"things were still kind of sober then. Anyway, I didn't turn into some badass vampire slayer on *my* eighteenth birthday. You gotta own it, girl."

I just shrugged, not quite sure I felt all that different than I had the day before, at least where vampires were concerned. I mean, yeah, I had my mark now and the bracelet. Still, it felt more like an easing-in type situation at this point. One by one, the pieces falling into place.

All this buildup leading to my eighteenth birthday, as if everything was going to change—as if *I* was going to change—just because I'd reached the magical age. Maybe I'd been worrying over nothing.

"Where are y'all staying, anyway?" I asked, eager to change the subject.

"Same hotel as Aidan and Dr. Byrne. Aidan arranged all the rooms and everything. We're flying out tomorrow afternoon, though. Sophie, Max, and Marissa are headed down to Saint Bart's. Oh, and Tyler, too."

"What? You're kidding, right?"

"Nope," Cece said. "I think something's going on with his mom.

He didn't want to go home, and since he and Max are roommates and all . . . well, you know. It just made sense."

The idea that Tyler might be working his way through my friends—first Cece, then Kate, then Sophie—made me uncomfortable. On the other hand, he'd gone on only one or two casual dates with Cece, and as far as I could tell, there wasn't anything going on with him and Sophie.

At least, not yet.

Cece obviously sensed my hesitation. "You don't think he and Sophie . . . you know?"

"I don't know," I said with a shrug. "Do you? I mean, it's not like it matters, right?"

Cece leaned back in her chair, folding her arms across her chest. "I think she's secretly into him but afraid to tell us. Which is too bad, because I think she'd be good for him."

"Sophie is the redhead, right?" Whitney asked, and Cece and I nodded. "Yeah, I've noticed the way she watches him. I'm pretty sure she's crushing hard."

Cece gave me a pointed look. "See? Tyler just needs to step up and—oops, speak of the devil. On your left," she warned as Tyler approached our table.

"Hey, birthday girl," he drawled, reaching for my hand. "Come dance with me."

"You think you can handle me?" I asked with a grin.

"Well, why don't we find out?" he shot back.

Laughing, I took his hand and followed him out to the center of the floor.

An hour later, I returned to the table where I'd stashed my bag and shoes and collapsed into a chair, exhausted. I'd been dancing nonstop, making my way around the dance floor from group to group.

Mostly, Aidan just watched, claiming me only for the slow songs. But when he held me in his arms, the heated look in his gaze promised more—*much* more. I couldn't stop thinking about that silk blindfold in his pocket, his teasing words about *later*. My skin tingled all over, just thinking about it.

As far as I was concerned, later couldn't come fast enough. I was feeling brave—reckless, even. My mind wandered back to that day in his room, the day he'd returned. Skin against skin, his body beneath mine.

I had to pick up a glass of water from the table and press it against the side of my face to cool my heated cheeks as I considered the possibilities.

Just then, Matthew dropped into the seat beside me, his eyes shadowed with concern. "Hey," he said. "Having fun?"

"Yeah, I'm having a great time. Why?"

He shook his head. "I don't know. I thought I felt . . . a disturbance in the force or something. You suddenly felt . . . *off* to me."

Oh, man. I sure hoped he couldn't read my mind now that I'd turned eighteen. We probably should have tested it earlier, while we were out getting my tattoo. The last thing I needed was Matthew knowing what I'd been thinking about just before he sat down.

"I'm sure it's nothing," I said with a shrug, going for casual. "The party's great. It looks like everyone's having fun, right?"

"Wait," he said, going suddenly still, his gaze fixed on my bracelet. "Was it doing that before?"

I glanced down at my wrist, suddenly aware of a sharp, burning sensation. Even more ominous, my bracelet's center stone, one of the bloodstones, seemed to be swirling, the black and red roiling like an angry storm cloud. "That's not good," I muttered.

"What does it mean?" Matthew asked, his gaze meeting mine.

I swallowed hard before replying. "It means vampire. *Bad* vampire."

I stood so abruptly that my chair tipped over backward. Quickly, I reached for my shoes and slipped my swollen feet into them. "Look around," I said. "Make sure everyone's here, accounted for. We've got to keep everyone inside."

"That vision," Matthew said quietly, his thoughts traveling the same route as mine. "Jack."

We both scanned the room, searching for his tall, athletic frame, his blond hair. "I don't see him," I said.

Matthew shook his head. "Me either."

"Let's find Kate, then," I said, pushing my way through the crowd, Matthew at my heels. I found her sitting at a table on the edge of the dance floor, holding her cell phone in one hand. "Where's Jack?" I called out breathlessly, bracing my hands on the back of a chair. "C'mon, Kate, where is he?"

She looked up and shrugged. "I don't know. We had a fight. I think he might have gone outside for some air."

I turned toward Matthew and saw my own terror mirrored there in his eyes.

"Shit," he muttered under his breath. "Listen, Kate. You've got to stay here, but if you see Jack, you make sure he stays put, understand me? You *cannot* let him go outside. This is important, okay? I'm talking life or death here."

"What's going on?" she asked, her voice rising shrilly. "Violet?" Her pale blue eyes were wide as saucers, her bottom lip trembling. "You've got to tell me what's happening!"

I shook my head. "There's no time. Just . . . if you find him, don't let him go outside." The heat against my wrist intensified, the bloodstone glowing now. "Crap, Matthew, we've got to hurry!"

"Let's go," he said, taking my hand.

From across the room, I saw Aidan watching us, saw his eyes narrow a fraction.

What's wrong? he asked telepathically.

Follow us out, I answered, hurrying to keep pace with Matthew's longer strides. *We've got to find Jack. Now!*

I had no idea how much of a head start we had, how much warning the Daughter's Eye provided. I knew only that we had to hurry. I led Matthew through the tables toward the rear exit, the one marked "emergency exit only." As soon as we stepped outside and skimmed down the stairs, Aidan caught up with us.

"Vampire," Aidan said, jerking his chin upward, his gaze scanning the horizon. "Not Luc. A stranger."

I held up my wrist, showing him the glowing reddish black stone. "We already figured that out. And holy crap, I don't have my stake."

Matthew crouched down, pushing up one pant leg. "I've got you covered," he said, retrieving a lethal-looking stake from a sheath strapped to his calf. "But you're supposed to be carrying one at all times," he snapped. "This isn't a game, Violet."

Gratefully, I took the weapon from him, wrapping my hand around the smooth, satiny shaft. "I know. I'm sorry."

I watched in silence as he unbuttoned the top few buttons on his shirt and reached inside for his baselard. I felt it then, the energy between the dagger and my stake, like a pulsating force.

"Which way?" Matthew asked me.

I took a deep breath and looked around, unsure. Directly behind us stretched the club's driving range and golf course. Over to the right was the pool. To our left, there was nothing but dense woods.

And a vampire, my senses told me. "That way," I said, tipping my head toward the woods.

Matthew raked a hand through his hair. "Damn it, just like the vision. I don't like this. Where the hell is Jack?"

"We'll find him," I said, taking a deep, calming breath. "We *have* to, before it's too late."

"Jack!" came a high-pitched voice off to our left, echoing off the trees.

Our heads all swiveled toward it in unison.

"Okay, what was that?" Matthew asked.

"Oh no." My heart sank in recognition. "That was Kate. How did she get out there?" I cupped my hands around my mouth. "Kate!" I hollered, but there was no response.

"Let's go," Matthew said, and we took off at a sprint.

We hadn't made it twenty yards into the moonlit woods before we heard a bloodcurdling scream from somewhere up ahead.

No! Please, God, no.

"We've got to move faster," Aidan said, grabbing my hand and stopping me dead in my tracks. "My way, Vi. Hold on tight." He held out his other hand toward Matthew. "Dr. Byrne, you too."

Matthew looked slightly confused, but he took Aidan's hand anyway. And then . . . the entire world seemed to tumble, a dark kaleidoscope of sensations.

In the blink of an eye, we were there, in the clearing I'd seen in my vision. A female vampire stood not ten feet away, clutching a body to her chest, its neck bent at an improbable angle.

What happened next was so quick, so instinctual, that I could barely believe it. With a flick of his wrist, the baselard flew from Matthew's fingers right into the vampire's left eye.

She tossed the body aside with a grunt and reached blindly for the dagger, trying to pull it from her damaged eye. Without wasting a single second, I sprinted toward my target, my stake lifted high. A scream ripped from my throat as I brought it down with as much force as I could muster.

Straight through her heart.

I cowered, covering my ears as the vampire let out an inhuman-sounding shriek and then went quiet. She collapsed in a heap on the ground, her one undamaged eye staring unseeing at the sky as blackish blood pooled around the shaft of the stake that protruded from her chest.

At once, my bracelet went cool against my wrist as I lay there panting, entirely spent.

"I'll destroy it," Aidan said, dragging the vampire's corpse away, toward the edge of the clearing while Matthew knelt over the crumpled form that remained. I couldn't look, couldn't bear to see who was lying there with their life's blood soaking the grass.

Please, not Kate.

And then I heard voices, calling out to us. Footsteps growing louder. Next thing I knew, they were there surrounding us—my friends. I backed away, one hand covering my mouth as my stomach roiled in my gut.

"Someone call 911!" Matthew shouted, and I watched numbly as Tyler pulled out his cell phone and started stabbing the screen.

"C'mon, we're losing her!" Matthew cried.

Tyler was yelling into his cell. Whitney was beside him, feeding him information about our location.

It was happening exactly as I'd seen it. I began to hyperventilate as Matthew ripped someone's shirt into long strips—

Joshua's, I noted, seeing him standing there in nothing but a thin T-shirt now.

Matthew knelt over the prone form on the ground, pressing the wads of cloth against the victim's neck to stanch the bleeding. Cece was there, leaning on Sophie's shoulder crying.

And Jack . . . Jack was kneeling beside Matthew, sobbing. "Stay with us, Kate! You've got to stay with us. Don't leave me, damn it."

I could smell the blood now—way too much blood. I gagged once, twice before my knees buckled and I fell to the ground, struggling to catch my breath.

Instantly, Aidan was back, there by my side. "They're doing everything they can," he said soothingly. "Help is on the way."

"You've got to do something," I said, my voice rising in desperation. I clutched the front of his shirt with both my hands, shaking him as hard as I could.

Kate was dying. Dying! But Aidan . . . Aidan could save her.

I struggled to my feet, dragging him with me. "You've got to do it, Aidan. You've got to turn her. Now!"

He shook his head, his eyes slightly wild. "What are you talking about?"

"Save her," I sobbed. "Turn her. It's her only chance."

"I can't do that, Violet."

"Yes, you can. You've got to. Don't you see?"

"Are you mad?" His voice was a harsh whisper now. "I would never sentence anyone to suffer this existence. Never."

"Kate!" Jack cried out, his voice breaking on the single syllable. "C'mon, you've got to fight. Stay with us. Please, Kate!"

In the distance, a siren wailed.

"Please, Aidan," I begged. "Please. Before it's too late."

His cool gaze met mine, chilling me to the bone. "I'm sorry, Violet. I can't. I won't."

A sob tore from my throat. I slapped a hand over my mouth, stifling it as I turned away from him. I stumbled back toward my friends just in time to see Matthew drop his chin toward his chest in defeat, his blood-covered hands resting on his thighs.

"She's gone," he said.

20 ~ Dead Wrong

I'm not sure how I made it through Kate's funeral without losing my mind—how any of us did, really. The last week of break had been nothing short of a nightmare. Only, there'd been no waking from this one, no sigh of relief when the alarm sounded and you found yourself tucked safely in bed.

My sorrow was unrelenting. I'd screwed up; I'd somehow sent Kate out to suffer what should have been Jack's fate. How had I missed the clues? True, I hadn't expected to find my friends in Atlanta during break. I had expected this vision to take place closer to home. The semiformal attire had made me think prom, maybe. The filled-out, fully leaved trees suggested later in the season, at least in New York. I'd thought there was still time to figure it out.

I'd been wrong. *Dead* wrong. And Kate had paid the price.

Thanks to Aidan's mind tricks, the Atlanta police, along with Kate's family, were convinced that some random, depraved murderer had killed her in a particularly gruesome manner. A botched robbery, they theorized. After all, rich kids wandering out in the woods around a posh country club would be easy targets. That explanation was good enough for them.

But those of us who knew the truth, well . . . we'd have to live with it for the rest of our lives.

School had offered us an extra week's time off, but we'd all been anxious to return, to be together again. The first day back, they'd called us all to the school's counselor's office, even Matthew. I know they were trying their best, but talking about it didn't help. Not for me and certainly not for Jack.

Jack, who had headed back inside the club after receiving a frantic text from Kate that night. Only he hadn't bothered to text her back to tell her he was coming, and so she'd gone out looking for him.

And I would never, ever forgive myself for that.

My cell, set to vibrate, buzzed beside me. Patsy. With a sigh, I connected the call.

"Hey, Mom." I lay back on my bed, staring up at the ceiling.

"Hey," Patsy said. "So, how are you doing?"

"Fine," I lied. "I mean, I'm hanging in there."

I heard her sigh. "I really wish you'd taken the school up on their offer and stayed home a few more days. It's just too soon after something like that."

"Well, I talked to the school counselor yesterday." I figured that would satisfy her.

"Oh, that's good. Okay." I could hear the relief in her voice. "I . . . um . . . I kind of need to talk to you about something important, but I know it's not really a good time."

Uh-oh. What now? "It's fine," I said. "What's going on?"

"Well, this is kind of big. It's quite a shock, even for me."

"Okay. Go on," I prodded.

"Paul's asked me to marry him," she blurted out. "And I said yes."

"Wow. That's . . . great," I said lamely. "Congratulations."

"There's more," she warned, and I braced for it. "We're moving to Australia. In June, right after your graduation."

"You're *what*?"

"I know it seems sudden, but we've been talking about it for a while now. And . . . well, I figured you'd probably want to go straight to Paris and get settled once you graduate anyway, so—"

"Wait, what do you mean, Paris?" I sat up, glancing over at the calendar on the wall, realizing with a start that April first—

decision day—had come and gone. My heart began to race, my palms damp now. "Do you know something I don't?"

"Didn't you check the university's website on the first of the month? I thought you told me—"

"I totally forgot to check. Are you saying the official acceptance came in the mail already?"

"Yes! The American University of Paris. I thought you said it was your top choice."

"It *is* my top choice." At least, it *had* been. The last couple of weeks had made decisions like this one seem irrelevant.

"So . . . are you excited?"

"Of course! Paris. Wow, I just can't believe it. I guess I sort of pushed it to the back of my mind. You know, with everything else . . ." I couldn't bring myself to finish the sentence.

"Of course, honey. I know it's been a tough time. She was your friend, after all, and it was just so horrible, so random. It could have been any one of you. I just hope they catch that sick bastard."

But they wouldn't, of course. This was one murder that would remain unsolved.

"Anyway," Patsy continued after a heavy sigh, "the lease isn't up here until the end of September, so you've got plenty of time to pack up your stuff. And . . . I know Australia's far away, but you can come visit us anytime you want. Seriously, Violet."

I was glad for the change of subject. "I . . . yeah, of course. So . . . when are you getting married?"

"We haven't decided yet, but it'll be really low-key. Just City Hall or something." In other words, I wasn't invited. "Wait, can you hold on a sec, Violet? Actually, I better take this call. I'll try you back later, okay?"

"Sure," I answered.

"Thanks. Love you!" she chirped.

"Love you too," I said, then ended the call. I set aside my cell, my thoughts spinning.

On the one hand, Patsy moving to Australia would make things so much easier. I'd be able to go to Paris and do whatever Mrs. Girard asked of me without any questions. There'd be no one around to check in with. No one to lie to.

But on the other hand, Patsy was the closest thing to a parent I had left, and Australia was far away—literally on the other side of the globe. I was going to miss her.

And then there was the news about my acceptance letter. I hurried over to my laptop, needing to see for myself. A few clicks later, and there it was—application status: accepted. I wondered if Aidan had remembered to check.

I started to reach out to him telepathically and then stopped myself. We'd barely spoken since that awful night in Atlanta. He probably thought I was still angry with him for refusing to turn Kate, but I wasn't.

I was ashamed of the way I'd acted, horrified that I'd asked him to do something so terrible. At the time, I'd seen it only as a way to save Kate. To cheat death. I owed him an apology.

Aidan?

Silence. I stared at the clock, waiting for him to respond. A full minute passed. Then another.

Hi, he said at last. *You settled in yet?*

Yeah. Can we meet somewhere?

I'm in my room. Why don't you just come here?

I hesitated. *Are you sure? Won't we get in trouble?*

Honestly, Vi, I don't think Mrs. Girard cares what we do anymore.

That was good enough for me. *Okay, I'll be right there.*

I'll leave the door unlocked.

When I stepped inside his room ten minutes later, Aidan was sitting at his desk, his golden head bent over a book. He turned toward me as I shut the door, a wary expression on his face. Behind me, I heard the lock click into place.

"Hey," he said softly. "How are you doing?"

"Better than Jack," I answered with a shrug. He was back at school, an empty shell of himself. He kept his distance from the rest of us, just going through the motions. But it was clear that his heart wasn't in it, and who could blame him?

"I shouldn't have told him about the vision," I said. I'd saddled him with unnecessary guilt—with the knowledge that she'd sacrificed herself for him.

"You only told the truth." Aidan closed his book but remained seated, studying me closely. I could feel the hurt radiating off him in waves.

Tentatively, I took a step toward him. "Aidan, I . . . There's so much I have to say to you. I'm just . . . I'm going to take down the wall around my thoughts, okay? It'll be easier."

I saw his eyes widen a fraction. "Are you sure?"

I nodded, dropping the barrier.

His cool gaze met mine, his head tipped to one side in concentration. I could feel it now, the invasion of my mind, like invisible tentacles that poked and prodded. I forced myself to allow it, to concentrate on my remorse, my shame.

Aidan's poker face was severely lacking—I could see his every reaction to my thoughts mirrored in his features.

"Okay?" I asked once I was convinced that he understood.

"It's more than okay, Vi." He rose, closing the distance between us.

I let out a sigh as he wrapped his arms around me, his lips pressed to my forehead.

"We're good, then?"

He nodded. "We're good. If you can forgive me for missing the funeral, that is."

"I wasn't surprised you took off, not after the way I treated you."

"It wasn't that, Vi. It was Mrs. Girard. She didn't think it was safe, that's all. She's convinced that whoever that vampire was, she was after me. An assassin."

"Because she knew about the whole *Dauphin* thing?"

"Probably. Our enemies know that Mrs. Girard is protecting me—they know something's up. They've heard whispers about the *Dauphin*, and they want to remove the threat. Mrs. Girard is convinced this isn't the end of it, that they'll keep sending out scouts—individual assassins—even before there's full-scale war."

"But why assassins, if they know the *Dauphin* can't be destroyed by one of their kind?"

"Apparently, that's the one part of the legend that Mrs. Girard and Luc withheld from the rest of the Tribunal. That's their trump card. Obviously, Dr. Blackwell figured it out, but they think that knowledge died with him and Julius and those two females."

"So what do we do?"

"For now, we sit tight. Mrs. Girard has upped security—there's a full force of guards around Winterhaven at all times now."

I suppressed a shudder. "Vampire guards?"

He nodded. "They're not a threat. Your bracelet is still glowing white, right?"

I glanced down, noting the now-familiar sight of the glowing moonstones. The bloodstone was totally unaffected. Whoever these vampires were, they were on our side. I let out a sigh of relief. "It's white. We're good."

"Of course, if you ask me, this security force is sending our enemies a clear signal that they're right—that I *am* being protected. That I'm a key player in Mrs. Girard's scheme. That I am the *Dauphin*. But they didn't ask me."

"So you're not allowed to leave campus anymore?"

"No. I'm on total lockdown here. That's why I wasn't at the funeral. But I should have been there for you. It must have been . . . awful."

I inhaled sharply. "It *was* awful. I can't even stand thinking about it. Can you just . . . I don't know . . . help me forget? Just for a little while?"

"I can try." He gathered me close, hugging me tightly. "Do you need to be somewhere, or can you stay?"

"I can stay. What'd you have in mind?" I teased, desperate to lighten the mood.

He released me then, peering down at me with one raised

brow. "Oh, really now. Going there, are we?" he asked, laying the British accent on thick.

I couldn't help but laugh. "You just sounded *so* much like an aristocrat. I feel like I should curtsy or something."

He swept one hand in a grand gesture. "Hey, don't let me stop you. I'm all for girls falling at my feet."

"Now you're starting to sound like Tyler," I said, rolling my eyes.

"Minus that annoying Texas drawl, I should hope."

"Hey, I'm a Georgia peach, remember?" I laid on my accent as thick as possible, drawing out each syllable. "There ain't nothin' wrong with a drawl."

Aidan sat on the edge of the daybed, holding out a hand to me. "Come here, then, Georgia peach."

I complied, settling myself beside him. I laid my head on his shoulder and sighed, feeling my tense muscles relax as I inhaled his familiar scent. "Thank you," I said, realizing just how much my mood had improved since I'd walked through that door.

"For what?"

"For making me smile. I needed that."

"It'll get easier, Vi. Just take it one day at a time."

I nodded. "I know." After all, I was no stranger to loss. Neither was Aidan. Maybe it was why we worked so well. "Do you mind if I put on some music?" I asked, reaching into my back pocket to retrieve my cell.

"Breaking the rules again, I see."

"I figured since I was already breaking a big one by coming to your room, I might as well go all out. Anyway, I'm obsessed with this song. Makes me think of you," I added, hitting play.

The opening notes of my current favorite song began to play—low, quiet. Melodious. A tambourine joined the acoustic guitar and mandolin as the tempo increased.

"Ugh, angsty Irish rock," Aidan said dismissively as the chorus began, and I looked up at him in surprise.

"They're not Irish," I said.

"Scottish? Welsh?"

I narrowed my eyes. "They're from Colorado. You don't like this song?"

"It has a boring beat," he grumbled.

"A simple beat," I corrected. "But the lyrics . . ." I trailed off, unable to put my thoughts into words. The lyrics were simply . . . perfect.

"I can't get past the beat to *hear* the lyrics," he said.

"Okay, whatever," I said, holding up my hands in surrender.

Aidan reached for my right hand. Turning it over, he ran the pad of his thumb over my now fully healed tattoo. "I'd almost forgotten about this. It really does look nice, doesn't it?"

I nodded. "I love it."

He released my hand, looking thoughtful now.

"What is it?" I asked.

His gaze met mine, and only then did I notice the faintest trace of red creeping in. The sight should have frightened me, but it didn't. "I'm sorry your birthday was ruined," he said at last. "I had such plans for after. Our own private party."

"I know." My pulse leapt, my mouth suddenly dry.

"Tell me, Vi," he said, his brow knitted as he trailed a finger down the side of my face. "Do you believe in the whole concept of soul mates?"

I shook my head. "Honestly, I'm not sure. I mean, you just threw me off there with that whole music thing," I added with a smile.

"I think most people misinterpret the concept," Aidan began hesitantly. "They expect that their soul mate will be just like them. You know, that a soft, gentle intellectual will fit only with another soft, gentle intellectual. Or a fiery personality can match only another fiery personality. But I think it's just the opposite, that soul mates are more like two sides of a coin."

"Oh, really?" I said, intrigued now. It was clear that he'd put a lot of thought into this.

The corners of his mouth twitched with a smile. "Yes, really.

And you and I . . . well, we're so very different, aren't we? And yet . . . that connection between us was almost instantaneous. You're the lightheartedness to my solemnity, the spontaneity to my careful planning, the light to my dark. If you're heads, then I'm tails. Together we're a whole. Maybe that's what a soul mate *truly* is."

My eyes were damp, I realized, swiping them with the back of my hand. "Do you have any idea how much I love you?" I asked.

He leaned toward me, his forehead against mine. "I've a pretty good idea of it," he said, his voice thick with emotion. "Which is why I should probably get you out of here."

I knew he was right, and yet I couldn't help but dip my head lower, brushing my lips against his mouth. I heard his breath catch in his throat, felt him clench his hands into fists by his sides. Still, I opened my mouth against his, needing to taste him, my soul mate.

I was breathless when I finally pulled away, my skin flushed all over, my lips slightly swollen and bruised. Lifting one trembling hand, I traced his bottom lip with my index finger, wincing as I made contact with one sharp, elongated canine.

"I could really use that cure right about now." Aidan groaned, a hint of desperation in his voice.

"Have you fed lately?" I asked.

"Yeah. That's not the problem, I'm afraid." He closed his eyes, taking several deep, calming breaths.

It was those dual needs, I realized—bloodlust tied to desire. He wouldn't risk biting me again.

"Time to change the subject, then." My mind cast about for a solution. And then I remembered. "Paris! Patsy said my acceptance came. You know, from AUP. What about you? Did you check online?"

"I totally forgot," he said. "Anyway, what's the point? Now that I've agreed to this whole *Dauphin* thing—"

"Because we're going to cure you, that's why. Go on." I waved a hand toward his laptop. "Check right now."

Just like that, the red receded from his eyes, his teeth fully normal now. He rose, making his way to the desk. Leaning over it, he opened his laptop's browser and logged on to the university's application system. A few clicks of the mouse later and he turned back toward me. "Looks like I'm in too," he said without a trace of emotion.

I let out a sigh, a flicker of hope igniting in my chest. For now, I'd just go along with the assumption that everything would work out—that he'd do his *Dauphin* thing, set the vampire world back in order, and return to Paris, where we'd have his cure waiting. That was the plan, and I was sticking to it.

"So," I said, unable to suppress a smile. "Let's talk about living arrangements in Paris. Roommates, right?"

At first I thought he was going to continue to argue with me over the futility of the situation. So I nearly wept with relief when he returned my smile instead. "Did I ever mention that I own an apartment in Paris? In the seventh *arrondissement*, right near AUP. A very nice view of *La Tour Eiffel*."

I sucked in a sharp breath. "You're kidding, right?"

He shook his head. "Not kidding. Roomie," he added with a grin.

"Hey, I've got an idea," I said. "Remember how we talked once about going on a graduation trip? You know, to Brompton Park. Your old house," I added unnecessarily, as if he didn't know.

"You really want to go there?"

"Definitely. Let's *all* go. Cece and Sophie and Marissa. The guys too. I think we could all use a little vacation after . . . well . . ." I swallowed hard. I couldn't say her name, couldn't bear to bring it up again. "We can pool our money and rent out the house for a week. What do you think?"

"I think it's a great idea," he said with a nod. "If it'll make you happy."

"Very happy. Here"—I reached for the mouse on his laptop—"go to the UK Trust website and look it up. Let's see when it's available."

He quickly typed in a search and opened the page. I watched as he clicked through, opening up the calendar. My heart sank when I saw the red X's. "Crap, it's booked the week after graduation. But look, not the week after that."

"You want to go talk to your friends? Have them ask their parents and check on airfare. Don't worry about the house—I'll have my agent in London make the arrangements."

I eyed him dubiously. "Your agent in London? What does that even mean?"

"That you don't have to worry about securing the house," he answered with a laugh. "I'll make some calls now."

"Okay. I'm going to go see if I can catch everyone before dinner." I leaned down to press a kiss to his forehead. "And thank you. This is going to be awesome."

21 ~ It's Gotta Be You

"Jenna Holley is *what*?" I asked, my voice rising shrilly.

Sophie sank onto Cece's bed with a sigh, her eyes red and swollen. "Moving into my room. Right now."

"Bu-but why?" I stammered. "It's only a couple of months until graduation. Anyway, what about Marissa?"

"I asked Marissa if she wanted to move in." She unzipped her hoodie and shrugged out of it.

"And?" I prodded.

"And she said no. You know, the whole empath thing. It makes her uncomfortable to be around other people all the time, vulnerable to their emotional state. Blah, blah, blah."

I shook my head, confused. It didn't make any sense. I mean, okay, I guess I could understand Marissa's point, although some empaths chose to have roommates. Max was living with Tyler now, after all.

But why would they assign Sophie a new roommate so close to the end of the year? And why Jenna Holley, of all people?

"Well, what happened to Jenna's roommate?"

Sophie shrugged. "I don't know. I think she might have transferred to Summerhaven at the end of the semester or something."

"I just don't understand what difference it makes. It's not like they needed to free up a room or anything."

Sophie's hazel eyes filled with tears. "Mrs. Girard said she didn't think it was a good idea for me to be living alone right now."

I kind of had to agree with Mrs. Girard there. I couldn't even imagine having to stare at the empty side of the room that was Kate's on an everyday basis. As it was, we all avoided Sophie's room now, unable to bear it. Sophie needed company—needed someone to fill that empty space. But Jenna Holley?

"Maybe you should try talking to Marissa again," I suggested. "It's not like it'll kill her to have a roommate—"

"It's too late—Jenna's already moving in." She sighed heavily.

"Well, you know you're welcome here anytime. Seriously,

you only need to go to your room to sleep, right? You could even leave a change of clothes here if you wanted. Shower on our floor."

"I guess. Or I could just suck it up. How many weeks are left?"

I glanced up at the calendar on the wall. "Ten or eleven, maybe? Wait, have you gotten any acceptance letters yet?"

Her mouth curved into a smile. "Princeton."

"Princeton? That's great, Soph! Wasn't that your first choice?"

"Yep. I'm still waiting to hear from Dartmouth, but I think my mind is made up."

"Wow," I said. "I knew you'd go Ivy."

"I just can't believe you're going to Paris. It's so far away."

"I know. But you'll come visit, right? I mean, it *is* Paris." And Sophie's parents had plenty of disposable income.

"Sure. And you'll come back to New York, too, right? You've still got Aidan's town house, and Princeton's just a train ride away."

I shook my head. "I don't understand why Aidan won't take his house back. You know, now that *he's* back. It just feels weird, keeping it in my name and all."

"That boy's a funny one. Dr. Byrne thinks he's made another breakthrough, by the way. With his cure," she clarified. "He's pretty sure we'll have it by the end of the semester."

"I hope he's right," I said, but I refused to get my hopes up.

I'd heard it before, too many times. The closer they got, the more impossible it seemed.

"Hey, have you booked your plane ticket for England yet?" Sophie asked.

"Yep." Just as I expected, Patsy had been fine with the idea of a trip to Europe with my friends. She'd given me her credit card number to book the flight, calling it a graduation present. "Cece and Josh did too. What about you?"

"Just yesterday. I guess we can somehow try to get seats together once we get to the airport. I left my seat selection blank for now."

"Yeah, me too."

Sophie reached for her backpack. "We should probably get started on our homework."

"Probably," I agreed, even as my thoughts returned to our original topic of conversation. "But . . . what are you going to do about Jenna?"

"What *can* I do, Violet? It looks like I'm stuck with her."

"Okay, so why the lab?" I leaned against a black-topped table watching Matthew as he dug around inside a drawer. He'd sent me a text asking me to meet him there rather than his office for our usual Saturday-morning rendezvous.

"It's just an idea I had," he said. He set several items on a tray and then turned to face me. "I know it sounds kind of weird, but I'd really like to take a sample of your blood. Just to see if I can pinpoint anything out of the ordinary that might serve as a *Sâbbat* marker or something. Do you mind?"

"No, I guess not." My gaze strayed to the hypodermic needle lying on the tray beside two test tubes and a piece of narrow rubber tubing.

"I'm told I have a gentle touch," he offered with a smile.

"Yeah, sure. You know I can't stand the sight of blood, right?"

"Said no one ever while dating a vampire," he quipped.

"Very clever. Ten points to Gryffindor."

Matthew reached for a pair of rubber gloves and slipped his hands inside, securing them with a snap. "I've always thought of myself as more of a Ravenclaw." He tipped his head toward one of the stools on the far side of table. "You want to sit for this?"

"I probably should. Less distance to fall when I faint." I trudged around the table and took a seat, offering up my right arm.

"You're not *really* that bad, are you?" he asked as he swabbed the inside of my elbow with an alcohol pad.

"Almost." I took a deep breath, exhaling slowly as I gathered my nerve. "Okay, let's get this over with." I turned my head, staring at the clock on the wall while he inserted the needle into my vein. True to his word, he was so gentle that I barely even felt the prick. "Why two tubes?" I asked, trying to make distracting conversation.

"There are a lot of different things I want to test." He fell silent for a while, and I continued to stare at the clock, watching the second hand make its lazy circuit. "Okay, I'm just about done," he said at last. I was vaguely aware of the sensation of the needle being removed, and then he pressed a cotton ball against my skin, bending my elbow to hold it in place.

"Wow, that was quick. Do I get a Band-Aid, Dr. Byrne?"

"Of course you do." He held up two. "SpongeBob or Disney princesses?"

"Seriously?" I shook my head. "I'll take SpongeBob. I'm not even going to ask what you're doing with princess Band-Aids."

He tossed away the cotton ball and replaced it with the bandage. "Done. Okay, now what? Do you want to go back to my office for a bit?"

"Sure, why not? Maybe you can talk me through a replay of one of my visions, one that still hasn't happened yet."

His gaze met mine, a muscle in his jaw flexing perceptibly. "The one where you saw yourself kill Aidan?"

I swallowed hard. "Yeah, that's the one. You haven't seen it yourself yet, have you?" It was weird to think that he sometimes experienced my visions—it made me feel somehow . . . exposed.

And yet it could be helpful. I almost wished he *would* see this particular one, mostly to save me the heartbreak of describing it to him.

"Haven't seen it," he said. "Just let me put this stuff away, and we'll give it a try."

Five minutes later, I settled into the chair across from his desk. His office was warm, comfortable. It didn't take long for Matthew to lull me into a trance-like state as I concentrated on the familiar ticktock of the clock.

An unfamiliar room. Plush carpet beneath my feet, robin's-egg blue with a dark brown pattern—scripty curlicues and little birds. There was a window, I noticed this time; beyond the panes of glass, I saw green. Green, rolling hills. A willow tree. I tried to look around for more clues, but I was crying too hard, deep gulping sobs that racked my entire body.

"You have to do it, Vi," a voice pleaded. Aidan. I turned to face him, horrified. "Please, I beg of you," he continued on. "It has to go into my heart. You can do it; I've taught you how. Don't let me down, not now. You promised."

"No," I said, wanting it to stop. "Please, no. Don't make me, Aidan. I can't do it."

"Yes, love. You can. Right here." He tapped his chest, above his

heart. "There's no time to waste. You must do it now. Now," he repeated, his tone urgent.

"I can't," I cried. "I can't do it. How can you ask me to?"

"Because I love you, Vi. I love you, with all my heart. It has to be you—don't you see?"

"No!" I screamed, suddenly back in Matthew's office. I was shivering violently, my teeth clattering as I tried to catch my breath. "I can't watch it again. I can't."

Instantly, Matthew was on his feet, hurrying around the desk to wrap me in his arms. "It's okay, Violet. I've got you."

22 ~ Gross Misinterpretation

McKenna, I want you to pair up with Smith for this exercise." Coach Gibson tipped his head toward the piste. "Demonstrate correct form for the rest of the class, why don't you."

Dutifully, I took my place opposite my opponent. I didn't see much point, really. Fencing was a winter sport; we were done for the year. For us seniors, our high school fencing careers were over. You'd think Coach would let us sit back and take it easy—that he'd focus on the underclassmen instead.

Apparently not.

He gave the signal, and Suzanne and I began the exercise. There were no sounds save that of our shoes squeaking against the mat, of the clanging of our foils as they met.

Once we finished demonstrating, I pulled off my mask and wiped the sweat from the sides of my face as the rest of the class took up their foils.

Suzanne set her own mask on the floor and then laid a hand on my shoulder. "Hey, I'm really sorry about Kate. I would have gone to the funeral, but we were in California. I just . . . well, I wanted you to know. That's all," she finished lamely.

"Thanks," I said, my voice thick. Why did she have to bring this up? Why now?

"God, I feel so bad every time I see Jack Delafield," she continued on, oblivious to my discomfort. "He's such a mess. I can't believe he's back at school. I mean, I heard they'd just gotten back together and all. And then for something like this to happen?" She shook her head. "Did she really get attacked outside your birthday party? I mean, I don't want to pry or anything, but that's the rumor."

"I—uh—yeah." I couldn't speak. Could barely breathe. I had to get out of there. Now. "I've got to . . . I mean, will you tell Coach that I had to leave early? Meeting with my GC. I forgot."

Suzanne's eyes widened. "Oh. Okay. I didn't upset you or anything, did I?"

I just shook my head, then busied myself collecting my gear.

As the rest of class continued the exercise, I made my way over to the cubbies and grabbed my bag.

I heard Coach Gibson call out my name just as the door slammed shut behind me. I hurried down the stairs with no idea where I was going. It didn't matter, not really. I just needed air.

Afraid that the coach might send someone after me, I picked up my pace, jogging away from the building at a brisk clip, my bag banging against my side.

The chapel, I decided. Of course—no one would bother me there. I quickened my pace as my destination came into view above the treetops. A couple of minutes later, I hurried inside and made my way through the vestibule and down the aisle, toward the rear-most pews.

Panting, I slid into a seat. I'd only just caught my breath when the door banged open behind me. I turned, startled to find Tyler there, making his way toward me. "Hey, you okay?"

"I'm fine," I answered. "Needed some air, that's all."

He moved closer, leaning against the edge of the pew now. "Well, something must've happened in there to make you run out the way you did. What's going on, Violet?"

"It's just . . . something that Suzanne said." I took a deep, calming breath. "I think she was just trying to be nice. You know, about Kate."

"Ah, I see." He slid onto the pew, scooting in beside me. "The old 'I'll pretend to be comforting when I'm really just digging for details' kinda thing?"

"Yeah. Pretty much. I just—I don't want to talk about it. Not to anyone who wasn't her friend, who wasn't there that night. I know that's probably weird."

He reached for my hand. "Nah, not weird at all."

I squeezed my eyes shut, forcing back tears. "I can't help but think about that night—replay it over and over in my head. I barely even talked to her. She was busy with Jack, and I . . ." I trailed off, shaking my head. "I'm trying to remember the last thing I said to her. It was something like 'wait here—don't go outside.' If I had known those would be the last words I'd say to her—"

"Don't," Tyler said, squeezing my hand. "Just don't, okay? You're going to drive yourself nuts. There was no way you could have known. No way you could have prevented it."

"I *should* have known. If I hadn't been so distracted—"

"It was your fucking birthday, Violet. Look, I know you feel responsible. I get that. Trust me. I've played a few rounds of 'what if' in my head too. What if I'd fought a little harder for her; what if she'd been with *me* that night instead of Jack." He brushed his thumb over my knuckles, his head bowed over our joined hands.

"I realize I didn't know her as long as you did—as long as the rest of you did. But I liked Kate, Violet. Really liked her." He lifted his gaze to meet mine, and I was shocked to see that his clear green eyes were glistening with tears.

"I know you did," I said, even though I hadn't realized how much until that very moment. "I'm sorry. I was being selfish. I didn't even think about you—about what you might be going through."

"She was fun. Uncomplicated." A single tear rolled down his cheek. "I miss her."

I did the only thing I could think to do then—I gathered him in my arms, allowing him to press his face against my breastbone as I stroked his hair. "I miss her too," I said. Soon his tears had dampened the front of my shirt, but I didn't care. He needed this. We needed it. I was clinging to him desperately, holding on to the one person whose guilt might just match my own, who understood that tangled mess of emotions swirling inside me whenever I thought of Kate.

Several minutes passed in silence as we sat there holding each other, sharing our grief. Outside, the bells pealed to signal the end of sixth period. A crow cawed loudly—once, twice. Somehow, we didn't hear the door to the chapel open. We missed the approaching footsteps.

"Violet?"

I shoved Tyler away with a gasp, stunned to see Aidan standing there at the end of the aisle, just outside the vestibule.

Watching us.

The pain etched into his features was undeniable as his expression shifted from disbelief to anger in a heartbeat.

I realized then that pushing Tyler away had been a bad move on my part. It made me look guilty, like I'd been caught doing something that I shouldn't. *Crap.*

"Listen, man," Tyler said, turning toward Aidan with a grimace. "This is not what it looks like."

"Oh, yeah?" Aidan said, his voice so level and cool that my blood turned to ice in my veins. "Because it *looked* like you two were all over each other."

Tyler held up two hands in surrender. "Seriously, dude, don't be mad at her. She was just comforting me."

"Shut up, Bennett," Aidan said. His eyes were beginning to go vampiric, rimmed in red now. I was afraid to look at his incisors. This was a very bad combination, a dangerous one—jealous teenage boy plus overprotective vampire. I needed to neutralize the situation, but how?

"It was *all* me, man," Tyler pressed on foolishly. "I came after her, just to make sure she was okay, and then I started bawling like a pussy. She was just being nice."

"Oh, I have no doubt that you were just waiting for an opportunity to make your move," Aidan said with a shrug. "I've always suspected you have a thing for her."

Tyler rose and slipped into the aisle facing Aidan. "Why don't we talk about this later, after you've had a chance to calm down? I don't like the way your eyes look right now. Violet, maybe you should get out of here."

Did he think he was protecting me? From Aidan? He was the one who was going to need protection—any minute now if he didn't shut up.

"You're making it worse, Ty," I managed to say. "Just go, okay?"

"I'm not leaving you here with *him*." Tyler swept an arm in Aidan's direction. "He may be your boyfriend, but dude's a vampire. An angry one," he added under his breath.

In the blink of an eye, Aidan had him by the throat, pressed up against the chapel's wall ten yards from where they'd been standing just a second before.

I was on my feet in an instant, because this . . . this was not going to be a fair fight. "Let him go, Aidan!"

He ignored me. Tyler was gasping for breath now, his eyes beginning to bulge. He was no match for Aidan's superhuman strength; no mortal was.

Fear racing through my veins, I reached for Aidan's shoulder.

"Let him go!" I repeated. "He was telling you the truth—we weren't doing anything."

Aidan just ignored me, squeezing tighter instead. Tyler's face was ashen now.

In full panic mode, I began to tug at Aidan's arm, forcing him to turn and look at me. His terrifying red gaze met my steady, pleading one. "You're going to kill him," I said forcefully.

Inexplicably, he cried out in pain, releasing Tyler and cradling the hand that had been around Tyler's throat.

Tyler slumped to the ground in a heap.

"What did you do?" Aidan gasped, flexing his hand.

I could only gape at the sight, barely able to believe it. Aidan's hand was somehow misshapen, his fingers curled and bent at impossible angles. Yet, as I watched wide-eyed, his hand began to morph back to normal in a matter of seconds—just like that.

"Molecules," Tyler choked out, propped up on one elbow now. "I moved 'em around. You know, when you lost your focus."

"You can do that?" I asked breathlessly, my gaze shifting from Aidan's hand to Tyler and back again. "Holy hell!" Maybe it would have been a fair fight, after all.

And that's when Aidan leaned down and punched him, right in the face.

* * *

Tyler's face was a mess—he'd refused to go to Nurse Campbell for treatment—and Aidan wasn't speaking to me. Which made art history class the next day *so* much fun. They sat on either side of me now, bristling, while the gossip raged on around us.

I tried to imagine how I'd feel if I caught Aidan with his arms around another girl—if he'd shoved her away guiltily the second I stepped into the room and then claimed that he'd only been comforting her. Just thinking about it made me feel sick—made my head pound, my stomach lurch queasily.

I glanced over at Aidan's stony face, wondering if he was actually paying attention to what Dr. Andrulis was saying. His expression was entirely unreadable. If he noticed me watching him, he gave no indication of it.

I let out a frustrated sigh. Enough was enough. It was time for a little telepathic chat.

Can we please talk after sixth period?

He didn't move a muscle. *There's nothing to talk about.*

C'mon, Aidan. You know he's just my friend.

He remained as still as a statue, staring straight ahead. *Seriously, Vi? You two were all over each other, for God's sake.*

This wasn't going well. *Your room, then. Right after class.*

The silence in my head was deafening.

"Hey," Tyler whispered on my other side. "Violet?"

Irritated, I snapped my head toward him. "What?"

He held out my pen. "You dropped it."

I snatched it from him with a scowl, reminding myself that he had no idea that he'd interrupted a conversation. "Thanks," I whispered, trying to shake off the hostile vibes radiating from Aidan's direction.

The next fifteen minutes were pure agony. I almost wept with relief when the bells began to ring.

"Should I wait for you?" Tyler asked, looking uncomfortable. "You know, to walk over to fencing together?"

I busied myself with my bag, unable to look at his swollen, discolored face without feeling guilty all over again. "No. Go on without me. Actually, would you mind telling Coach that I'm not feeling well? I might walk over to the infirmary." It was only a half lie, since my head was pounding and I was out of Advil.

"Sure," he said. "Okay, um . . . later."

Aidan had started toward the door without me. I actually had to grab my bag and sprint toward him, catching up with him just as he stepped out into the hallway.

And then Jenna stepped into our path. "If it isn't the little lovebirds," she said, her voice dripping with venom.

"What do you want, Jenna?" Aidan asked, sounding bored.

"A run tonight, if you don't mind. It's a full moon."

"Is it? I hadn't noticed."

She narrowed her eyes at him. "Just be there. You wouldn't want me to go all wolf without a babysitter now, would you?" Her gaze slid over to me. "If you can manage to separate yourself from your little pet long enough, that is."

"Whatever. You know there's an entire security force out there watching the woods at night, right?"

"Yeah, and you better tell them to keep their distance, or else I won't be responsible for any damage I do. I'll see you tonight. Usual time and place." With that, she turned and flounced off.

23 ~ Like Sand Through the Hourglass . . .

"How'd you do on the history test?" I directed at the back of Aidan's head. He was sitting at his desk across the room, while I leaned nervously against the door.

"Fine" was all he said in reply. No elaboration, nothing.

"We, uh, probably need to get together with Joshua and Tyler at some point to finish up our art history project. You know, the *Girl Before a Mirror* thing. And the sculpture one, too."

"I knew what you meant." He opened up his laptop and reached for the mouse.

I took a few steps toward the center of the room, standing a few feet behind him. More than anything, I wanted to hurry over to him and wrap my arms around him. Instead, I held myself in check, fearing his rejection.

"Did you turn in any of your paperwork for AUP yet?" I asked, my voice shaky. "I think the housing form is due soon. If we're waiving student housing, we're supposed to tell them where we'll be living. You know, give them an address."

His only response was a curt nod as he continued doing whatever he was doing on his computer. He wasn't staying on any website long—it looked like he was just randomly clicking from site to site, just to appear busy.

"So, you're just going to sit over there and ignore me?" I asked, sinking onto the edge of daybed with a sigh.

He nodded. "That was the plan."

"C'mon, after all we've been through, we're going to fight over *this*? I told you it was nothing. He was crying about Kate, Aidan. Seriously. What was I supposed to do?"

"How about *not* put your hands all over him?" I couldn't see his face, but his voice was laced with jealousy.

I took a deep, calming breath. "This is crazy. You know that, right? Tyler is my friend, nothing more. And he's helping with *your* cure, by the way."

"What's that supposed to mean? That I should thank him by

giving him carte blanche to feel up my girlfriend whenever the mood strikes him?"

"It wasn't like that, and you know it. You're just being difficult. What can I possibly say to make you believe me?"

"How about giving me a little time? Some space, maybe."

"Are you serious?" I asked incredulously. This was a complete and total overreaction on his part. It didn't make any sense. "Where's this really coming from, Aidan? Because this isn't you. You don't do the jealous boyfriend thing."

He let out a heavy sigh and then finally swiveled in his chair to face me. "I think you need to figure out what you want, Violet. What you need. *Who* you need. There are no guarantees with me—I told you that."

I just stared at him, stunned by his words. He dropped his gaze, but not before I saw that same haunting emptiness I'd glimpsed before.

"I can't believe you're saying this," I finally managed.

He busied himself with some papers on his desk, avoiding my gaze. "Yeah, well, I can't believe I saw you with Tyler Bennett's hands all over you, so I guess we're even."

I rose on shaky legs and headed for the door. "I don't need time or space to think about anything. I know exactly what I want. Maybe *you're* the one who needs to do some thinking. Figure out what it is that *you* want." I paused to catch my breath, one hand on the doorknob. "Have fun with your dog tonight."

Without waiting for his response, I stormed out into the corridor, making sure the door slammed shut behind me.

I headed outside, my pace brisk as I walked aimlessly across the quad. I decided to head toward the river, my breath coming faster as I jogged down the path, desperate to clear my head.

Faster and faster I ran, my sneakers pounding against the pavement as I raced past the chapel. With each step, my anger seemed to dissipate, replaced with disappointment instead.

When I reached the bench at the end of the path, I paused, resting my hands on my knees as I caught my breath.

I rose, swiping the sweat from my forehead with the back of one hand. If he needed time, I'd give him time. Clearly, there was more to it than simple jealousy over a misunderstanding. Maybe he was scared. Worried. I knew he thought that he was putting me in danger, so maybe he was acting out of some sort of misplaced guilt. Whatever the case, I wasn't going to let him push me away so easily.

A calm determination settled over me as I started back toward the dorm, my pace slow and easy now.

When I finally made it back to my room, sixth period had ended and Cece and Sophie were already there, sitting side by side on Cece's bed with textbooks in their laps.

"Warning, Sophie," I said sourly. "Your roommate is going wolf tonight."

"Uh-oh," she said, setting aside her book. "Does that mean Aidan has to babysit?"

"Yep." I dropped my bag onto my desk. "Lucky him."

"Bad day?" Cece asked with a frown.

"You have no idea. I have a headache, too."

"You want to lie down for a little bit?" she offered. "Sophie and I can go to the lounge."

"No, but thanks. I've got homework."

"Wouldn't it be nice if we didn't have to do any more homework? I mean, now that we've already been accepted to college and everything."

My gaze shot up at once, taking in Cece's impish grin. "Oh my God! You got an acceptance today, didn't you?"

"Tulane. Full merit scholarship."

"That's awesome!" I hurried over and wrapped her in a hug. "Wow, I'm so happy for you. And . . . any news on Joshua?"

"Duke—his first choice. He's totally psyched." She waved one hand in dismissal. "Don't worry. We'll figure it out. I mean, if it's meant to be, it'll be, right? Anyway, tell her your news, Sophie."

"You got into Dartmouth?" I asked her, remembering that she was still waiting to hear from them.

"Yeah, but I already accepted at Princeton. Guess who else?"

"Someone else is going to Princeton?" I asked, confused now.

"Not just anyone," Cece said cryptically. "Go on. Tell her!"

Oh my God. "Not . . . ?"

"Tyler," Sophie confirmed with a nod. "Crazy, right? I didn't even know he'd applied there."

"So . . . is this a good thing?" I asked.

She chewed on her lower lip as she considered the question. "I don't know. Probably not, right?"

"Depends, I guess," I hedged. "But seriously, Princeton? Tyler's grades are *that* good?"

"I know, right?" Cece plopped back down on her bed. "I wonder if one of his parents went there or something."

"I don't know, but his grades really *are* that good," Sophie said. "At least, that's what Dr. Byrne says."

"Oooh, Matthew," Cece said, wiggling her fingers at me like she always did when his name came up. "By the way, what's up with Aidan? He seemed a little . . . uh . . . *frosty* earlier."

"Oh, you know . . . he's just being moody." I cleared my throat uncomfortably, hoping they wouldn't question why my cheeks were suddenly red.

"Hey, don't forget Friday is senior ditch day," Sophie said, mercifully changing the subject. "We're supposed to meet at the cemetery at sunrise."

Cece mock shuddered. "That's so creepy."

"But it's Winterhaven tradition, right?" I asked. "The cemetery and then Sunnyside."

"Yeah, but it's so lame." Cece rolled her eyes. "I mean, Winterhaven delivers bag lunches to Sunnyside. Technically, that makes it a school-approved field trip."

"Yes, but an unchaperoned one," Sophie reminded her.

"Ooh, so naughty!" Cece was laughing now. "Think of all the trouble we could get into. You know, at an old cemetery and a historic site."

"Uh-oh," I said. "Matthew."

"What about him?"

"There's no way he's going to let me go off campus without him, not after what happened in Atlanta."

"Seriously?" Cece asked.

I nodded. "Seriously."

She groaned loudly. "Well, forget the unchaperoned part, then."

"I just won't go, that's all. I'll stay here with Aidan." Because there was no way Mrs. Girard would let him go. It was too dangerous, even during daylight hours.

"But you have to go, Violet. I mean, we don't have that much time left together as it is." Sophie's eyes filled with tears. "There's just this and then prom and graduation."

"We've got the trip to England, too," I reminded her. At least, I hoped we still did, what with Aidan being mad at me and all. My own vision was swimming with tears as I fit myself between the two of them.

Cece shook her head. "Oh no. Don't start. 'Cause if the two of you do, then I'm gonna start bawling my eyes out."

I wrapped an arm around Cece; Sophie laid her head on my shoulder.

Just then, the door banged open. We all looked up to see Marissa standing there in the doorway, looking like she was about to cry too. "What's going on?" she asked, her gaze sweeping the room.

Sophie's breathing was ragged now as she reined in the tears. "We're running out of time together."

"I thought . . . never mind." Marissa shook her head. When Cece held out a hand to her, she hurried over to the bed and joined in the group embrace.

"I'm going to miss you guys so much," Cece sobbed, her face buried in Marissa's hair now. "What was I thinking? I'm going to be all by myself at Tulane!"

"But you've got family in New Orleans," I reminded her. "Your grandma and cousins . . ."

She shook her head. "It's not the same. Marissa and Max are both staying in New York. Violet and Aidan are going to Paris. And you'll have Tyler at Princeton," she directed at Sophie. "Even if he *is* a manwhore. But me? I've got no one."

"We can Skype every day." Sophie sniffled.

"Yeah, a group video chat," I agreed. "Every night."

Cece shook her head. "You're going to be in Paris, remember? Nighttime for us will be, like, butt crack of dawn for you."

"More like the middle of the night," Sophie corrected.

I reached for a tissue and dabbed at my eyes. "So, we'll find a time that works for everyone. Maybe not every day, but at least once a week, okay?"

Sophie nodded, reaching for my hand. "Agreed."

"Agreed," Cece echoed, adding her hand to the pile.

We all looked expectantly toward Marissa. "Agreed," she said. "What, did you think I wouldn't?" She rolled her eyes as she placed her hand on top of ours.

Still, I couldn't help but think how drastically things were going to change, and soon. Sophie was right—all we had left was prom and graduation and our trip to England.

Just a matter of weeks.

24 ~ I Spy

Never mind," I said, shaking my head. "This was a bad idea."

Cece sat up in bed. "C'mon, aren't you curious? I'll just project out there quickly and see what's going on and then I'll come right back. Five minutes, tops."

I chewed on my bottom lip, torn. On the one hand, I wanted to know what happened when Jenna went wolf—and exactly what role Aidan played in it. But on the other hand, I was asking Cece to do something that was against the COPA. Plus, I didn't want to be the kind of girlfriend who spied on her boyfriend.

Still . . . I was curious. "You're sure you don't mind?" I asked her.

"Totally. Anyway, I've done it before—gone astrally strolling through the woods at night. Remember?"

I nodded, recalling the last time she'd spotted Jenna and Aidan together, arguing. At the time, we hadn't known Jenna's story and hadn't realized what was going on.

"I guess," I conceded. I wasn't worried about her getting expelled—not anymore. The snow I'd seen in my vision was long gone, replaced by the lush green of late spring. "But don't go for long. I can't stand seeing you lie there while you're projecting. It totally freaks me out."

"Now you know how I feel when you're having a vision," she shot back.

"Okay, okay." I held my hands up in mock surrender. "You better get going before I change my mind."

With a grin, Cece scooted down on her bed, lying back on her pillow with a sigh. "Why don't you . . . I don't know, read a book or something? No hovering."

"No hovering," I repeated, hurrying over to my own bed. "Got it. I'll text Whitney, see what she's up to."

"Turn the sound off, though. I need quiet."

"I know. Sheesh." I flipped the volume switch on my cell to off. "There. Now go."

I tried not to watch as Cece began the process of deep breaths and slow exhalations. A couple of minutes passed in relative silence, and then I couldn't help but peek.

She was entirely still, a peaceful look on her face. My gaze slid down her body, looking for a twitch, a tremble—any sign of life. There was none. She might have been a statue, carved from stone. Clearly, her astral self was gone.

A shiver raced down my spine. I had to take a couple of deep breaths myself as I fought the urge to go over to her and shake her. I still didn't quite understand exactly how this astral projection thing worked, but I couldn't help worrying about what would happen if she somehow couldn't get back to her body. She'd assured me over and over again that there was no danger of that, but it didn't assuage my fears, not entirely.

I ran a finger over my cell's slick screen, debating whether or not I should actually text Whitney. With my luck, the second we got into a conversation, Cece would come back. It seemed best to just wait patiently, but the longer she was gone, the more nervous I became.

Setting aside my cell, I rose and padded over to the window, pulling back the curtains to gaze out at the starry night. The full moon hung high in the sky, casting a silvery glow across the lawn and the treetops beyond.

They were out there somewhere, Aidan and Jenna. I hated the thought of them together. Still, I felt stupid for sending Cece out to spy on them. I resisted the urge to look over at the still form lying on the bed—just an empty shell. I wanted to shake her, to tell her that I'd changed my mind. Instead, I leaned against the window, pressing my forehead to the cool glass, and took a deep, calming breath.

In through my nose, out through my mouth. The glass fogged, obscuring my vision as the minutes ticked by. Slowly, one after another, until I didn't think I could stand it any longer. *Hurry, hurry.* I tapped my foot impatiently, wanting to retrieve my cell so I could check the time. How many minutes had passed? Ten? Fifteen? I'd totally lost track.

Careful to keep my back to Cece's body, I shuffled over to my bed and retrieved my cell, then hurried back to the window. I glanced down at the screen with a huff of frustration—only seven minutes had passed. Not nearly enough time for her to have seen anything worthwhile.

I had to distract myself. Keeping the volume off, I checked my e-mail. Then my text messages. Then my social networks. With nothing else left to do, I tapped open a game.

"I'm baaack," came Cece's singsong voice behind me just as the game loaded.

Relief washed over me as I turned toward her, watching as she sat up and reached for the bottle of water beside her bed.

She took several long chugs, the plastic crinkling noisily as it emptied. "Whew, I'm thirsty," she said, wiping her mouth with the back of one hand.

I clicked my cell's volume switch back on and tossed the phone to my bed. "From the projecting?"

"Nah, from the Mexican food at lunch," she answered with a laugh.

I drummed my fingers on my thighs. "So?"

Her brows drew together. "So, what?"

I gave her a pointed look. "Aren't you going to tell me what happened out there?"

"Oh, right. Well, first off, I wish I could scrub my eyeballs. Did you know that she strips *naked* before going wolf?"

"Yeah, I know." Aidan had told me that last year.

"And she's certainly not shy. The little skank stripped down to nothing, right there in front of Aidan."

Of course she did.

Cece winced. "I probably shouldn't have told you that."

"No, it's fine." I took a deep breath, gathering my courage. "What did he do?"

"You really want to hear this?"

"I have to," I said. "Go on."

She shrugged. "He just watched. I mean, he didn't look like he was turned on or anything," she added hastily. "He was just, you know, standing there watching. With his arms folded, looking kind of bored."

"Uh-huh. Go on."

"So Jenna does her little striptease and then picks up her clothes and walks over and hands them to him. He's still just kind of watching her. His eyes were on her face the whole time, I swear."

I wasn't entirely sure I believed her, but I motioned for her to continue.

"And then she says, 'You know, for a vampire you're not that bad.' And then she kinda . . . I don't know . . . runs a finger down the side of his face."

I closed my eyes and took a deep breath.

"You said you wanted to hear this," Cece said haltingly.

I swallowed hard. "I do. Continue."

"So she says, 'I don't have to run tonight.' Aidan didn't say anything, so she adds, 'I'm not fragile like your little pet. You could bite me, if that's what it takes to turn you on. I'd heal as soon as I shifted.' I have no idea what she meant by that."

"I guess shifting speeds up the healing process for her or something," I speculated, fighting the urge to hunt her down and rip her limb from limb. "So what'd he say to her little proposition?"

Cece glanced down at her hands, suddenly unable to meet my eyes.

Uh-oh.

"Just tell me," I whispered.

"Fine. Just . . . don't shoot the messenger, okay? You're the one who made me spy on them."

"Tell me," I repeated.

"He said, 'Maybe later.' And next thing I know, Jenna drops to the ground. It was crazy, Violet. It's like one second she's her, and the next she's this . . . this . . . *creature*. But her eyes"—she shuddered—"they were the same."

"Maybe later?" My mind was stuck on Aidan's reply—the details about her shifting seemed irrelevant now. "You're sure that's what he said?"

She fiddled with her earrings. "Pretty sure. Not a hundred percent, but . . . yeah, I think that's what he said. And then . . . well, Jenna-the-wolf just took off running. Aidan sort of wadded up her clothes and went and sat on the bench at the edge of the woods. That's when I came back."

"I think I'm going to be sick." I headed for the door.

Cece half rose from the bed. "Wait, where are you going?"

I didn't stop to answer her. Instead, I hurried out to the bathroom next door, stopping at the sink to splash cold water on my face.

What was this—payback? Or was there more to their relationship—his and Jenna's—than Aidan had let on? I couldn't help but think the latter, since he had no idea that Cece was there, watching and listening. And without an audience, well . . . what kind of payback was that? What was the point if I didn't know about it? Was it possible that he'd been lying to me about Jenna all along? What other explanation *was* there?

This time, I really *was* going to be sick.

Fifteen minutes later, my face washed and teeth brushed, I shambled back to my room. Cece was sitting on my bed, my cell clutched to her ear.

"Yeah, she just walked in now," she said. *Matthew*, she mouthed, pointing to the phone. "Here, I'll let you talk to her."

She held out my cell, and I took it with still-shaking hands. "Hello?"

"Are you okay?" he asked without preamble.

"Yeah, I'm . . . it's fine."

"It doesn't feel fine. I got a really strong sense from you just now. Something's not right."

"Yeah, well . . . some things aren't *Sâbbat*-related, you know. This is just . . . a relationship issue. Private stuff." My cheeks were flaming now.

"With Aidan, you mean? Then it is *Sâbbat*-related, Violet. Anything to do with a vampire is."

I shook my head, even though he couldn't see me. "Not this. I promise, okay?"

"Can you meet me in my office in ten minutes?" he pressed.

"No! Do you know what time it is? It's after lights-out. I can't just sneak off to your office."

"Your mark is fine? What about your bracelet?"

I glanced down at my wrist. "They're both fine. Seriously."

I heard him exhale loudly. "Okay, then. If you're sure."

"I'm sure. You need to chill—you're stressing me out here."

"Well, how do you think I feel? God, Violet. I suddenly felt physically ill, like someone was ripping out my insides." His voice was sharp, his frustration evident.

I had no idea that my mental state affected him quite so strongly. "I'm sorry, Matthew. I sometimes forget how connected we are."

"It's okay. I just hope—"

I heard a muffled voice in the background. "Is everything okay?" A *female* voice.

"Everything's fine," came his reply. "I'll let you go," he said, louder now.

I glanced over at the clock on my bedside table. It was well after midnight. What was he doing with a woman in his room after midnight? "Is that Charlie?" I asked, my voice rising.

"I'll talk to you tomorrow" was all he said before abruptly ending the call.

I stared down at my silent phone in surprise. "That was weird," I said, glancing up at Cece's questioning gaze. "Don't ask."

"Are you kidding? I mean, the dude sounded frantic. I only answered your phone because he wasn't giving up, by the way. It started ringing the second you walked out, and he just kept calling, over and over again. Hope you don't mind."

"Of course I don't." I slumped onto my bed, my heart still pounding. "I guess our connection is getting stronger. But it's so weird—it's only one way. You know, him reading my emotional state, but not the other way around. I guess he thought I was in mortal danger or something."

She shrugged. "I guess so."

"And," I added, drawing it out for emphasis, "there was someone there with him. A woman. I'm assuming it was the mysterious Charlie. You know, the one who apparently isn't his girlfriend but is somehow there in his room with him after midnight. On a school night."

Cece pursed her mouth, looking thoughtful. "Well, how do you know he was in his room? Maybe they were somewhere else."

"Good point." I hadn't even considered that. "He must have been on campus, though, because he wanted to meet in his office in ten minutes."

Cece rolled her eyes. "Can you imagine if you got caught? How in the world would you explain that one? 'Oh, yeah . . . I know he's a teacher, and a really, *really* hot one, but he and I are just good friends. It's not a booty call, I swear.'"

I tossed a pillow at her, laughing now. Leave it to Cece to lighten my mood, even at a time like this. I was going to miss her *so* much. That thought alone wiped the smile right off my face.

"You okay?" Cece asked.

I sighed heavily. "I love you. You know that, right?"

"Hey, right back at you, girlfriend."

"You better call or text me, like, every day."

"You know I will. And hey, I can do my semester abroad in Paris. Junior year."

"You better. You won't even need student housing—you can stay with us." My voice broke on the last word. *Us*. Was there still an 'us'? I wasn't sure, not after what I'd heard tonight.

Even when Aidan had been off at the Tribunal, he'd somehow felt closer than he did right now. What was happening to us? The future that had once seemed so certain, so solid, despite the improbability of him getting his cure, now seemed ephemeral, like a hazy mist that was looping and curling on the breeze, just out of reach.

"Are you going to tell me what's going on with Aidan?" Cece asked, as if she could read my mind. "Because even *I* know this is out of character for him. He hates Jenna. I'm sure of it. And you two have been somehow off for the past few days. Even Josh noticed, and he's pretty clueless about that kind of thing."

My inner debate over whether or not to tell her the truth lasted all of five seconds. "Suzanne said something to me during fencing class the other day. About Kate. I don't know why I got so upset, but I ran out and Tyler came after me. We started talking about her, about how much he liked her, how much we missed her. We were just . . . I don't know . . . sitting there holding each other."

Realization dawned in Cece's eyes. "Oh, sweet Jesus. Aidan caught you, didn't he?"

"Bingo."

"Oh, man. I guess that explains Tyler's busted face. But you told Aidan what was going on, right?"

I nodded. "Yeah, but right now he's not listening to what I'm saying. He's too busy sulking."

"Well, this sheds new light on what I saw out there tonight, doesn't it? Maybe he was just trying to get back at you."

"If he were trying to get back at me, wouldn't it be better to do it right in front of me? He has no idea that I know about this, Cee. Remember?"

"Oh, yeah. Right."

I glanced over at the window, the view unchanged beyond the panes of glass. "Do you think it's 'later' yet?"

"Later? Oh . . . right." She shifted uncomfortably on the bed. "You're going to worry about this all night, aren't you?"

"Yup," I answered with a nod.

"Any chance you're going to get any sleep?"

I shook my head. "Nope."

She rose, reaching for her robe. "Okay, then. I'm going to the lounge to get us some coffee. Snacks too?"

"Definitely." I reached for my purse and dug out a couple of crumpled dollar bills.

She waved away my offer of money as she pulled on her fuzzy bunny slippers. "No, this one's on me."

A bittersweet smile tugged at my mouth as I watched her thump off down the hall toward the lounge. It was going to be a long, sugar-and-caffeine-fueled night. But I knew without a doubt that if anyone could help me through it, Cece could.

25 ~ Enough Already

Since I had to skip senior ditch day on Friday, I decided to watch the sun rise from the loft in the chapel instead. As soon as Cece left, joining the horde of whispering seniors gathering in the East Hall lounge, I slipped on a pair of running shorts and a T-shirt and jogged across the dark, silent campus.

By the time I reached the last set of steps to the loft, I was breathless. I swiped at the thin sheen of sweat on my forehead with the back of one hand, then hustled up the ladder, pulling myself onto the wooden platform with a heaving sigh.

Only, I wasn't alone.

"What are you doing here?" Aidan asked, turning to face me. "It's senior ditch day. You're supposed to be at the cemetery."

"Seemed like a better idea to stay here," I said with a shrug. "Otherwise, Matth—Dr. Byrne," I corrected, "would have insisted on tagging along. I figured that wouldn't make me very popular."

"Won't your little friend be terribly disappointed?"

"Won't Jenna?" I shot back. My jealousy had grown and festered since that first sleepless night. Each day since, I'd become angrier and more confused, my feelings a tangled mess of insecurity and self-righteous fury.

Aidan turned back toward the wall, but I could see his jaw working, the muscles flexing as he stood rigidly with his hands fisted by his sides. Several seconds passed in silence.

"I suppose that means your little spy reported back to you," he said at last.

My heart did a little leap against my ribs. "What do you mean?"

"I think you know exactly what I mean. I have preternatural senses, remember?"

"You mean . . . you knew?" I stammered.

He turned back toward me, his face an implacable mask. "I was fully aware of Cece's presence there in the woods."

"So you . . . what? Wanted to punish me?" My swelling rage was constricting my windpipe, making white spots dance before my eyes. "Is that it?"

His eyes narrowed a fraction. "Is that really what you think of me?"

"What else am I supposed to think?"

He waited a beat before replying. "That I was trying to make you jealous by acting like a complete and total ass."

Hurt, shock, surprise, relief—it all battled inside me. "You have *got* to be kidding me."

"It was a stupid, immature thing for me to do, Violet. I know that now. But I was seething with jealousy, and—"

"For nothing!" I shook my head. "We weren't even doing anything."

"And you know what's really killing me, Violet? As much as I want to hate him, I can't help but think you'd be better off with him. Especially now, with assassins crawling out of the woodwork. Did you know that the guards have intercepted three in the past two weeks alone? Right outside Winterhaven, coming for me. You'd be safer with him. With Tyler."

"But I don't want to be with Tyler. He's just a friend—there is *nothing* going on between us."

"There's nothing going on between me and Jenna either."

I turned away from him, tears flooding my eyes. "This isn't even remotely the same. She was *naked,* in case you didn't notice."

I heard him sigh. "For the record, that wasn't the first time

I've seen Jenna naked. It's quite routine, though she makes my skin crawl. I suppose it's something biological—you know, a vampire-werewolf thing. Regardless, I promise you I get no pleasure from it."

"Just shut up," I muttered. Hearing that he saw her naked regularly did *not* make me feel any better, even if the sight of her did make his skin crawl. Which I doubted, considering how freaking gorgeous she was. There was no way I could ever compare, not in the looks department.

He reached for my shoulder, turning me around to face him. "Can we stop fighting now? Please? It's ripping my heart out." His voice broke on those last words, making my own heart twist painfully in my chest.

The truth was, I didn't want to fight anymore, either. I just wanted things back to normal.

"Please forgive me, Violet," he continued. "I should have trusted you, believed you. I should have tamped down the beast inside of me."

I swallowed hard. "I can't believe I actually thought you and Jenna . . ." A shiver snaked down my spine. "I mean, seriously."

He hung his head, shuffling his feet against the dusty floorboards. "I'm sorry I was such an ass. I'll do anything—whatever it takes to make it up to you."

I couldn't stay mad at him, not any longer. "Okay, okay. Apology accepted. Consider yourself forgiven."

"Thank you." His blue-gray eyes met mine. "Now please come over here and put me out of my misery. I'm not sure I can stand it another second."

I hurried into his embrace, pressing my cheek against his chest as he wrapped his arms around me, holding me tight. I let out a sigh of contentment as his lips moved against my temple.

"Have you any idea how much I love you?" he asked, his voice a hoarse whisper now. "I bloody well thought it would kill me, keeping you at arm's length. I can't do it, Violet. Never again."

"I know," I said, tipping my chin up to meet his gaze. "Just kiss me, okay?"

He did. Somehow, we ended up tangled together on the floor as he kissed me deeply, thoroughly, hungrily. I arched my body against his, wanting more, wanting to be swallowed up entirely.

"When are they coming back from Sunnyside?" he asked, his lips leaving mine just for an instant before finding them again.

"Doesn't matter," I somehow managed to say. "We've got all day."

He pulled away, smiling down at me. "Ditch day. Right. God, we need a blanket or something."

Scrambling to his feet, he found the box in the corner that

held a stash of blankets and throw pillows. I just stared at the square window above me, the sky a perfect blue beyond the glass.

"You're smiling," Aidan noted, standing over me now. "I haven't seen that in far too long."

"I was just thinking how normal this is. You know, the fight and all. For once it wasn't about something supernatural or anything like that. It didn't have anything to do with you being a vampire or me being a *Sâbbat*. You called it 'juvenile,' but that's what it should be, right? I mean, no matter how long you've lived, you're really just seventeen. You acted like a normal seventeen-year-old would. I think . . . I think maybe we needed that. It's like . . . I don't know . . . just so *human*."

"And *that's* why you were smiling?"

I sat up, scooting over to allow him room to spread out the blanket. "Yeah, I guess so. I mean, that and the fact that we can stay here making out all day long if we want. We're not expected in class, and there's no one here to come looking for us. At least, not until after lunch."

"What about Dr. Byrne?"

I shrugged. "What about him?"

"You must have told him you weren't going off campus with the rest of the class. So . . . did you tell him where you were going instead?"

"Uh-oh," I said, realizing the problem. Matthew was hyper-attuned to my emotional state. And if my emotional state got all . . . aflutter . . . would he feel it? How would he interpret it? Worse, would he start combing the campus, looking for me, when I didn't answer my cell phone?

"Why 'uh-oh'?" Aidan asked, on his knees beside me now.

A plan formed in my mind. "Is there any way you can . . . you know, pop into my dorm room real quick and get my cell phone for me? I need to call Dr. Byrne and tell him where I am." *And who I'm with,* I mentally added. Embarrassing as it was, Matthew would probably figure out what was going on once he started reading me, if he knew I was here with Aidan. I cringed at the thought, but what choice did I have?

"Of course. Is it on your desk?"

"Yeah, I think so. Plugged into the charger."

"Okay. Sit tight. I'll be right back."

He was, in a matter of seconds. He handed me the phone with a smile.

"Okay, that is just *so* weird," I said. "You know that, right?"

"Do you want to know how it's done? Technically speaking, I mean?"

I envisioned a lengthy, scientific-term-laden explanation and shook my head. "Not really, to tell you the truth."

He looked a little hurt. "Well, don't say I didn't offer. It's really quite fascinating."

"I'm sure it is, science boy. But give me five seconds to call Dr. Byrne, and let's pick up where we left off from before, okay?" I pulled him closer, reaching for his hand and pulling it toward my stomach. "I'm pretty sure your right hand was here," I said, laying it against the bare skin between my waistband and the hem of my shirt. "And mine was—"

"Make your call," he said impatiently, his eyes darkening with desire. "Quickly."

I was feeling more than a little sheepish the next morning when I stepped into Matthew's office for our weekly coaching session. Under the weight of his gaze, I made my way to the chair across from his desk and sat, fiddling with a loose thread on the hem of my sleeve.

He cleared his throat uncomfortably. "We might as well get this over with. You know, like ripping off a bandage."

"Go for it," I muttered, bracing myself.

He regarded me coolly, his hands folded on the desk in front of him. "You had a good time yesterday, I take it."

My cheeks immediately flooded with heat. "Ugh, this is *so* not fair."

"Trust me, in this case I'd have to agree." His cheeks were almost as red as I imagined mine were.

"Just what did you sense?" I asked, suddenly overcome with a morbid curiosity that, mercifully, vanished just as quickly as it had appeared. "Never mind. Don't tell me. I don't want to know."

"Good, because I sure as hell don't want to tell you. But I *am* starting to wonder if I should have a little chat with Aidan."

I rolled my eyes. "Oh my God. Please don't. This is embarrassing enough as it is. And . . . trust me, okay? You don't need to be worried."

"No offense, but that's kind of hard to believe after the read I got from you yesterday."

My cheeks burned hotter still. "Can't you just . . . I don't know, turn it off or something when I'm with Aidan?"

He leveled a glare in my direction. "Can you turn off your visions?"

"Okay, never mind. I get it."

The truth was, Aidan and I had pushed the limits yesterday. If it weren't for the fact that he was a vampire and I was a *Sâbbat,* well . . . maybe it was a good thing that we were. We'd gotten a little careless and a lot carried away. But then, I was eighteen now and Aidan, well . . . he wasn't a virgin. Besides, we were genuinely in love. I started feeling giddy all over again, just remembering the way he'd . . .

"Can you please stop that?" Matthew snapped, pulling me from my thoughts.

I rose on shaking legs. "Okay, I'm leaving."

"Why?" he countered. "It doesn't make a difference if you're sitting right there in front of me or not. You know that."

With a groan, I slumped back into my seat. "Great. So I have to watch what I'm doing—or even thinking—so that it doesn't affect you, but you can do whatever the heck you want with Charlie in your room in the middle of the night?"

"What are you talking about?"

"The other night. When we were on the phone. I *heard* her."

Several seconds passed in silence but for the ticktock of the clock on his desk. "Not that it's any of your business," he said at last, "but we weren't in my room. We were in the lab."

"The lab? What were you doing in the lab together?"

"Charlie is a biochemist. We were working on something. And obviously not having nearly as much fun as you and Aidan were in the loft yesterday."

I winced as his words hit their mark. "Why don't you tell me about Charlie, then, instead of keeping her a big mystery. It's only fair, don't you think?"

He leaned back in his chair, his hands folded behind his head. "Okay, what do you want to know?"

"I don't know," I said with a shrug. "How did you meet her? What's she like? Stuff like that, I guess."

"I met her my junior year at MIT, and we've been close ever since. Actually, we both went to Winterhaven, but not at the same time—she's a few years older than me. Her father's a teacher here. I think you had him last year for history."

"Dr. Penworth?"

Matthew nodded. "Charlie's the reason—or at least I *thought* she was—that I took this post at Winterhaven. She did her PhD at Columbia, and I wanted to stay close by."

"So she *is* your girlfriend," I said, ignoring the ridiculous and unexpected stab of jealousy.

"Charlie knows about the whole *Megvéd* thing," he hedged. "She knows she can never come first in my life."

"You didn't answer my question," I pointed out.

"Because there is no answer to it. My relationship with Charlie is what it is. She knows that if a better offer comes her way, she's welcome to take it."

"Wow, that's awfully noble of you."

He shrugged. "What else can I do? It's not like I have a choice—not really."

I was dying to know if they were sleeping together, but I knew I couldn't ask. It would be crossing a line, for sure. Still, I couldn't help but wonder.

"You said she's a biochemist?" I asked instead.

"Yes, a brilliant one. She's still at Columbia; she's got her own life, her own work."

"So, what were you doing in the lab together?"

"She's helping me with Aidan's cure. And . . . well, I don't want to get your hopes up, but things are looking pretty good. I'm cautiously optimistic that we'll have it by graduation. I just wish there was some definitive way to test it beyond the cellular level. Anyway, is there anything else you want to know?"

"I guess that about covers it," I said, even though it didn't, not really. Like a true scientist, he'd omitted anything about feelings. He hadn't said if he loved her, or if she hated me for coming between them. "I'd kind of like to meet her, though."

"I don't think so," he said, shaking his head.

Which probably meant that she wanted to rip mine off. "Well, this has been enlightening."

"Though not very useful, as far as coaching sessions go."

"Oh, please. Why do we even pretend that they're still coaching sessions? We're just hanging out. Might as well call a spade a spade."

"I suppose you're right. So . . . has Aidan told you about the attacks?"

My pulse leapt with alarm. "What attacks?"

"In Eastern Europe and somewhere in Asia. Unexplained deaths—a rash of them. Wounds to the victims' necks."

"Where did you hear this?" I asked.

"From Aidan. I guess this Luc character told him—you know, his scary-looking new bodyguard. Between these civilian attacks and the assassin that came after Aidan in Atlanta, well . . . things are definitely escalating. What's going to happen if this war breaks out before school ends? Have you given any thought to that?"

I shook my head. "I'm just hoping that it doesn't. But if it does, well . . . I assume Mrs. Girard will somehow excuse me from finals and grant me my diploma, even if I'm not around to finish the semester, right? I mean, she's the one making me play a part in all of this."

"Wait, that reminds me . . ." Matthew rose from his chair and went to a cabinet against the far wall, where he rummaged around for a bit. When he returned, he had something in one hand—a vial of some sort. He moved to stand just in front of me. "I've been meaning to test something out on you."

"Okay," I said warily.

In one swift movement, he removed the cap.

Immediately, my senses exploded. My right wrist burned; my entire body seemed to vibrate. Glancing down, I saw that the blackish red bloodstones on my bracelet were roiling angrily, glowing now.

Two words flooded my consciousness: *Vampire. Destroy.*

In an instant, I had my stake in my hand, poised to strike.

"Whoa!" Matthew said, ducking behind his desk. Hastily, he recapped the vial.

Just like that, the sensations disappeared. Gone. *Poof.* "What was that?" I asked, dropping the stake to the floor by my feet.

Matthew looked a little pale. "Infected vampire blood, along with a tissue sample. That was some reaction, though. I didn't even see you reach for your stake."

I tipped my head toward my bag. "It was in there."

"Yeah, but you moved so fast. *Too* fast. Next time you need to take a second to establish the connection with me first, okay? You would have struck on your own, with no coordination. We're a team, remember?"

"Well, next time warn me before you go sticking vampire blood under my nose like that! Where did you get it, anyway? It isn't Aidan's."

His eyes widened a fraction. "You can tell it isn't Aidan's?"

"Yeah." I held up the wrist with the bracelet. "White stones, good vampire. Red stones, bad vampire. It's pretty simple. Anyway, I don't get all wiggy when it's a good vampire. Especially if it's Aidan."

"I had him take this sample from the vampire we slayed in Atlanta," he said, pointedly avoiding any mention of Kate. "The female. Before he burned the corpse."

I just nodded, trying to ignore the painful lump that had formed in my throat. I would *not* let myself think about Kate. Not now.

He rubbed a palm against the dark stubble on his cheek, looking thoughtful. "Anyway, it's interesting that you reacted so strongly. I guess that means it's either something in the blood or in the tissue cells that sets you off. The vampire doesn't have to be alive. Of course, I use that term loosely in this case."

"Well, that's just fascinating," I said sharply. I was still shaking all over, thanks to his little test. Adrenaline, I supposed.

"Can we try it one more time? Only this time, the second you sense it, reach out for me psychically, okay?"

"I'm not sure I know how," I said truthfully. "You mean telepathically?"

"Try using the same mental muscle you use to put up the wall around your thoughts. Does that make any sense to you?"

"Yeah, I guess," I said, resigning myself to the experiment.

Clearly, Matthew thought this was an important skill to hone.

"Okay, ready? I'm going to uncap it again."

I nodded. "Ready."

Just like before, I had my stake in my hand, moving to strike a mere second or two after he'd removed the cap. There had been no time to reach out to him psychically, no time to think or do anything at all, except react.

It was only on the fourth try that I managed to pause long enough to flex my psychic muscle. *Megvéd*, I thought, pushing the word from my mind in much the same way as I reached out telepathically to Aidan.

And then I felt what seemed like a *click* inside my head. Suddenly, he was there. Matthew. Inside my consciousness.

Vampire. Destroy. The words were a command this time, spoken directly to Matthew, but with no discernible effort on my part. I couldn't explain it, not even if I tried. There were no words to describe the connection. We were simply . . . one.

I reached for my stake; he unsheathed his baselard, all in the blink of an eye. If he feinted left, I went right, and vice versa. We moved in perfect unison, not like separate bodies, but like two parts of a single one, anticipating each other's every move, bolstering it.

And then he recapped the vial. I felt him disengage from me

psychically, just like that. I felt off, like I had vertigo or something. I collapsed into the chair behind me with a gasp, trying to regain my equilibrium.

Across from me, Matthew looked equally dazed. "Wow," he said, raking a hand through his hair. "That was . . . intense."

It took me a second to catch my breath. "Yeah. I think we got it that time."

"I guess so." He set down the vial, his hands trembling slightly. "You think we can do that at any time? Or just when there's a threat?"

"You're asking me?" I shook my head. "I'm totally in the dark here. I know nothing. I don't even know what the hell that *was*."

The corners of his mouth lifted into a smile. "I'd call it pretty damn awesome, wouldn't you?"

I had to admit it was.

26 ~ Dancing Queen

Prom night at Winterhaven was much the same as prom night anywhere else. After a day of primping and preening, the seniors donned their tuxes and cocktail dresses and piled onto a coach bus headed for the big event—in our case, a beautiful hotel fashioned after a castle that sat high atop a hill overlooking the Hudson River.

The evening began with a formal, sit-down dinner followed by dancing. The only difference between others proms and ours was that everyone attending Winterhaven's had to sign a special COPA rider that outlined additional rules and punishments specific to this special, off-campus event.

Apparently, there had been problems in the past. With only

two weeks left before graduation and college plans already set, the threat of expulsion didn't hold much weight for some, it would seem. So in order to secure a ticket to the Winterhaven prom, you had to make a special trip to the headmistress's office to read and sign the rider. Of course, the special circumstances also meant that everyone attending had to be a student at Winterhaven—in other words, no outside dates.

Not that this affected too many people, but I knew of at least one girl—a senior on the fencing team with me—who had to go dateless because her boyfriend went to one of the hill schools in Riverdale.

Regardless, I was certain that I had the hottest date possible. I glanced over at Aidan, sitting beside me in his tux, and thought for sure that he was the most beautiful boy I'd ever seen. He'd opted for a white dinner jacket instead of black, and it suited him perfectly, made his eyes look like clear aquamarines in the flickering candlelight.

He'd used some sort of product on his hair to tame the golden waves, but one single curl had escaped, falling across his forehead. I resisted the urge to reach over and brush it back, deciding that it gave him a careless, boyish air that fit the circumstances.

More than anything, I was glad that Mrs. Girard had let him come. Luc was here, of course—Aidan's own personal bodyguard.

At least a dozen additional vampire guards were stationed around the perimeter of the grounds, keeping watch. At the first hint of a threat—real or imagined—Aidan would be whisked back to Winterhaven. He'd had to agree to that before Mrs. Girard would allow him to come. Well worth it, I decided. Even if it meant Luc was lurking in the shadows, following us everywhere we went.

Aidan leaned toward me, his breath warm against my neck. "You want to go outside and get some air?"

"Are we allowed?" I asked.

"No one said I had to stay inside," he answered with a shrug.

I nodded, pushing aside my half-eaten slice of cheesecake, and rose to follow him out. I couldn't help but admire the decor as we wove our way toward the exit, the room a labyrinth of tables, chairs, and bodies. The prom committee had chosen black, white, and red as the night's color scheme, and the result was truly elegant. The round tables were draped in black, the chairs covered with crisp white linen. A tall, rustic candelabrum stood in the center of each table, holding white pillar candles in various sizes. Long-stemmed red roses were twined around the base and arms, filling the room with their scent. The overall effect was magical, like something out of a fairy tale.

And I felt like a princess in my chocolate-brown chiffon dress. I'd accessorized it with French blue—strappy sandals and a simple wrap. Aidan's mother's aquamarine and diamond necklace—the one he'd given me last year for Christmas—completed the outfit.

The jewels were heavy against my throat, fit for a viscountess. I didn't feel worthy of them. They were far too valuable, too precious for a school prom. But seeing the happiness—the love, the pride—shining in Aidan's eyes when he saw me wearing them told me I had made the right choice.

As soon as we stepped out onto the stone patio, I paused, glancing back inside. "Wait. I'd better tell Matthew where I'm going. You know, just so he doesn't get all twitchy if he can't find me."

I saw Aidan roll his eyes, though he tried to hide it by turning away from me. "Fine," he said. "Do you see him anywhere? He was sitting over there with the other chaperones."

I peered through the glass in the door, my gaze scanning the staff table in the room's corner. Matthew's seat was empty now. "That's weird. I don't see him. Oh well. We can't stay out long, anyway. I think they're doing king and queen soon, and I've got to be there to cheer for Cece when she wins."

Winterhaven was progressive in many ways—we didn't have cheerleaders or a homecoming court, much less a homecoming queen. But some of the old-school traditions remained, including the presentation of prom king and queen, voted on by the senior class. There were actual crowns and scepters, or so I'd been told, and the king and queen led off the night's dancing with the opening slow song, also chosen by the seniors. I was pretty sure that Cece had it in the bag, though who would be voted king was anyone's guess.

"Feeling confident in your roommate, I see." He reached for my hand, bringing it to his lips.

"No one else has a chance," I said with a laugh. "Anyway, she looks like a queen tonight."

"The both of you do. *My* queen," he said with a mock bow.

I leaned in to him, resting my head on his shoulder. The sun had only just set, leaving the sky a colorful canvas. Indigo, gray, orange, pink painted the sky in wide, rolling bands. Down below, the town's lights were twinkling, matching the first stars up in the sky. In the distance, the river stretched and twisted. Across it spanned the Tappan Zee Bridge, brightly lit against the river's still, dark waters.

The breeze stirred, lifting the tendrils of hair from the sides of my face, cooling my skin, and I let out a contented sigh. "It's a beautiful night, isn't it?"

"Beautiful," Aidan agreed, but when I glanced up at him, I saw that he was looking at me, not the view. My heart did a little giddyap, my skin tingling all over.

"Have you ever been to a prom before?" I asked him.

He shook his head. "No. Never. You?"

"This is my first."

"Good," he said, his fingers trailing down the column of my neck, eliciting a shiver. "A first for us both. I feel as if I'm at a ball, stealing away my paramour for a forbidden kiss."

I held my breath as his lips slanted down toward mine. His kiss was soft and gentle and sweet, leaving me aching for more.

"Let's go down to the lawn," he said, his voice low and silky smooth. "Perhaps we'll find a hedgerow maze to get lost in."

Wordlessly, he led me down the wide steps to the flagstone path below that wound through the hotel grounds. We'd taken only a few steps when I stopped, dead in my tracks. Matthew stood a dozen or so feet away, with a woman. And they were arguing—loudly.

"It's just that I don't like surprises. You know that," he said. "You should have told me you were coming."

"Then it wouldn't have been a surprise," the woman said sharply.

Charlie. It had to be Charlie.

"You're putting me in an awkward position," Matthew said. "I'm supposed to be chaperoning. Not . . . with a date."

"Technically I'm here with my father. I'm *his* date. This is about *her*, isn't it?"

Matthew shook his head. "No. I just don't think it's a good idea."

"Look, Matt, if you're willing to give up everything for her, don't you think I at least deserve to meet her? Can't you at least give me *that*?"

For some inexplicable reason, I chose that moment to test our connection. I reached out to him psychically: *Megvéd*. There was that click again, and then he was there, right inside my head. For a split second, our consciousnesses merged. I could feel everything he felt—panic, discomfort, confusion. And then just like that, he disengaged.

As if in slow motion, he turned toward me. The woman followed his gaze, her eyes meeting mine, and then she looked back to Matthew.

His face said it all.

"Aren't you going to introduce us?" the woman asked, a brittle smile on her face.

I launched myself into action, hurrying over to where they stood in silent standoff. "Hi, I'm Violet," I said, forcing a neutral tone into my voice. "You must be Charlie. I've heard so much about you!" I held out a hand to her, and she took it, pumping it twice before releasing it. "Oh, and this is Aidan. My boyfriend," I added pointedly, offering him my best besotted-girlfriend smile.

"It's so nice to finally meet you, Violet," Charlie said. "Obviously, I've heard a lot about you, too."

She was tall in heels—almost as tall as Matthew. Her hair was pale blond, pulled back into a neat French twist, and her eyes were the same light blue as Kate's had been. She looked older than I'd imagined. Older and more sophisticated.

And she loved Matthew—I could sense it. Really loved him, in a desperate kind of way. I'd never felt so low in all my life.

Because I was the one keeping them apart. She'd never have him all to herself—*ever*—and there wasn't anything I could do about it. No amount of reassurances, of promises that my heart belonged elsewhere, would change that. As much as I liked to think that I was in control of my own destiny, there were some things that fate controlled—like centuries-old blood-borne legacies that couldn't be denied, no matter how hard we tried or how badly we wanted to ignore them.

Just then my cell, which I'd stowed away in my little purse, let out a screeching chirp. "Sorry. I need to get this," I said, digging it out and glancing down at the screen.

Where are u? the text read. *They're about to do king and queen!*

"We have to get back inside," I said to Aidan. "It's crowning time."

He just nodded, clearly anxious to extricate himself from this uncomfortable little tableau.

"It was really great to meet you," I directed at Charlie as I stuffed my cell back into my bag. "Maybe we can . . . I don't know . . . go out to dinner or something after graduation?" It was a stupid suggestion, but I was floundering for something appropriate to say.

"It was good to meet you too," Charlie said.

"We'd better hurry," Aidan said.

I made it back just in time to clasp Cece's hand and give it a squeeze before they called her name, declaring her prom queen. The room erupted in cheers as she made her way to the center of the dance floor and accepted the sparkling tiara.

Standing beside me, Joshua wolf-whistled loudly as Queen Cece made her curtsy, scepter in hand.

"She looks beautiful up there," I told him, nudging him in the ribs.

"She looks amazing," he agreed.

"And now for the presentation of our prom king," the announcer said.

I rose up on tiptoe, trying to see who had the mic. It was Suzanne Smith, I realized, head of the prom committee. I made a mental note to congratulate her on a job well done.

"As this year's prom king, the senior class has chosen . . ."

A lengthy drumroll followed, during which I glanced over at Joshua, looking hopeful.

"Not a chance," he shouted over the din. "Who would vote for a shifter?"

". . . Aidan Gray! Come on up and join your queen, Aidan," Suzanne chirped cheerfully.

"Well, this is awkward," Joshua quipped while Aidan just stood there, looking a little stunned.

"Go on," I urged, giving him a little shove forward. "You just got promoted—from viscount to king."

I had to stifle a laugh as Aidan was crowned, looking about as stiff and uncomfortable as anyone possibly could. The senior ballad was announced, Cece and Aidan were shoved together, and the dancing finally began.

And, okay, a teeny-tiny part of me was jealous to see the two of them up there dancing—my boyfriend and my best friend. But I had to admit that they looked spectacular together. Cece's silvery white dress set off her dark skin and hair flawlessly, a perfect foil to Aidan's fair, golden-boy looks. It almost looked planned, as if they had coordinated their outfits and everything.

Halfway through the song, Suzanne took up the mic and invited the rest of us to join in.

Joshua tapped me on the arm. "I guess you and I . . . I mean, why not, right?"

I tried to look coy. "Are you asking me to dance, Josh?"

"Well, you know, I just thought since my date is a little occupied at the moment. With yours."

"Let's go, then." I reached for his hand, dragging him out onto the dance floor.

"I'm not a very good dancer," he warned as I wrapped my arms around his neck.

I couldn't help but laugh. "There's not much to it. Just rock back and forth."

"Okay, but this is just weird," he muttered. "With you, I mean."

"Hey, thanks a lot! At least you're taller than me now." I had to look up to see his face. "Way taller. Wow. What happened to you?"

"Just a late bloomer, I guess." He shuffled around so that he had a better view of Aidan and Cece in the center of the throng. "Damn, why do they have to look so good together?"

I turned to look over my shoulder at the pair of them gliding elegantly across the floor. Aidan met my gaze and winked. In return, I blew him a kiss.

"Are they *waltzing*?" Joshua asked. "Seriously?"

"Just hang on. It'll be over soon and you can reclaim her.

Sheesh, you don't hear me complaining. I'm going to lay my head on your shoulder for a second, okay? Try not to flinch too much."

His mouth curved into a smile. "Are you using me to make him jealous? I don't approve."

"I love this song. Shhh, let me enjoy it." My head still resting on Joshua's shoulder, I sang along as we swayed awkwardly.

When the song finally ended, Suzanne reclaimed the mic. "Let's get this party started!" she shouted, and the DJ obliged with some pumping bass.

A relieved-looking Joshua released me just as Aidan and Cece hurried over to us. "Switch!" Cece commanded.

And then she and Joshua were gone, swallowed up by the crowd.

"I missed you," Aidan said, ducking his head down toward my neck. His lips tickled the skin beneath my ear, making me shiver.

"What is your thing with necks?" I teased. "I swear, you'd think you were a vampire or something."

"Very funny. You want to dance?"

"Yes, but pictures first. I don't want to be all sweaty." I led him away, toward the far corner of the room, where the formal portraits were being taken. Every couple of seconds, the flash went off, temporarily blinding me as we approached.

"Look, there're Sophie and Tyler in line. Max and Marissa too.

Hurry. Let's catch up with them before someone else gets in front of us."

Tyler asking Sophie to prom had been an unexpected surprise. I just hoped he didn't screw it up. I was glad to see that, for now at least, Sophie was smiling happily. She looked like she was having fun.

"Hey," I called out, joining them in line just as Sophie and Tyler stepped up to have their pictures taken.

"If it isn't the king himself," Marissa said. She looked beautiful in a short, magenta strapless dress with a peplum, paired with black patent Doc Marten boots. Max had coordinated his accessories with a matching bowtie and cummerbund and had dyed the tips of his spiky hair—all a bold magenta.

"Wow, Max," I said, eyeing him up and down. "You're really rocking that punk-formal look. Juilliard isn't going to know what hit them."

"That reminds me," he said. "Don't forget to e-mail me your friend's name. That ballet chick. I'll look for her at orientation."

"Yeah, and give me her cell number," Marissa said. "I'll text her as soon as I'm settled in the dorm. We can hang out."

Come fall, they would all be together—Max and Whitney at Juilliard, Marissa downtown at NYU. I was glad that Whitney would have someone to show her around the city, to introduce her to people. I was just sad that that someone wouldn't be me.

"Next," the photographer called out, and Max and Marissa switched places with Sophie and Tyler.

"There you are," Sophie said. "I was looking for you at the crowning. I didn't see you anywhere."

"We went out for air and just barely made it back in time."

"Good thing you did," Tyler said. "Can't have the king miss his own coronation."

For a moment there, the air crackled with tension. *Just ignore him*, I told Aidan telepathically.

"But hey, man, congrats on that." Tyler paused, looking Aidan straight in the eye. "We're good now, right?"

Several seconds ticked by in strained silence. Finally, Aidan nodded. "We're good."

"Next," the photographer bellowed.

Aidan and I started toward the camera, but I stopped midway, an idea forming in my mind. I turned back toward my friends. "We need a group shot when Aidan and I are done. Someone go find Cece and Josh, quick!"

I saw Max and Tyler dash off while Aidan and I struck our first pose for the camera.

"Okay, little lady, turn a bit more to your left. That's it. Chin down. Smile, you two." *Pop.* We tried several different stiff, awkward poses before Tyler and Max returned with Cece and Joshua in tow.

I motioned for everyone to join us, and we all squashed together, arms looped over shoulders and around backs. Aidan was on one side of me, Sophie on the other. I glanced around at my friends, laughing and smiling as the flash popped, thinking I'd never been happier in all my life. This was perfect . . . well, as close to perfect as it could ever be without Kate. Still, something felt slightly off, but I wasn't exactly sure what. And then I caught sight of Matthew in my peripheral vision.

"Hey, Dr. B.," Tyler called out, motioning with one hand. "Come on. You should be in this too."

"Yeah," Sophie said, moving over to make room for him between us. "C'mon, you go right here."

Tears burned behind my eyelids as he squeezed in, an arm thrown carelessly over my shoulder. Now it felt right, I realized as the flash began to pop again. Just so—with Aidan on one side of me, my *Megvéd* on the other. And around us, the best friends anyone could ask for. If only I could bottle this moment in time, capture it for eternity.

We were all together, minus Kate and Jack. Together, but never again whole. As the final flash popped, a single tear slipped down my cheek, captured digitally for all time.

27 ~ The End of the Road

I glanced up from the pile of notes in my lap when Cece walked into the room, looking exhausted. "Are you finished?" I asked as she collapsed onto her bed with a groan.

"Yep, done. Finally. What about you? Just that one final left?"

"Yeah, first thing tomorrow morning. I'm going to be cramming all night long. You might want to go stay with Marissa."

"Nah, I'll keep you company. I can sleep all day tomorrow. Well, that and start packing."

"Don't even say it!" It was only a matter of days before graduation, before we all packed up and left Winterhaven for good. Just thinking about it made me feel sick to my stomach. "Anyway, how'd you do?"

"Fine, I guess. The essay question kicked my butt. I'm just so glad it's over."

"Hey, don't rub it in." Beside me, my cell began to ring. "Ugh, it's Patsy. Probably calling to tell me she's not coming to graduation, after all," I said sourly, then connected the call. "Hey, there. What's up?"

"Just calling to see how finals are going," she chirped.

"Really well. I've got my English test tomorrow, and then I'm done."

"What about the calculus test you were so worried about?"

"I think I aced it, thanks to Aidan." He'd quizzed me relentlessly, until I could work every problem backward, forward, and sideways. "My history paper's turned in, and we got an A on our final art history project, so it's looking pretty good."

"I knew you'd do just fine," Patsy said. "Listen, I know I said we'd be there Friday night for graduation, but something's come up at work."

Of course it had. "Don't worry about it," I said. "Really."

"But you'll be in New York next week, right? Before you leave for London? We'll get to see you then."

"Sure," I said. "But look, I'm probably going to stay at Aidan's when I'm there in the city, okay?" Since it was *my* place now, technically speaking. Of course, Patsy didn't know that, but still. It occurred to me that, at some point, I was probably going to have to tell her. Then again, maybe not. Not with her halfway around the world in Australia.

"But we'll get together for dinner or something, right? We'll take you both out somewhere nice to celebrate your graduation."

She was making this *way* too easy.

"That sounds good. Actually, I better get back to studying now."

"Okay, sweetie. Good luck. And I'll be thinking about you Friday night. Paul too. He sends his love."

"Thanks," I said. "Talk to you later."

I ended the call and set down my phone with a sigh.

"She's not coming?" Cece asked.

"Nope. Big surprise, right?" Still, I was disappointed. There wouldn't be a single person there to cheer for me when I walked across that stage and took my diploma. How pathetic was that? Aidan and I were lucky that we had each other, since neither of us had anyone else.

"I just don't get that woman," Cece said, shaking her head.

"Yeah, me either. It doesn't matter, though. I just wish Gran could come." She'd wanted to, and I'd had several long talks with Melanie, her home health aide, debating it. Melanie had finally spoken with Gran's doctor, who had failed to give his support, and that had been that. Gran wasn't happy, but I'd promised to come visit them in Atlanta before I went to Paris.

"Well, my grandma's coming up from New Orleans, and all the aunts and uncles and cousins too. It's going to be a zoo. I won't have any time to hang out with you guys while they're here. Which is annoying, because it *is* our last weekend."

"Yeah, but it's not good-bye, remember? Just a week, and then we'll be in England together."

"I can't wait," Cece said. "I wish Aidan would let us all chip in on the house, though."

I shook my head. "He says it's taken care of. The Trust people know he's a relative of the original family, so . . . I don't know. Maybe they worked out a deal or something. I think we're getting to use rooms that aren't usually open to the public. Something like that."

"That's so cool. Just imagine if they knew the truth—the prodigal son, returned. A freaking *century* later. Anyway, what about Dr. Byrne?"

"What about him?" I asked.

"I assume he's going with us, right?"

I nodded. "Looks that way. I'm sure Charlie is thrilled."

"I actually feel kind of bad for her. I mean, it's probably hard to understand this thing between you and Dr. Byrne if you're not a part of it, you know? And then you've got to add in the fact that he's a teacher and you're a student and, well . . . it must be weird for her. That's all I'm saying."

"See, that's why you're so popular," I said, shaking my head in amazement. "You can always see things from other people's perspectives. What do they call it? Empathy?"

"Hey, you gotta feel for the chick," she said with a shrug.

"Trust me, I do. I swear I do. It's just . . . I think she *really* hates me." I winced, remembering the cold look in her eyes when we'd met.

Cece gave me a pointed look—lips pursed, one brow raised. "Wouldn't *you* hate you? In her position, I mean?"

"Heck, yeah. Of course I would. That doesn't make it any more pleasant, though." I glanced down at the notes surrounding me, a painful reminder of my upcoming final. "I really should be studying."

She nodded, rising and reaching for her bag. "Okay, I'm supposed to meet Josh at the café, anyway. You want me to bring you back anything?"

"Yes, something sweet. That, and a mocha. Actually, make it a peppermint mocha." The peppermint would help soothe my pretest nerves.

Cece's face lit with a smile. "You got it, girlfriend."

I sighed heavily as the door shut behind her. Just one more final—I could do this. After all, I was a tough, vampire-slaying, tattooed, going-off-to-live-in-Paris kind of girl. What was a measly English final in the face of all that?

With a groan, I got back to work.

Friday night came all too fast. The past few days had been a blur—checking grades, packing trunks, waiting for the end to come.

And now it had. I shifted uncomfortably on the hard pew, waiting for my name to be called.

Sophie's valedictory speech had been brief but inspiring, the perfect combination of serious but funny. How was I going to make it through each day of class at AUP without her there beside me?

As student body president, Cece had made a speech too. All those New Orleans cousins and aunts and uncles had hooted and hollered when she was finished, making her blush, and all I could think was how awesome she was—the perfect roommate. Fate had been so kind to me.

And Aidan, well . . . when I'd seen him walk across the little stage erected at the front of the chapel and take his diploma from a smiling Mrs. Girard, it had seemed so real. Like somehow all the schooling he'd received before now was meaningless—that *this* graduation was the one that really counted, that marked the true beginning of the rest of his life.

The rest of them who'd been called up before me alphabetically—Max, Tyler, Cece, even Jack—seemed so distant now, somehow just out of reach. I felt numb, disengaged—

"Miss Violet McKenna."

It took me a second to recognize my own name. Beside me, Shannon McKenzie nudged me in the ribs. I rose, making my way to the end of the pew vaguely aware of the sound of cheering and whistling behind me, where the parents and family were seated. I glanced back, surprised to see Patsy and Paul on their feet, smiling in my direction.

What the heck?

"Congratulations, *chérie*," Mrs. Girard said, handing me my diploma with a smile. How easily she slipped into the role of cheerful headmistress, I realized, taking the leather case and tucking it beneath my arm as I made my way back to my seat.

The procession continued on—Joshua, then Marissa a few minutes later. I clapped for them all, trying not to notice the empty spot between the *R*'s and the *T*'s where Kate Spencer should have been. Finally, they called out Amy Zuckerman's name, and then the microphone fell silent.

The chapel's pipe organ began to play the alma mater, and at last we tossed our caps into the air with a flourish. And then it was over. High school was done, a chapter in my life complete.

Aidan found me even before I'd made my way out into the crowded aisle. "I didn't think Patsy was coming," he said, taking my hand.

"I didn't either." I shook my head, feeling a little dazed as I followed him out of the chapel and onto the lawn, where a brightly lit reception tent had been set up. The trees surrounding the lawn were strung with twinkle lights, and paper lanterns lit the path. The sky was clear, the air surprisingly balmy for early June in the Hudson Valley—a perfect night to celebrate under the stars.

"There she is!" came Patsy's voice, just behind me. I turned to find her there, smiling broadly. "Look at you," she said, wrapping me in a hug. "You look so grown up. Your father would be so proud of you right now."

"I can't believe you're here," I said. "You said you weren't coming."

"I wasn't sure we could make it, and I didn't want you to be disappointed. And then when I found out we *could* come . . . well, I wanted to surprise you." She held up her left hand, wiggling her fingers dramatically.

Immediately I noticed the gold band on her ring finger. "What? When?"

"This past weekend. Nothing big, just at City Hall. We'll have a reception once we get to Sydney."

"Wow," was all I could manage.

"Congratulations," Aidan said, mercifully stepping in and offering his hand. Patsy took it and then pulled him into an awkward hug. "It's so good to see you. It's been so long, hasn't it? Oh, Paul, this is Aidan Gray. Aidan, this is my husband, Paul Layton. My second husband. Current." She was babbling incoherently now, obviously caught in the web of the Aidan Effect.

"Why don't we go get something to eat?" I asked, trying to distract her. "I think they're serving dessert."

"Sounds good," Paul said. "Lead on."

Minutes later, we got our plates of cookies and assorted pastries and found a table, while Paul went off to fetch drinks.

Before I sat, I unzipped my lavender graduation gown and stepped out of it, revealing the simple white sundress I wore beneath. Aidan had already removed his own gown—silver for boys—and wore rumpled khakis and a plain white button-down shirt with a deep violet-colored tie.

"Don't know how to work an iron, I see," I quipped, reaching over to straighten his tie.

"Who has an iron at boarding school?" he asked with a chuckle, leaning down to kiss the tip of my nose.

I wasn't going to admit that *I* did—it was just one of my many neuroses. Cece always teased me about it, especially the time she caught me ironing a stack of underwear.

"You're not having anything, Aidan?" Patsy asked as soon as we sat, noticing the blank spot where his plate should be.

"No, I'm not hungry. Big dinner," he lied, patting his stomach.

I reached across the table for a napkin, and Patsy laid a hand on my wrist, trapping my hand against the table. "Wait, what's this new ring you're wearing?" She glanced from me to Aidan and back to me again. "Is there something the two of you need to tell me?"

I shook my head. "No, it's just a gift. You know, like a . . . umm . . ."

Help me out here, I pleaded telepathically.

"I think they call it a promise ring," Aidan supplied.

Thank you.

"It's pretty," Patsy said, lifting my hand to examine it more closely. "It looks like an antique—a really precious piece, actually."

I gave Aidan a desperate look.

He cleared his throat uncomfortably. "Yeah, I found it at one of those antique stores. You know, the junky kind. I thought it suited her."

"Well, you have a good eye. I bet some poor soul had to pawn it for cash and the store didn't quite realize what they had. I think that happens a lot these days."

"Yeah, probably," I murmured. "Oh, look, here comes Paul with the drinks." Thank God.

Just as he slid back into his seat, Mrs. Girard appeared at our table. "Mr. Gray, if you don't mind, I need a quick word with you."

Just like that, his eyes seemed to shift from blue to a stormy gray, his mouth set in a hard line. "Of course. If you'll excuse me for a moment."

I watched him go, my mouth suddenly dry. I reached for the iced tea Paul had set in front of me, nearly draining the glass in a single gulp.

"Wasn't that the headmistress?" Patsy asked.

I just nodded, a knot of fear forming in the pit of my stomach.

"You don't think he's in trouble or anything, do you?"

"I'm sure it's nothing," I said, forcing myself to smile brightly. "Go on, eat. You don't have to wait."

As Patsy bit into a pastry, I watched Aidan follow Mrs. Girard to the edge of the lawn, right to the spot where I'd slain Julius, I realized with a shudder. Luc joined them, his dark hair gleaming under the bright moonlight.

I couldn't make out what they were saying—they were much

too far away for that. They gave away nothing with their body language either. All three stood stock still while they talked, their bodies rigid. My anxiety soared with each passing minute, and I found myself looking around for Matthew.

He was nowhere to be seen.

Luckily, Patsy and Paul had lapsed back into conversation while they ate, oblivious to my growing discomfort. I decided to give it another minute or two, and then I was going to have to go find Matthew. I wasn't quite sure why, but something about this felt off, and I didn't even have my stake with me.

"So, are y'all staying in Tarrytown tonight?" I asked Patsy, mostly to distract myself.

She shook her head. "No. I wish we could, but we've just got so much to do to get ready for the move, right, Paul?"

He just nodded.

"Actually"—she glanced down at her watch, the one my father had given her so many years ago—"as soon as we're done eating, we should probably head back. I hope you don't mind."

A wave of relief washed over me. "No. It's fine. I've still got a lot of packing and people to say good-bye to."

"Do you want me to send a car for you on Sunday?"

"No. I'm pretty sure Aidan's already ordered a car," I said, drumming my fingers on the table. Truthfully, I had no idea if he had or not. But now I would make sure that he did. Or maybe Matthew could give us a ride. It didn't matter—we'd figure it out later.

"Hey," came Aidan's voice behind me, nearly making me jump out of my skin. He moved to stand behind me, both hands resting on my shoulders as he leaned down toward my ear. "Can I talk to you for a second? It's nothing," he directed at Patsy and Paul. "I'll bring her right back. I promise."

They nodded in unison, looking a little woozy. Clearly, Aidan had used one of his mind manipulation tricks on them.

Without another word, I rose and followed him back inside the empty chapel.

"What's going on?" I asked as soon as we stepped out of the vestibule. I didn't like the look on his face—his eyes had taken on that empty look, his jaw clenched tightly.

"We've got to go," he said without preamble.

My heart began to race, my palms dampening. "What do you mean, go? Go where?"

"Paris. Pretty much right away. They're gathering for a fight, and they need their *Dauphin*."

"Who's gathering for a fight?" I asked, confused.

"The Propagators. They're all headed to the Tribunal headquarters, prepared to seize power. To put one of their own in the Eldest's seat."

I clenched my hands into fists of frustration. "I don't understand. Why now?"

"I don't know. I thought we'd have more time."

I took a deep, calming breath. "Okay, so we go. We get this over with, whatever it is. Bu-but what about England?" I stammered, my resolve weakening. "We're supposed to go the week after next."

A muscle in Aidan's jaw was working furiously. "You'll get your trip to England. I'll make sure of it."

"Well, what am I supposed to tell Patsy?" I asked, floundering now. "And Matthew. I've got to tell Matthew. He's got to come too. I need him."

"We've got an hour, tops. Nicole has the plane waiting at a private airport nearby. Leave your trunks and just gather whatever you need for a few days, okay, Vi? I'll find Dr. Byrne and tell him what's going on. It's his choice if he wants to come with us or not."

"Okay," I said numbly. "I'll go tell Patsy I'm not feeling well. Or—or that you're not feeling well, and I'm taking you to the infirmary. And then I'll just be in my room, changing and getting my stuff ready."

He nodded, reaching for my shoulders, his fingers digging sharply into my bare skin. "I'll meet you in your room as soon as I can. I never should have gotten you into this, Violet. I am so very sorry."

The stark desolation in his gaze was sobering. He thought this was it for us—the end of the road. But it wasn't; it wouldn't be. Not if I had anything to do with it. "You can't protect me from this, Aidan. It's what I'm meant to do. What you're meant to do. It'll work out; it's all going to work out," I said calmly, assuredly.

Only, I wasn't sure who I was trying to convince more . . . him or me.

28 ~ Leaving on a Jet Plane

I had never been on a private jet before. I had to admit, a girl could get used to it. Plush leather seats, a flat-screen TV, cashmere blankets—it was definitely posh, even if I was too terrified to actually enjoy any of it.

Because this wasn't any old private jet—this was the Vampire Tribunal's jet, and we were on official business. Technically, there *was* no Tribunal at present; it had been disbanded while the fight for the Eldest raged on. Still, Mrs. Girard retained control of their assets—including the plane—and she was ready to make her move.

My friends had *not* been happy when I'd told them I was leaving and why. There'd been very little time for good-byes, but

I'd assured them that I would be back in time for the trip to England. I only hoped it was the truth.

I glanced up at Matthew, who was sitting directly across from me and Aidan, facing us. He looked remarkably calm, all things considered. He had a book open in his lap, but I couldn't tell if he was actually reading it, or just pretending to. When we'd boarded, he'd offered to sit somewhere else, to give Aidan and me some privacy. But I wanted him close by, where I could see him.

Even though my bracelet's moonstones glowed benignly instead of the more ominous bloodstones, I still didn't trust Mrs. Girard and Luc, not completely, and not with my *Megvéd*.

Aidan and I had to tell Mrs. Girard about my connection with Matthew when we'd insisted that he join us. She'd seemed genuinely surprised and not at all pleased that we'd kept it from her. I counted that as a personal victory. My secrets were mine to keep until I was ready to share them. Besides, Mrs. Girard didn't own me—she didn't own any of us. She wasn't even Matthew's boss anymore; he'd turned in his resignation weeks ago, effective today, the last day of the term.

So he could follow me to the ends of the earth, I supposed. Poor Charlie.

"We still have several more hours until we land," Aidan said, interrupting my thoughts. "You should try to get some sleep. Dr. Byrne too."

I glanced over at the window, forgetting that the plane came equipped with permanent blackout shades. There was nothing to see, no indication of the hour outside the window, no view of the night sky or the ocean below.

"I don't think I could sleep if I tried," I said, nervously twisting the ring on my finger. Not on a plane full of vampires, even if they were the friendly variety. And not with the unknown danger that lay ahead of us.

Mrs. Girard had prepped us once we'd taken off, filling us in on what was going on. It didn't sound good—Propagators gathering in Paris, along with leaders from a few Eastern sects who sided with them. The message was clear: Come and get us, if you can.

And so we would, or die trying. I'd agreed to the plan, the price of Aidan's freedom, so there was no backing out now.

Just freaking great.

At the time, it hadn't even occurred to me that I was pledging Matthew to the fight too. If something happened to him, if something happened to Aidan—

"It's going to be okay, Violet," Matthew said, his steady gaze meeting mine. "I don't know how, exactly, but we're going to succeed, okay?"

I sat up straight in my seat, my heart pounding now. "You've had a vision!"

He nodded, looking strangely grim. "I've seen enough to know we come out safely on the other side of this."

I took a deep breath, considering his words—and the ones left unspoken. He'd seen more, something bad. That was the way our visions worked. "What else?"

"It doesn't matter; let's deal with this threat first."

"You can't just—"

"I need more details," he interrupted. "A replay when I can actually focus on it. There's time. Just . . . trust me on this."

From the tone of his voice, it didn't seem like I had a choice.

"Anyway, Aidan's right. We should get some sleep." He set his book on the table in front of him and then retrieved the blanket from the empty seat beside him, unfolding it and laying it across his lap.

"I'll keep a close eye on everything," Aidan assured me, reaching for my hand. "I promise."

"Maybe if I listen to music," I said, reaching for my cell phone and earbuds.

Aidan leaned toward me, his lips close to my ear. "Remember that song you played me? The one with the slow, marching beat? Try that; I bet it'll put you right out."

I shot him a glare. "I love that song."

"I know you do," he said with a grin.

"You're lucky I adore you," I shot back, then shoved my earbuds in and pressed play.

Not a day goes by that I don't give thanks that you do, he answered inside my head, drowning out the song's opening notes. *Now go to sleep, love.*

I hadn't thought it possible, but I must have dozed off. The next thing I knew, the landing gear rumbling beneath my feet jolted me awake. The lights in the cabin were low; I had no idea if it was night or day. Across from me, Matthew was still sleeping, his arms folded, his features slack. He looked peaceful, far younger than his years, a shock of dark hair falling across his forehead.

I sat up stiffly, an uncomfortable crick in my neck where I'd been leaning against Aidan's shoulder. "We're landing already?" I asked, yawning.

"I'm afraid so. How'd you sleep?"

"Like a rock," I said.

Matthew woke, straightening in his seat. "We're there?" he asked sleepily.

"Just about," Aidan said. "I talked to Nicole while you two were sleeping. When we land, the three of us are going to my apartment to wait. Nicole and Luc are going straight underground, gathering forces. When they've chosen the spot for the confrontation, we'll join them, drawing the enemy to us."

I nodded, unable to speak.

"Are you ready for this?" he asked me, just as the plane bumped against the ground.

"How long do you think we'll have? At your apartment," I clarified. "Before they send for us."

"Not long. A matter of hours."

"That's it?"

He nodded. "That's it. We need to get you and Dr. Byrne something to eat right away."

"What time is it?" Matthew asked.

"Hard to tell with no windows, isn't it?" I glanced down at my watch. "Just after four in the morning, New York time. So that's, what? Ten a.m. in Paris? The sun will have risen already—how will they get around?" I asked, assuming that Mrs. Girard and Luc hadn't taken the elixir that made it possible to withstand the sun.

But crap, Aidan *had* taken it—which meant he was going into a fight with his abilities compromised. Again.

"Don't worry," Aidan assured me. "They have their ways. Paris has an extensive underground footprint, you know. It's why the city is so popular with vampires. Tribunal Headquarters is really an entire network—safe houses connected via the Metro system and unused tunnels and chambers. It reaches far out into the countryside."

"Wow, they should include that in the travel brochures," I said sourly. "'We've got vampires, all the way out to the burbs.' That'll get the tourists flocking."

Aidan just shrugged. "It's true of most cities with a large subway system. London, New York, São Paulo, Prague, Moscow, Seoul, Tokyo, Hong Kong."

"Remind me to avoid those cities from now on," Matthew said with a frown.

The plane rolled to a stop, and Mrs. Girard made her way to the front, pausing as she passed us. "You know the plan, Mr. Gray. There's a car waiting to take you to your apartment."

He just nodded, reaching for my hand and helping me to my feet.

I wondered where, exactly, we'd landed. A private airport, I imagined, but surely we'd still have to go through customs or something.

Turns out we did, but there wasn't much to it, just a single agent who barely glanced at our passports before waving us along. We followed Luc and Mrs. Girard down a ramp and through a door that led to a garage, where two long, dark cars were waiting. Somehow, our bags had already made it off the plane and were being loaded into the trunks by liveried drivers.

Silently, we climbed into the rear car. Just like on the plane, Aidan sat beside me, Matthew directly across, facing us. The first thing I noticed was that a panel completely blocked my view of the driver, and the windows on the sides and back of the car were entirely blacked out—which was odd, because it hadn't looked that way from the outside.

Curious, I tapped on the glass.

"We don't need this," Aidan said, hitting a button on a panel above our heads.

There was an electric whir, and the dark panels on either side of the car slid down, revealing normal windows. "They're reflective from the outside," Aidan explained. "So, looking in, you can't tell the windows are blacked out."

I suppressed a shudder. "That's so creepy. How far outside Paris are we?"

"About an hour, if the traffic's light."

Matthew took out his cell phone, glancing down at the screen with a scowl. "If you guys don't mind, I need to check my messages," he said, looping a headset over one ear.

"Go ahead," I said, scooting closer to Aidan.

Aidan reached for my hand, lacing his fingers through mine as the car slid out of the garage and picked up speed. "Are you scared?" he asked, his voice low.

"A little. I don't know. I mostly feel resigned. A little relieved too, if that makes any sense. I've been dreading this day for so long—knowing that it would come, but refusing to let myself think about it. But if what Matthew said is true—you know, his vision—then I'll just be glad to have it over and done with."

He glanced down at our joined hands for a moment and then raised his gaze to meet mine. "You're assuming that whatever we do today will fulfill our obligation to Nicole and her cause. I'm afraid I don't think it's that simple."

"Well, why not? If you end this war—"

"How am *I* to end this war?" he asked, his voice rising. "There's no proof that this *Dauphin* legend is true. And even if it is, my role isn't assured. For all we know, the man who raised me is my biological father, after all. This is madness, Violet."

"You *make* them believe it. Listen to me," I urged, squeezing his hand. "You've got Mrs. Girard's army behind you and me and Matthew beside you. It doesn't really matter if those other vampires can destroy you or not, because I'm not letting them." I took a deep breath, gathering my thoughts. "You tell them that you're the *Dauphin*, and you make sure they believe it. You can do this. I know you can."

"You've that much faith in me?" he asked, leaning forward till his forehead rested against mine.

"I do," I answered. "You just need to have faith in *me*. In Matthew and in his vision."

"I love you, Vi," he whispered, his breath coming faster now, mingling with mine.

"I know." And then I kissed him, completely forgetting Matthew's presence there in the car with us until I heard him clear his throat loudly.

"Sorry," I said, drawing away reluctantly. "Everything okay?" I asked Matthew, seeing that his scowl had deepened.

"Oh, you know." He stuffed his cell phone back into his pocket. "Just a half dozen or so messages from Charlie, wondering where the hell I am."

"Uh-oh," I said, hating the unfairness of it all. "What are you going to tell her?"

"I have no idea," he said sharply. "Can we talk about something else? Maybe . . . I don't know, combat strategy or something? Since we'll have to all work together this time."

That was enough to distract me throughout the rest of the drive into Paris.

* * *

Aidan's apartment was pretty much exactly what I'd expected—large, exquisitely furnished, and comfortable. It took up the building's top two floors on the side facing the Eiffel Tower, the second floor reached by a spiral staircase.

We'd stopped to pick up an oh-so-not-French lunch of cheeseburgers and fries—*Le Royal Deluxe et des frites*—a few blocks away, and after a quick tour of the apartment, sat at the long, rectangular farmhouse table eating. At least, Matthew and I were eating.

Aidan had disappeared back upstairs. I could hear him banging around above us as I slowly chewed my food, hoping my nerves would allow me to keep it down.

"So, this is where you're going to live, huh?" Matthew took a sip of his drink, watching me over the rim of his cup.

"Apparently. It's pretty nice though, right?" I glanced around, admiring the copper pots and pans hanging from the ceiling. "Awfully swanky for student housing."

"And big," Matthew added. "I think I counted three bedrooms besides the master suite, plus a formal living room and that little nook he called a parlor. There was a library on the second floor too. It's got to be two or three thousand square feet, at least. What does he do with it all?"

"I suppose you're going to ask us to rent you a room," I joked, then immediately wished I could take it back when I saw the stricken look on his face.

I didn't have time to question him, because Aidan came back in then, carrying a sword.

"What are you doing with that?" I asked, watching as he took it over to the counter and laid it down with a *clang*.

"I think I have some silver polish somewhere," he said, digging around the cabinet beneath the sink.

"You're going to polish a sword? Now?" I finished my last fry, crumpling the container and tossing it in the bag. "Anyway, where'd you get that thing?"

"It's been in the family for years," he answered, still searching through the cabinet. "It's quite old, really, but it'll do."

"For what?" Matthew asked.

"If I'm to be the point man, out front, I need a weapon," Aidan explained. "It won't kill a vampire, obviously, but it'll stop one long enough for the two of you to flank in and do your thing. Anyway, we'll need one for later. To separate—"

"—the head from the body," I finished for him. "Yeah, I remember. Is it sharp?"

He nodded, running a hand down the length of the blade. A ribbon of red appeared on his palm, dripping grotesquely down his wrist as he reached for a towel. "Perfectly so. It just needs to be shined up a bit." Wincing, he wiped away the blood. "That hurt."

"I'm sure it did," I said, watching in amazement as the deep gash healed itself in a matter of seconds, right before my eyes.

Matthew nodded appreciatively. "That's a nice trick."

"Isn't it?" Aidan examined his hand, looking pleased.

I exhaled quickly. "Okay, what now? I mean, after you're done polishing your sword?"

Aidan shrugged. "We wait. This might take me a while, though."

"Great," I said, feeling as if I might jump out of my skin. I had to do something, occupy myself somehow. Otherwise I was going to lose it, just sitting around twiddling my thumbs. "I think I'm going to go sit on the balcony upstairs and read my e-mail, then. Or . . . maybe I'll check out the library first, if that's okay."

"Hey, *mon appartement est votre appartement*. This is your home, come fall."

He sounded *way* too cheerful, I decided. As if he were putting on a front, playacting for my benefit—trying to pretend like everything was okay, when it wasn't. How could it be?

"You mind if I come with you to the library?" Matthew asked, tossing the rest of his lunch in the trash.

"Course not." I stood and headed for the door, taking my drink with me. "Come find us when you're done polishing your sword, okay, Aidan?"

He nodded. "I won't be long."

But I knew he would be. He wanted to be alone; I could sense it. Whatever his reasons were, I'd have to respect them, even if I didn't like it.

And I didn't, not one bit.

"C'mon," I said to Matthew. "Let's go see if he's got anything good to read."

29 ~ Visitors of the Unexpected Kind

Ow!" I cried out. "My wrist." I glanced down at my bracelet, horrified to see the blackish red bloodstone glowing hotly against my skin. "No. Oh no. Aidan!"

He was beside me in an instant. "Look," I said, holding up my wrist.

He glanced toward the window, where the moon had risen high in the sky.

There was no way of knowing if this was a single assassin, or a larger threat. But there *was* a threat—there was no doubting that.

Megvéd, I called out telepathically, establishing the connection with Matthew. Without even trying, I relayed the information to him in a split second.

I wasn't sure what room he'd been in—if he'd been in the library reading, or if he'd gone to bed. It didn't matter, though. He had no trouble finding me.

We were ready, the three of us. Aidan with his ancient sword, me with my stake, and Matthew with his baselard. The three of us stood in the center of the master bedroom, an immobile unit as we waited, listening. Aidan's senses were better than ours, and it didn't take him long to figure it out. "The balcony," he said. "Two of them—maybe three."

In the blink of an eye, Luc appeared before us. "Vampires," he said, his dark eyes narrowed.

"Yeah, we got that," I said sharply. "Thanks."

"A scouting party, I think," Luc added, ignoring my jab.

"There's not much room to maneuver on the balcony," Matthew said. "We choose better ground, then draw them to us."

"But where?" I glanced around the room, taking in the luxurious furnishings. "Here?"

Aidan shook his head. "Not here. There's a park nearby. It's gated—it'll be locked. We go there."

"You take Violet," Luc said. "I'll get him." He tipped his head toward Matthew.

Panic made my breath hitch in my chest. "Wait, no! You can't split us up. Aidan, take us both—like you did in Atlanta."

"It's okay, Luc. I can take them both."

"What if they don't follow us?" Matthew asked.

Aidan's eyes hardened. "They will. Grab on, both of you."

We did.

The horrible sensation was brief. A hiss and a pop, and I opened my eyes to find myself standing in a leafy park that was completely shrouded in darkness save for the hazy light of the moon.

Once again, I reached out psychically to Matthew, establishing the connection between us—horrified that, at some point, I'd let it drop.

We formed a semicircle, the four of us, waiting.

It didn't take long. Two vampires appeared seemingly out of thin air, a male and a female. They were both tall, dark haired, and dark eyed. "We've come only to talk," the female said, her voice heavily accented. "To see who this boy is that Nicole Girard keeps so close to her heart. Her most favored creation, yes? But why? What is so special about this boy, this vampire?"

"Who sent you?" Luc asked, stepping forward as if he were our leader.

"Why, we came on our own accord, of course."

Breach her mind, Matthew urged. *See if she's lying.*

I have to drop my connection with you to do that, I argued.

Just for a moment. Search her mind; see what her intentions are, he insisted.

"You've brought friends, I see," the female said. "Mortals. Do not fear us. We talk, that's all."

I didn't trust her. More important, my bracelet didn't trust her. I did what Matthew asked.

It took me only a split second to see her plan. The male would take out Luc and hold Aidan captive; the female would kill Matthew and me. The "talk" was just a distraction. Of course.

Megvéd. Just like that, he knew everything I knew. We sprang into action.

The female first—she was our greatest threat. With her removed, the male would be indecisive, unsure.

Matthew's baselard flew through the air, straight into the female's eye. She shrieked, and Luc moved to protect Aidan while I leapt forward and plunged my stake into her heart.

The female went down with an inhuman cry that silenced itself as her body hit the ground. Matthew retrieved our weapons as I wheeled toward the male, who had somehow gotten one beefy arm around Aidan's neck. Luc slammed the pair of them to the ground, struggling to free Aidan and gain his feet before the male came after them again.

They were moving so fast, I could barely follow the fight. Someone had to immobilize our enemy long enough for Matthew and me to do our job, but right now he was nothing more than a blur, a constantly moving target.

And then something—some*one*, I realized—jumped right on top of Matthew. I heard him grunt, the breath knocked from his body as he slammed against the ground, face-first.

"Just a lowly mortal," the vampire growled, moving off Matthew's body so that he could flip him over, neck exposed. "He's no match for me."

"No, but I am." Adrenaline surged through my veins as I lifted my stake high in the air and launched myself at him. Just as I expected, the vampire turned toward me, his body angled just enough for me to accurately skewer his heart with my stake in one clean stroke.

I saw surprise widen his dark eyes at I hit my mark, and then his body went slack, slumping to the ground beside Matthew's prone form.

Terror paralyzed me as I just stood there and stared at my *Megvéd*—my protector—lying so still and quiet. *Please be okay. Please, please.*

Luc was beside him in an instant, his fingers on the pulse at his throat. "He's fine. Just knocked out cold."

Thank God. Oh, thank you, thank you.

"Aidan, get them both back to the apartment. I'll stay and finish off the corpses—just leave me that sword."

I turned to find Aidan standing there, looking pretty much unscathed. "You have matches?" he asked Luc.

Luc nodded. "Yes. Now go. We don't want to draw unwanted attention."

Aidan reached for my hand. "I can't take you both, not with Dr. Byrne unconscious. He'll be dead weight. I'll take you first and come back for him."

I pulled away from his grasp. "No. Him first. I can wait."

"He's better off here with Luc for now," Aidan argued. "Otherwise, I have to leave him alone while I come back for you."

I swallowed hard, realizing he was right. Of course. Nodding my assent, I reached for Aidan's hand. "Let's go," I said. "Make it fast."

An hour later, we all sat around Aidan's kitchen table, Matthew holding an ice pack to his head. His face was bruised, several shades of purple and blue, but otherwise he seemed okay.

"We're sitting ducks here," Aidan said. "This is crazy. How long until Nicole calls for us?"

"Soon," Luc said. "And until dawn, there's an entire squad of guards surrounding the building. You'll be safe."

"Well, where were the guards before?" I asked sharply. "Maybe they could have prevented that whole fiasco back there."

Luc's obsidian eyes met mine. "The sun had only just set. Besides, we had not expected an ambush. My guess is that they were telling the truth about acting on their own, not following anyone's orders. Two rogues, thinking that they might be rewarded generously for bringing Aidan to our enemies."

I glanced over at the window above the sink and shuddered. "Well, whatever they were, I'm willing to bet there's more of them out there."

"The guards will keep watch throughout the night. The Wampiri haven't yet arrived, and they're the only ones of our kind who can hunt during daylight hours. You'll be safe. I promise you."

I turned toward Aidan. "Why are we trusting him?" I asked. "Seriously. This is one of the vampires who locked you up, who helped torture you. And we're supposed to trust him to keep us safe?"

Aidan let out a sigh. "I trust him, Violet. I do."

Luc offered me a tight smile. "If it'll make you less uneasy, feel free to breach my mind. I'm certain you'll be assured by what you find in my thoughts."

"No, thank you." I rose, pushing back my chair. "Fine. If you say we're safe, I'm going to sleep. I'm exhausted, and I want to be ready for whatever comes next. Matthew, you should . . . I don't know . . . probably try to stay awake or something, right? I mean, you probably have a nice concussion there. Aidan, can you keep an eye on him?"

"Of course. You go lie down. Luc will post a guard outside the bedroom window. Get some rest, okay?"

That was it? He was simply dismissing me, sending me upstairs like a child?

With a huff, I stormed upstairs toward the master bedroom. Truthfully, I had no idea why I was so mad. I was frustrated, I guessed. Scared. No one had expected a fight before the fight.

I was so tired, I didn't bother to change into pajamas. I just collapsed onto the bed and pulled the covers up around me. Before I knew it, I drifted off into oblivion.

There was a loud knocking somewhere. I sat up, disoriented. The sun had risen, the first lavender light of dawn slanting across the bedcovers. Something that sounded like a doorbell chimed, sending shivers up my spine.

I flung off the covers and leapt out of bed, hurrying downstairs as fast I could. Aidan and Luc were already there, moving toward the door.

"Who is it?" I asked breathlessly. "Not more of them. Please tell me it isn't more of them."

"I doubt it," Luc said. "They wouldn't be out during the day."

"Where are the guards?" I asked.

"Gone until sundown." Luc tipped his head toward me. "Let her answer it. You can't expose yourself like that."

"I'm fine. The elixir, remember?"

"Which you should not have taken, not with the threat we're facing. You need all your capabilities."

"My capabilities are good enough. Anyway, they can't destroy the *Dauphin*, remember? At least, that's what you keep telling me."

"She gets the door," Luc growled.

"I'll get the door," I said, slipping between them just as the doorbell chimed once more.

"Your stake," Aidan said, handing it to me.

"Gee, thanks. Coming," I called out, hurrying into the foyer with the length of smooth hawthorn clutched tightly in my right hand. My bracelet was fine—no glowing stones, except for the white ones. Harmless. We were safe—I hoped.

Aidan unlatched the lock, and I reached for the brass door handle and turned it, opening the door just the slightest crack as I peered out. "Who is it?" I asked.

"Bonjour!" came a familiar voice.

What the heck? I threw open the door, gaping at the sight before me. Tyler. Oh my freaking God, it was *Tyler*. Cece. Sophie. Joshua. Marissa.

"Sorry. Max couldn't come," Marissa said. "His parentals were not very accommodating."

"Wh-what? How?" I stammered.

"My aunt works for Air France," Marissa said with a shrug. "She managed to hook us up with a last-minute standby."

"I can't believe this," I said, blinking hard. *I must be dreaming—still upstairs, tucked cozily in bed.* Except . . . I was pretty sure I was awake.

"Hey, bestie," Cece said with a smile. "Did you really think we were going to let you guys fight this battle without us?"

I just shook my head, completely flummoxed.

"This is a bit unexpected," Aidan said, stepping up beside me. "But please, do come in."

30 ~ The *Dauphin*

"We've been summoned," Aidan said, glancing up from his cell.

My heart leapt into my throat, my stomach lurching uncomfortably. We'd been sitting silently side by side on the little velvet divan in the master suite for more than an hour, my body fitted alongside his as we waited for the call.

And now I would've given anything to ignore it, to continue sitting there long into the night, Aidan's fingers stroking my hair as I listened to the rhythmic beating of his heart. Cece, Joshua, Sophie, and Marissa were all scattered about the room—Sophie in a chair by the window, reading; Cece and Joshua on the floor near our feet, playing a quiet game of Scrabble; Marissa on the bed, texting Max.

We were prepared. We'd spent the better part of the day formulating our plan, which Luc had communicated to Mrs. Girard. Tyler would actively join in the fight, as would Joshua and Marissa. Their gifts would come in handy. Cece and Sophie would remain at the apartment under the protection of a pair of vampire guards. As much as they hated to be left behind, we just couldn't find a way to utilize them.

Besides, Cece could project to the scene of the battle and report back to Sophie. There was a chance that her astral self might somehow distract our enemies. At least, that was her game plan.

Cece's body would remain safely here, under Sophie's watchful eye. And Sophie—well, her talents might be useful after the fight was over. To assess the damage.

"Someone go tell Tyler and Dr. Byrne," Aidan said, disentangling himself from me and rising to stand stiffly. "I'll meet you all downstairs in five minutes."

"I'll tell them," I said, standing on shaking legs and making my way to the library in a daze.

"It's time" was all I said, my voice quavering.

They both looked up at me, their faces matching masks of fierce determination.

Tyler rose stiffly and, with a nod in my direction, made his way out to join the others. Matthew reached for his shoulder harness and silently strapped it on. Far more elaborate than the one he usually wore, this one held four blades, two at the ready beneath each arm. He'd spent the better part of the long afternoon practicing pulling them from their sheaths, one after another, in rapid succession. "You've got your stakes?" he asked as he guided me out of the room, one hand pressed against the small of my back.

I nodded. "Downstairs, in the kitchen." One for the sheath strapped to my leg and two more for my new shoulder harness. I felt like something out of *The Matrix* when I wore them all at once. All I needed was a black leather duster.

"Just let me stop in the bathroom first. Tell everyone I'll be down in two minutes, okay?"

Matthew nodded and hurried down the spiral staircase as I stepped inside the hall bath and locked the door behind me. It took me several tries to pull my hair back into a neat ponytail and secure it with the hair band I'd been wearing around my wrist.

Once I'd finally accomplished it, I took a moment to catch

my breath, staring at myself in the mirror, shocked by the image looking back at me. There were dark circles under my bright green eyes, eyes that were too big in a much-too-pale face. I looked like a terrified kid, I realized, not like a kick-ass vampire slayer out to save the world.

I dropped my gaze, unable to bear looking at my cowardly self another second. I just needed to splash some cold water on my face, I decided. That would help. But I was shaking so badly that I fumbled with the faucet, my hand slipping and knocking the bottle of expensive, scented hand soap into the porcelain basin.

Giving up, I gripped the sink tightly, trying desperately to pull myself together.

"Violet?" Aidan called up. "It's time—the car's here."

This is it. You can do this.

One more deep breath and then I unlocked the door and stepped out into the hall. "I'm coming."

A half hour later, the stretch limo dropped us off at a Metro station in the second *arrondissement,* where we took a train three stops before getting off and slipping through a door that eventually led to a long, stone-lined tunnel lit sporadically by fixtures that gave off a dull, yellowish light.

I had no idea how Aidan knew where to go, but we followed him without question down the tunnel and up a set of stairs, which took us to a large basement of some sort. We crossed the basement and went through a door, then down another set of stairs that led into yet another tunnel, this one narrower than the one we were in before, but more brightly lit.

About a hundred yards in, Aidan paused, facing the wall. "It's right about here," he said, running a hand along the stones that made up the wall.

I didn't see anything. "What's here?"

"The door." He continued to run a hand along the stones, at last stopping and turning to face us. "Here it is," he said. "Just give me a second."

I looked at Matthew quizzically, but he shook his head. "I don't see a door there," he said.

"Yeah, you sure 'bout that?" Tyler looked equally unconvinced.

"You can't see it because your senses aren't nearly as sharp as mine," Aidan said. "I just have to press on this stone—this one right here."

I held my breath as he leaned against the wall. Eventually, there was a scraping groan and it began to give. "No mortal could open this, trust me," he said with a grunt.

The seemingly invisible door swung open, and in a single-file line, we followed Aidan through and into a huge, cavernous space that appeared to be a theater of some sort. To our left was a stage, about six feet off the ground and maybe fifteen or twenty feet deep. Enormous fringed gold velvet curtains were held back on either side of the stage. The area where the audience would sit was sort of cone shaped, narrower toward the front, but growing wider as you moved back toward the far wall.

There were two rows of long, wooden benches set out on either side of the stage, right up front, but all the other benches were stacked up against the walls, which were lit with enormous torches set high up—all glowing brightly now, casting flickering orange light across the dark stone floor.

"What *is* this place?" I whispered, a shiver racing down my spine. It felt ancient and a little bit evil.

"Ah, you made it," Mrs. Girard called out, startling me so badly that I stumbled back against Matthew. He steadied me, both hands on my shoulders as we turned to watch Mrs. Girard walk across the stage toward us with Luc at her side, her heels clicking loudly against the wooden floor. "And I see you've assembled your troops. You're just in time—they're already on the move. Guards!"

The shadows behind her began to move, taking shape. Several dozen male vampires made their way across the stage and down the steps on either side. They were all enormous, each and every one of them, and menacing looking, too. I was glad they were on our side.

Mrs. Girard and Luc followed them down, coming to stand beside us. "Let me speak first," she directed at Aidan. "And take this."

Luc held out something that looked like a long, sheathed sword.

"I brought my own," Aidan said, reaching for the strap thrown across his shoulders.

Mrs. Girard shook her head. "Forget that puny weapon. This sword is fit for a king."

She pulled it from its sheath, and I had to admit it was impressive with its jeweled hilt and engraved blade. "It is said to have belonged to Louis Antoine, Duke of Angoulême, last *Dauphin* of France," she said reverently. "And now it is yours, *mon chou*."

Aidan took it, admiring it. While he did so, Luc removed the weapon Aidan had brought with him, the one he'd so painstakingly polished, and handed it to Tyler. "You take this," he told him. "I've been told you're pretty good with a sword."

Tyler took it with a grin. "Indeed I am."

"Okay, guys," Matthew said, gathering us into a tight circle. "You know the plan. Marissa, you try to control the mood. Keep us calm and focused, if possible. Stay back behind the guards—a safe distance from the fight. Joshua, you'll help create a diversion when we need one. We can fight only one pair at a time—try to keep us covered. And, Tyler, just help out any way you can. See what happens when you shift their molecules around. If nothing else, use the sword."

"We've got this," Tyler said with his usual swagger.

Mrs. Girard's head snapped up at once. "They're here," she said. "Stay behind me for now, Aidan. When I present you, look them in the eye. Do not let them cow you."

I bristled at her implication. Aidan wouldn't cower, and neither would the rest of us. We were warriors—the Winterhaven Warriors.

Aidan turned to face me. *Whatever happens, Vi, I love you. Heart and soul, never forget it.*

Never, I answered. *I have faith in you. In all of us.*

And then they began to file in silently from the back of the space, filling in the shadows with their ranks.

Who are they? I asked Aidan.

Propagators, mostly. Females with their consorts. There's the leader of the Wampiri from Russia, and behind her, leaders of the ancient tribes, mostly from Eastern Europe and the Far East. And the rest . . . just opportunists, I suppose.

There were so many of them. My wrist was burning now—a sharp, throbbing pain—my bracelet's bloodstones glowing eerily alongside the moonstones. Without even thinking about it, my mind reached out for Matthew.

Megvéd.

And then he was there, inside my head. His mind was deadly calm, sharply focused. Binding my thoughts to his, I was able to find my center. A quiet determination settled over my consciousness.

Yeah, we had this.

Mrs. Girard stepped forward. *"Bonsoir,"* she called out loudly, her voice reverberating against walls. "I'm glad you've come. Tonight, the High Tribunal will be restored."

A female vampire stepped forward, clearly their leader. She was striking, tall and inhumanly pale, her blond hair falling in loose waves down her back. "You haven't the Eldest, Nicole Girard," she said, her voice sharp. "But we do. You have no authority here."

"On this night, we begin a new era of rule," Mrs. Girard argued. "I've something far more powerful than the Eldest, you see. I have the one with royal blood, the one who cannot be destroyed by our kind, the one who controls every breed of slayer, who will lead us into a peaceful era of coexistence with our mortal counterparts." She paused a beat for emphasis, smiling broadly now. "I have the *Dauphin*."

She turned and gestured toward Aidan, who strode forward without a backward glance, taking his place by Mrs. Girard's side.

The woman threw back her head and laughed. "Surely you jest, Nicole. Look at him—he's a just a boy, a male, the weaker of our species. He's no leader, no threat to us."

"You underestimate him, Galina. I suggest you tread carefully," Mrs. Girard warned.

On my unspoken command, Matthew and I moved forward in perfect unison, taking our places beside Aidan.

"And you've brought some mortals, I see," the woman called Galina said, her voice laced with amusement. "Are they a part of this new era, as well?"

Even before she'd finished speaking, the two male vampires who'd been standing behind her moved forward menacingly. I saw that one carried a sword, the other a brightly lit torch. One to behead, the other to burn—a vampire assassin squad. I had only to breach the mind of the one with the sword for a split second to know their intent—they were going for Aidan, not for me and Matthew. After all, what were two mortals to them but a minor nuisance, like a pair of harmless flies?

Instantaneously, I transmitted the knowledge I'd gleaned from the vampire's mind to Matthew, as well as my own plan of attack. A mere fraction of a second had passed—just the time it took to blink an eye—and we launched into action.

As the vampire on the left lifted his sword to strike, Aidan's flashed out, blade meeting blade in an ear-splitting *clank*. At that moment, Matthew's baselard flew through the air, into the eye of the vampire carrying the torch. When the vampire wielding the sword turned to see what had caused his companion to cry out, Matthew's second baselard hit its mark at the precise moment that I drove my stake through the first vampire's heart. I paused only a second before pulling my stake from the gaping wound.

And then, like a well-timed *pas de deux*, Matthew and I wheeled around each other so that I could stake the second vampire while he retrieved his baselard from our first victim's corpse.

A split second later, Aidan joined in our dance, slicing the vampires' heads off in two neat strokes while Matthew, who'd somehow managed to catch the torch before it hit the ground, laid fire to the bodies.

I watched with satisfaction as both corpses burst into all-consuming flames that somehow extinguished themselves in a matter of seconds, leaving nothing behind but a rotten stench and a pile of ashes.

There was a brief moment of stunned silence, and then chaos erupted, the din rising like the buzz of angry insects.

A second and third pair advanced on us as Mrs. Girard's guards pressed into action, encircling us and managing to hold back the rest of our would-be attackers while we efficiently dispatched two females and then two more males. Matthew and I moved as one, in perfect synchronicity, his blades flying, my stakes hitting their mark again and again while inhuman shrieks pierced the air.

In the center of the fray stood Tyler, his sword meeting several different blades, often at once. Like the gifted fencer he was, he managed to deflect or avoid each blow, ducking and twisting, wielding the heavy weapon as if it weighed nothing at all. He somehow managed to disable several pairs of would-be attackers as they headed toward Matthew, Aidan, and me. I could only assume he was messing with their molecules the same way he had with Aidan's that day in the chapel. I have no idea how he was able to do it while wielding his sword, though—talk about multitasking. I wondered if Marissa was somehow lending him a hand in the calm and focused department.

And then another pair broke through the line. A dense fog—created by Joshua, no doubt—cut them off from the rest of our enemies. Hidden from view, Matthew and I took them down, one right after the other. This scenario played out over and over again. The fog, the blade, the stake, Aidan's sword—it repeated itself like a loop as the beheaded bodies collected on the floor, just waiting to be burned into oblivion.

And then at last the howling mob retreated. They backed away, surveying the carnage from a safe distance as Aidan, Matthew, and I regrouped, our weapons held at the ready as Tyler and Joshua joined the guards to form a protective semicircle around us.

And then my heart leapt into my throat as Aidan stepped

forward, past the guards, his bloodied sword held aloft in victory. "I am Aidan Gray," he said, his voice loud and clear and sure. "I am your *Dauphin*, son of Edward VII, King of England. I alone control the *Sâbbat* and her *Megvéd*. The prophecy says I cannot be destroyed, not by my kind, and you've seen proof of that here today."

He strode back and forth as he spoke, his spine straight, his head held high. "I'm offering you a choice—we can continue this stand, destroying you one by one, sending you straight to hell where you belong. Or you can crawl back to wherever you've come from and tell your people what you've seen.

"Tell them this: Eldest rule is no longer," he said, his voice echoing throughout the chamber. "Nicole Girard, creator of your *Dauphin*, retains the title of chairwoman of the High Tribunal. Each tribe, each coven that has existed in accordance with the code of laws, will choose their representative to govern beside her.

"Mark my words—indifference to the law will no longer be tolerated. Executions will be swift and efficient. If anyone here doubts me, I suggest you challenge me now, on this ground." He paused, his gaze sweeping over what was left of them.

No one said a word.

"The rules are simple," he continued. "We coexist secretly and in peace with mortals. We avoid the kill when we feed. We eschew innocents. We create our own kind sparingly and with great care. If you cannot abide by this code, speak now and suffer my judgment."

From somewhere ahead and to my left, I heard a shriek of fury. A black-haired female appeared to fly forward, a blur that stopped short on the end of Aidan's sword. In an instant, Matthew's baselard flew through the air, into her eye, and I sprang forward with my stake, dealing the deathblow with practiced precision.

"Who's next?" Aidan taunted, removing the weapons from the corpse. He handed them to Matthew, who wiped them on the leg of his already-bloodstained pants before returning me my trusty length of hawthorn.

My body tense and rigid, I waited for the next attack, but none came. One by the one, the dissenters began to drop to one knee.

"My *Dauphin,*" came a whispered voice, and then another. And another. Another still. On and on it went until they were all kneeling—every last one of them. Even the one called Galina, her blond head bowed reverently.

Mystified, I looked to Aidan, unsure of his next move. I watched in wonder as he lifted his chin proudly in the air, looking every bit the young king they believed him to be and nodded.

"This is done," he said, his tone commanding. "Go now."

31 ~ Like Breathing Air

It was only when we'd stumbled back to Aidan's apartment near dawn that I noticed what a ragtag bunch we were. My hair had obviously caught fire at some point, a big chunk burnt off almost up to my chin on one side, and Matthew's eyelashes had been singed clean off. Both of us were sporting numerous bruises from head to toe, along with cuts and gashes that were just beginning to crust over.

Tyler, too, was covered in bruises and cuts caked with blood, and Joshua sported a deep gash along one cheek.

Aidan remained unblemished, though like Matthew and me, his blood-soaked clothes were ruined and his skin was coated with a thin film of putrid ash. So was his hair, which now looked a dingy sort of dishwater gray rather than its usual golden blond.

Only Marissa appeared unscathed. *Thank God.* I couldn't help but remember how Marissa had suffered in our fight with Julius, her throat ripped open, her skin deathly pale. I was relieved that the guards had kept her safe, that she'd come through this fight without a scratch. She deserved that. She'd earned it.

As soon as we walked through the door, Sophie and Cece came running toward us. "Thank God you're okay!" Cece cried. "I watched the whole thing—you guys were awesome!"

Sophie looked peeved. "Yeah, and I was stuck with the shell of her body and two scary-looking vampires. I had no idea what was happening till the very end, when Cece decided to come back here."

"Hey, I was busy causing distractions," Cece shot back. "Could you tell?"

"I noticed," Aidan said with a smile.

He had? He hadn't mentioned it, but then, he *had* been pretty occupied.

"Anyone need me to check anything out?" Sophie offered. "Any injuries?"

"You should look at that cut on Joshua's face," Matthew said, his brow knit. "He might need stitches."

Sophie nodded. "What about you, Tyler? You're a mess."

"Hey, you can check me out anytime you like," he quipped with a wink.

Sophie's cheeks pinkened. "Very funny. Okay, how about you all go get cleaned up, and I'll set up triage in the kitchen. Aidan, do you have any first aid supplies?"

He nodded. "I have no idea *why* I do, but yes. I'll go get them for you."

"Guys, I've got to get in the shower," I said, my knees suddenly weak. "Like, now."

"Go on up." Aidan gestured toward the stairs. "The master bath is all yours."

I made straight for it, stripping off my clothes and dumping them in a trash bin while the enormous claw-foot tub filled with water. Unfortunately, there wasn't a real shower—just one of those old-fashioned, hand-held thingies hanging on a hook, but it would have to do. A few minutes later, I sank gratefully into the steaming water, thinking that I'd never been as sore, as exhausted, in all my life.

Finding a bar of violet-scented soap—how had Aidan managed that?—I hastily ripped off the wrapper and began to scrub myself raw. I wanted to rid myself of every trace of the night's work, to scour the memories from my brain. It was always the same—I was perfectly fine while in *Sâbbat* mode, finding satisfaction, almost a thrill, as my stake hit its mark. But afterward, it hit me hard.

How many vampires had I destroyed tonight? Eight, ten, twelve? I'd lost count. I had to remind myself that I hadn't taken their lives, not exactly. Their mortal lives had already been ended in ways that had nothing to do with me. Besides, if I hadn't destroyed them, they would have killed me. Killed Matthew, Tyler, Joshua, Marissa. All of us.

I set aside the soap, my skin red and raw now. Holding my breath, I slipped beneath the water, submerging myself. I stayed there, my eyes squeezed shut, until I thought my lungs would burst—a test. Unable to bear it a second longer, I propelled myself upward, gasping for air the moment my mouth broke the surface. The survival instinct was too strong to deny, just as it had been last night—just as it would always be when I came face-to-face with a murderous vampire. I had to accept that, or I'd drive myself crazy.

Sighing resignedly, I reached for the shampoo, squeezing an untidy lump into my palm. It smelled good—vaguely tropical—but I cringed as I ran it through my lopsided, burnt-off hair. I wondered just how bad it looked.

"It's pretty bad," Aidan confirmed, once I'd finally gotten out of the tub and pulled on a tank top and a pair of pajama pants. "I think you'll have to get it cut. But as luck would have it, you're in Paris. Get some sleep, and then we'll find someone to take care of it."

I just nodded, exhausted as I climbed into the bed that would be mine come fall. I'd have to do something about the duvet cover, I decided, snuggling beneath it. It was way too masculine. The room needed something brighter—maybe a sage green in shantung silk.

My mind was just beginning to drift off when Aidan leaned down and pressed a gentle kiss to my lips. I reached up to cup his cheek, wondering suddenly what it would feel like with stubble. It was hard to imagine him any differently, since he remained perpetually unchanged.

He turned his face toward my hand, his lips against my palm. And then he froze. "You're bleeding," he said.

I sat up. "Where?"

"Your arm. It's deep. Why didn't you tell me? I would have sent you straight down to Dr. Sophie. She was having so much fun down there with antiseptic and bandages that I didn't have the heart to tell her that I could heal minor wounds myself."

I examined the arm in question. He was right; there was a gash on the inside edge of my right biceps, about two inches long. I must have opened it up when I'd scrubbed myself clean.

I shoved down the sheets and duvet, noting with a frown that I'd bled all over them. "Crap. I need to strip the bed and get these in the wash before they stain."

Aidan laid a gentle hand on my shoulder, restraining me. "Don't worry about it, not now. Here, just pull it back and I'll get you a quilt or something." He went to the cedar chest at the foot of the bed and dug around, then returned with a heavy chenille blanket. "This should keep you warm enough. Now, let me see your arm."

He sat down beside me, running his fingers lightly along the wound. "I'll take care of this," he said, his voice soft. "Go on. Lie back down."

I was too tired to resist, even if I'd wanted to. Besides, his method was way more appealing than stinging antiseptics and Band-Aids. Scooting down beneath the blanket, I settled my head on the plump, goose-down pillow and waited, my body taut with anticipation.

First he wiped away the blood with something cold and wet, dabbing gently, until the wound was entirely clean. And then he bent his head, his tongue against my skin now, making short, silky strokes that caused gooseflesh to erupt all over my body.

"Oh my God," I breathed. "Do you have any idea how good that feels?" A calm seemed to wash over me, my body relaxing against the soft mattress as he continued to lick me, his strokes longer now, the pressure increased as my eyelids grew heavy.

"There. It's healed," he murmured at last, but his mouth didn't leave my skin. Instead, he trailed kisses up toward my shoulder, across my collarbone, down to the dip between my breasts.

I arched against him, clasping the back of his head. My fingers tangled in the hair at the nape of his neck, guiding him lower, toward the exposed skin between the hem of my tank top and the waistband of my pajama pants.

"Violet," he protested with a groan, but his mouth obeyed. "This is . . ." *Kiss.* "We shouldn't . . ." *Kiss.*

And then, inexplicably, I yawned—a deep, breathless yawn wrought from sheer and utter exhaustion.

With a low chuckle, Aidan laid his head on my belly. "You need to sleep."

I nodded, stifling a second yawn as I did so. "Did everyone else go to bed already?"

"I think so, once they got their bandages." His fingers traced a path down my right side. "They're exhausted, just like you."

"What are you going to do all night?"

"I'll stay with you for a little while, but then I'm going to see Nicole. We need to discuss her expectations from here on out. I won't be gone long."

"You're sure it's safe?" I asked, stroking his hair. It was damp from his shower and back to its usual golden color.

"Entirely so. Should I make an appointment for you somewhere while I'm out? For your hair? For first thing tomorrow, maybe? You and your friends can have a girls' spa day or something like that."

"Sure," I said with a sigh. "That sounds nice, actually. When do you think we'll go back home?"

"I don't know—that's why I need to speak to Nicole. How many days do you need in New York to prepare for our trip to England?"

"We're still going?" I asked drowsily.

"Of course. I promised I'd take you, remember?"

I just nodded.

Lifting his head from my stomach, he scooted up in the bed and fitted himself beside me. *Heart and soul,* he said inside my head.

Heart and soul, I answered back, and then drifted off with a smile on my lips.

I opened the front door of Aidan's town house in Manhattan—*my* town house, technically speaking—to find Matthew standing there, his hands thrust into his pockets, a messenger bag across one shoulder.

His eyes widened when he saw me. "I'm still not used to the hair," he said, shaking his head.

I reached a hand up to my short, silky bob. "Yeah, me either."

"It looks good, though. It suits you."

"Thanks. What are you doing here? I didn't expect to see you till tomorrow at the airport."

"I just needed to talk to you about something; it won't take long. Can I come in?"

"Sure, of course." I moved aside. "Sorry about the mess. I'm still packing, if you can believe it. I'm just not sure what to take. The weather's apparently really fickle this time of year in Dorset—are you bringing a warm jacket, or just a raincoat?"

He didn't move beyond the marble-tiled foyer. "That's what I came to talk to you about. I'm not going with you to England."

"You're not? But I thought . . . I mean, you said—"

"I know what I said, but I was wrong. You don't need me. You'll be fine with Aidan."

"Oo-okay," I said, drawing it out, trying to figure out what had caused this change of heart. Because when we'd left Paris three days ago, he'd said he *was* coming with us.

Everything had been settled. Aidan had gone to Mrs. Girard and told her that her *Dauphin* was going on vacation, whether she liked it or not. He'd held up his end of the bargain, and now it was up to her to reestablish the Tribunal. She could get along without him just fine for a couple of weeks, he'd insisted.

And Matthew, in turn, had maintained that he couldn't possibly let me go to England without him, not when he wasn't one hundred percent certain that there was no longer a threat.

So we'd agreed that he should come. He wasn't going to stay at Brompton Park with us—that would have been too weird, a teacher crashing his students' grad trip. Instead, Matthew had booked a room in the nearest inn. The Cock's Crow, or something silly sounding like that, an old coaching inn above a tavern a couple of kilometers from the estate. Far enough away to give us our privacy, but close enough if a threat presented itself.

And now, the day before we were set to leave, he decided he wasn't going? It didn't make sense—not at all. There had to be more, some explanation—

"Your vision," I said. *Aha.* "The one you wanted to replay, that you didn't want to talk about. That's what this is about, isn't it? You think something bad is going to happen if you come with us."

He nodded. "Something like that."

"Well, isn't there anything else we can do to prevent it? What exactly did you see?"

His gaze met mine, his expression guarded. "It's better if I don't tell you, Violet. I know I say this way too often, but you've just got to trust me on this, okay? It's going to be fine. I want you to go and have a good time. You'll be safe. I promise you."

I shook my head, an uncomfortable feeling niggling at my brain. "I don't like this. Should we cancel the trip?"

"No, definitely not." He rubbed his jaw with the palm of one hand, his eyes suddenly damp.

What the *hell* was going on? Without really thinking about it, I started to reach out to him psychically, hoping to better understand what was going on.

"Don't, Violet. I won't let you. Just . . . come here." Abruptly, he held out his arms to me, and I allowed him to gather me in his embrace, his chin resting on the top of my head. "Go to England and have a great time with your friends, okay?" he murmured, his voice thick with emotion. "Just . . . be happy."

"I'd be happier with you there," I said, surprised to realize that it was the truth. The days we'd spent together in Paris—me, Matthew, Aidan, and my friends—had felt strangely perfect, despite any initial awkwardness. So much so that I'd actually considered asking Aidan if Matthew *could* rent a room from us, come fall.

Because I had to admit that I felt complete with the two of them on either side of me—boyfriend and big brother, lover and protector. "You won't change your mind?" I pleaded.

"Do me a favor and don't make this any harder on me than it already is, okay, Violet? This is the way it's got to be."

I nodded. "This doesn't have anything to do with Charlie, does it?"

"Nope." He took a deep breath and then pressed a chaste kiss to my forehead before releasing me. "Okay, one last thing. I need to talk to Aidan."

"Uh-oh. Why?" I eyed him suspiciously, imagining some super embarrassing talk about being "safe" and "using protection" while staying at Brompton Park.

"Clearly not for the reasons you're thinking. It's just something between him and me, Violet. I'd really appreciate it if you'd respect that."

"You're making this awfully difficult, you know that?" I let out a sigh. "Fine. I'll go get him. You want to wait in the living room? I've got to run over to Patsy's apartment to pick up some stuff anyway. I'll give you guys some privacy."

"Thanks," he said, lifting the messenger bag's strap over his head.

"Okay, I'll see you later, then." I paused at the bottom of the stairs, one hand resting on the end of the curved banister. Something was keeping me there, watching him, as if I were trying to solve a riddle.

But it was no use. His consciousness was closed off to me, his face entirely unreadable. I turned and started up the stairs.

"Hey, Violet?" he called out, and I stopped short, turning toward him expectantly. There was a pregnant pause, our gazes locked. "You're a remarkable *Sâbbat*," he said at last. "And an even more remarkable young woman. You're everything I hoped you'd be. Thank you."

My heart soared at the compliment. "You're not so bad yourself," I said with a smile. "Go on. I'll send Aidan right down."

32 ~ Prodigal Son

I glanced up at the portrait on the wall and then back to Aidan, who was standing beside me. The boy in the portrait was wearing tight beige pants with a ruffly shirt and a cravat, a striped vest, and a dark blue coat. Tall, shiny boots came up to his knees. The boy beside me wore only faded jeans and a simple white T-shirt, his feet bare.

Their wildly different attire hinted at the centuries that separated them. And yet somehow, inexplicably, they were one and the same.

"This is so surreal," I said, shaking my head. "You know that, right?"

He shrugged. "Imagine how it feels for me. I still can't believe you're here. It's like . . . my two existences have merged or something."

"In a good way?" I asked hopefully.

"Of course. Though I'm fairly certain you wouldn't have liked me very much if you'd known me then. I was an arrogant ass."

I took a step toward the portrait, studying his likeness more closely now. "You look pretty cocky, don't you? Like you owned the world. Like you were too good for everything and everyone."

"I think you pretty much nailed it. I sat for this one on my seventeenth birthday. I vaguely remember being annoyed."

"I like the outfit, though. What are those, breeches?"

"God, no," he said, sniffing derisively. "They're pantaloons. Far more fashionable than breeches."

"Well, maybe you could put on your *pantaloons* later and parade around a bit." I waggled my brows suggestively. "Who knows? You might get lucky. Dressed like that, who could resist you?"

"I *do* miss having a valet," he said, sounding wistful.

"Really?" I asked, surprised.

"No," he answered with a laugh. "I'm kidding. But you should feel free to help me dress for bed, if you'd like. You know, to make your visit to Brompton Park more authentic."

"Yeah, because a girl valet is *so* authentic. Nice try, though."

"Hey," Tyler called out from the bottom of the stairs. "Will you two stop gawking at the pictures of his lordship and get your asses down here? Max and Joshua are back with the beer and chips!"

"Beer and chips in the dining room at Brompton Park?" Aidan asked, shaking his head. "What has this world come to? Old Chiffers must be rolling over in his grave."

"Chiffers?"

"He was our butler, a fine old chap. Come. Let's go raise a glass of ale with our peers."

Laughing, I grabbed his hand and pulled him along beside me, down the wide, marble staircase and across the enormous great hall.

"I'll go see if they need any help in the kitchen," Aidan said, releasing my hand. "I don't want them breaking anything."

Cece looked up when I walked into the dining room. "Hey, where were you and Aidan?"

"Up in the minstrels' gallery," I said, pulling out a heavy chair and taking a seat. "There're some portraits of Aidan up there. You should go see them."

"You mean besides the one we saw online? The one with his sisters?"

"Yeah, a few more. There's one from his seventeenth birthday where he looks exactly the same as now. You know that mark on his face, just below his right eye?"

Cece nodded. "Yeah, that little scar."

"It's there in the portrait. He says he got it the day before his birthday, fencing with his sister. Without a helmet," I added. "Isn't that creepy?"

"Well, only because it was, like, a hundred years ago."

"Yeah, and he still has it now."

"Hey, guys," Marissa said, striding in. "Where's everybody else? I thought I heard Tyler squawking that Max and Joshua were back with the food."

"They are; they're about to bring it in." Cece hurried over to the door that opened out onto the great hall. "Sophie!" she called out, then turned back toward us. "She said she was going to the morning room. Isn't that just across the hall?"

"You're asking me?" Marissa answered. "I'm going to need a map to find my way around."

"Food!" Joshua bellowed, bursting into the room with Tyler and Max trailing behind him. "Get it while it's hot."

"And even better, beer!" Tyler added. "We're actually legal here in jolly old England. Can you believe that shit?"

"Kind of takes the fun out of it," Sophie said, wandering in just in time. "It's going to make our twenty-first birthdays so anti-climactic."

"Oh, I'll make sure it's climactic for you, baby," Tyler said, wrapping his arms around Sophie from behind.

Marissa wrinkled her nose. "Eww, you did *not* just say that."

Aidan came through the door carrying a stack of plates and silverware. "Careful with this stuff," he warned. "It's my grandmother's china."

"Your grandma's china?" Cece shrieked. "Are you crazy—it's got to be ancient! We can't eat on that. How'd you get it, anyway? You'd think it'd be locked up or something."

"Oh, it was." Aidan nodded gravely. "But I know the china safe's combination. Anyway, who better to use it than us? And besides, this is a special occasion."

"Hear, hear," Max said, raising a bottle of beer.

"Everyone gather 'round," Tyler ordered while Joshua handed out the beers. "A toast," he continued. "And then we eat, because I'm fucking starving here."

Max nodded his agreement, an arm wrapped possessively around Marissa's waist. "Nicely said, Ty. Nicely said."

"To us," I said, raising my bottle.

"To us," Cece echoed. "The Winterhaven Warriors."

Marissa raised her bottle. "To Sophie, our valedictorian."

"Smartest chick I ever met," Tyler added enthusiastically. "To my roomdog Max and his band—what is it you call yourselves?—who finally got themselves a real gig."

"The Screamers," Max answered with a grin. "Next month at the Mercury Lounge."

"To our elegant host, the Viscount Brompton," Sophie called out. "And his grandma's china."

Laughing, I glanced over at Aidan—who looked marvelously *in*elegant in his rumpled jeans and T-shirt. "To Matthew Byrne," he joined in, catching me by surprise. My heart twisted a little bit with regret. "Otherwise known as Dr. Hottie," he continued, "who wishes he could be here with us tonight."

Beside me, Sophie elbowed me in the ribs. "Hey, you told Aidan that we call him that?"

My cheeks burned guiltily. "What can I say? Occasionally I slip up."

"To Kate," Cece said, sounding solemn now.

"And Jack," Sophie added.

"And . . . I think that's everyone, right?" Cece raised her bottle high in the air. "Cheers!"

"Cheers!" we echoed in unison, clinking our bottles with gusto.

I glanced around the room at my friends as they scrambled for seats, thinking that I was perhaps the luckiest person alive. I took a mental picture of the moment, a still life of friendship captured on the canvas of my mind.

Tyler sat at the head of the table and reached for a plate. "Now rub-a-dub-dub, pass me some grub!"

Aidan shot him a deadly glare. "Violet, would you mind telling your little friend that he's sitting in my seat?"

At once, everyone turned to stare at him. We seemed to be holding our collective breaths, waiting.

And then Aidan smiled. "Come now, you didn't think I was serious, did you?" he asked with a laugh. "My seat is right here beside you, of course."

Smiling broadly, I leaned over and kissed him on the cheek.

"What time is it?" I asked Aidan while I perched on the edge of the bed, admiring the room. "My body is so confused." All this back-and-forth to Europe was wreaking havoc on my sleeping schedule.

"It's about two in the morning, local time. Are you tired?"

I shook my head. "Not really. So . . . this was really your room?"

"It was." He stood at the foot of the bed, looking around. "They've changed it around some, of course. That portrait wasn't there, for one." He indicated a painting above the fireplace. "The bed, though . . . it's the same. I assume the duvet is a reproduction, but it's an exact one."

The bed. This was *the* bed, I realized. The one from my vision—antique mahogany with four spindly posts. I'd seen it on the website, too—with the blue damask duvet trimmed in gold that I was sitting on now.

I tried to remember the vision, to remember what had seemed so ominous about it, but my memories were mostly hazy. It had been a long time since I'd replayed it. All I remembered was that Aidan and I were in the bed and that my hair was short. Like it was now. I hadn't even considered that when I'd gotten it cut. It wasn't like I'd had a choice, not with a big chunk of it burned off, anyway.

What, exactly, was going to happen if I got in this bed with Aidan? "Maybe we should sleep somewhere else," I said tentatively.

Aidan gave me a puzzled look. "I thought for sure you'd want to stay here. We could move you to the master suite, if you'd like. You can take my mother's bed."

Out of respect, no one had claimed his mother's rooms. His sisters' suites had been fair game, though. They were among the prettiest, with elaborate dressing tables and huge windows that opened out to the gardens below. Sophie and Marissa had immediately laid claim to those, leaving Cece to battle it out over the remaining rooms with Tyler, Joshua, and Max. Of course, the choices seemed endless—Brompton Park boasted an entire wing of guest suites.

"I don't know," I said. "Wouldn't that be a little weird for you, me sleeping in your mother's bed?"

"Not particularly," he answered with a shrug. "Anyway, it's up to you."

I gave the bed a sidelong stare, still unsure.

"Are you worried that I've . . . in this bed?" A faint flush stained his cheeks. "Never, not in this room, if that's what's on your mind, Violet."

"I wasn't thinking that. Of course, *now* I'm curious. If not here, then where?"

He leaned against the bedpost, watching me curiously. "Are you asking me where I lost my virginity?"

I closed my eyes, trying to banish the images. "Never mind. I don't want to know."

"Because back in those days, you—"

"Stop! Don't tell me. Just . . . forget that I said anything about it, okay? We're fine here. I don't want to have to move all my stuff."

"You know what I just remembered?" he said abruptly, pushing off the bed and walking over to the adjoining dressing room. "I wonder if it's still here."

I rose, following him. "If what's still where?"

He pushed the dressing table away from the wall and knelt down behind it.

"What are you looking for?"

"Can you hand me a pen or something? From the desk?"

"Sure," I said, walking back to the bedroom. But when I saw the pen—more like a quill, really—there on the desk, well . . . I wasn't going to give him that one. Instead, I went over to my purse and dug around, finding an old ballpoint on the bottom that probably didn't even work. "Here," I said, hurrying back and handing it to him.

I bent over him, watching in amazement as he pried loose a floorboard, then two more. When he'd exposed a hole in the floor about ten inches long by four inches wide, he reached inside and retrieved a rectangular wooden box.

"It's still here," he said, rising. "I can't bloody well believe it."

"Have you noticed that you slipped into full Viscount Brompton speech the moment we got here?" I asked. "I mean, I love your accent and all, but it's kind of freaking me out."

He ignored me, carefully lifting the lid and peering inside.

"Are you going to tell me what's inside your little box?" I prodded.

He looked up at me and smiled. "My secrets."

"Your secrets? Um, okay."

He took out a folded piece of paper, yellowed with age. "It's poetry, mostly, and dreadful, at that—chock-full of adolescent rage. I must have been fourteen, fifteen or so."

"Oh my God! You wrote poetry? You're going to let me read it, right?" I held out my hand. "C'mon, I'll be really careful."

"I've never shown them to anyone before. Not in all these years—more than a century."

"Please?" I wheedled, dying of curiosity now. "Just one?"

"You've been warned," he said after a pause. "It's painfully bad."

Gingerly, I took the fragile page from him. The first thing I noticed was that his handwriting was completely different—unrecognizable, really. Maybe it was his youth; maybe it was the old-fashioned pen he'd used, one that had to be dipped in ink. Whatever it was, it threw me for a loop. But not as much as the words I managed to decipher did.

We move as one

Together in union

Your breath cools my soul

Tenderness once forgotten

Leads to my explosive rebirth

Helpless, powerless

I give my heart to you

It lies crushed

Beneath the weight of your hatred

That was all I could make out, but it was enough for me to realize that it was about a girl.

"Wow," I said at last. "That's really beautiful. Here, let me see another one."

One by one, he unfolded the slips of yellowed vellum. I couldn't make out most of it, just a few lines here and there. Most were angry, I realized. *Really* angry.

"Whoever she was, I'd say it didn't go very well," I muttered.

He shook his head. "No, it didn't. I was very young."

"I just can't believe you wrote these," I said, carefully folding the last slip and handing it back to him. "You seem like a totally different person than you are now."

"I was spoiled, careless. I got angry if I didn't get exactly what I wanted."

"Meaning *her*," I suggested, and he just nodded. I didn't want to know who she was, hoped he wasn't going to tell me. I'd been impressed by his poems, but I was jealous, too. "Have you ever . . . you know . . . written a poem about me?"

"No. I haven't written anything in a very long time. These poems . . . they were a way to work through my anger. Writing about my feelings was cathartic, a way to exorcise my demons. I have no need for poetry now."

"Huh," I said, a little hurt. Which was silly, of course, but whatever. "Well, it's too bad you don't play guitar or piano. You'd make a good lyricist."

"Yeah, I could have pioneered the hard-core punk movement. You know, back in the 1890s. Given that Rachmaninoff a little competition."

"What else have you got in there?" I asked, peering inside.

He pulled out the remaining treasures. A yellow velvet ribbon. A button. A small golden thimble. Something that looked vaguely like a wooden acorn.

"Okay, a thimble *and* an acorn?" I asked. "What, are you Peter Pan?"

"It's funny," he said, shaking his head. "I know that each of these had some special meaning to me, but I can't quite remember what, not anymore. It's like . . . the memories are inaccessible. Just out of reach."

"I don't even know what this is," I said, holding up the acorn.

He rolled it around in his palm. "Just a trinket of some sort."

"So, what are you going to do with it all? Keep it, or put it back?"

"I think it should stay with the house, don't you?" He reached down to stroke my hair. "I'll put it back tomorrow. You look exhausted."

I nodded, leaning in to him. "I *am* pretty tired."

He set the wooden box on the dressing table and then led me back to the bedroom. I went over to my suitcase and pulled out my pajamas, my heart racing now. I had no idea why I was so nervous—we'd shared a bed in Paris without incident.

But *this* bed . . . I eyed it once more, my heart racing now.

When I glanced back at Aidan, he'd already stripped off his shirt. Which, of course, only made my heart beat faster.

Crap. That stupid vision. Unlike my usual glimpses of the future, this particular one hadn't shown anything terrible happening—nothing life-threatening, no maiming, no blood or broken bones. Still, I'd taken it as a warning, because they always were.

But maybe I'd been wrong. Maybe there really *was* nothing more to it than what I'd seen.

And what, exactly, *had* I seen? The two of us in bed together. Been there, done that. We were making out, but what else was new? And yes, sometimes when we did, his eyes turned red and his canines came out. But if he were going to actually bite me—pierce the skin and suck my blood—then wouldn't my vision have shown that, too?

I had to make a decision now, based on instinct alone. And my instinct was telling me that I was safe in this particular bed with Aidan.

That was good enough for me.

33 ~ Gone

"The house seems so quiet," I said, staring up at the ceiling above the bed. We'd left the curtains open, and the full moon cast a silvery light across our bodies. We lay there together, my head on Aidan's shoulder, one arm thrown across his bare chest. "Do you think they've all gone to bed?"

"Probably so. It's been a long day. I can't believe you're still awake."

"Well, so are you," I argued.

"Yes, but I don't have to sleep. You do. What's going on, Vi? You're so tightly strung right now, I could play you like a violin."

I let out a sigh. "Just thinking, I guess."

"Are you going to let me in on it?"

"Mostly about school in the fall. It's going to be so weird without everyone else." I was also thinking about those poems of his, but I wasn't going to mention that.

"It's a new chapter in your life," Aidan said philosophically. "One ends, another begins. You'll have many more."

"I guess. Anyway, you seem pretty quiet yourself."

"I suppose I *am* rather contemplative tonight" was all he said before falling silent.

And then my curiosity got the best of me. "You're not thinking about . . . well, whoever those poems are about, are you?"

"No," he said, shaking his head. "Well, not precisely."

I sat up sharply, gazing down at him with a scowl. "Well, which is it? You either are, or you aren't."

"I am, but not in the way that you think."

"Uh-huh. Go on."

"It's just . . . the relationships I had during my mortal life, they were so painful. I remember feeling raw, exposed, consumed. Angry, as you saw with those poems. But with you . . . I don't know, I feel almost peaceful. Most of the time, at least," he added, and I knew he was remembering that stupid misunderstanding with Tyler. "But even when I'm angry at you, I never really doubt us."

"So, what's your point?" I asked, my hackles rising. Because it kind of seemed like he was saying that he didn't feel as passionately about me as he did them. They consumed him; they inspired poems—I didn't.

He sat up, facing me. "See? This is exactly why I didn't want to tell you. I knew you'd interpret it that way."

"Well, how else am I supposed to interpret it?"

"What I was trying to say was that those relationships, they were toxic. Unhealthy. But with you . . ." He sighed, shaking his head. "What if it's got something to do with the vampirism? You know, changing my personality. What if I cure myself—become mortal again—and suddenly I'm that asshole again?"

"That's what you're worried about? Seriously? You don't even *have* the cure yet."

He shrugged. "Being here, in this house . . . it's making me remember my mortal life, that's all. I'm not sure I want to risk being that guy again."

"How 'bout we cross that bridge when we get to it, okay? I mean, look what happened the last time you tried the cure." I shook my head, trying to forget. "We've got four years of college ahead of us, and—"

"Let's not talk about this anymore, okay? You should get some sleep." He stood, reaching for his T-shirt. "I think I'm going to go for a walk or something. Maybe I'll feed. It's been too long; I'm probably pushing it."

"Wait. Don't go. Not like this." I scooted to the edge of the bed and reached for him. "C'mon, I didn't mean—"

"I know you didn't. I just need to clear my head."

I hated the tone of his voice—cool, detached. I had no idea what was going through his mind, but I had to take care of this now, before it was too late.

"Aidan? Please, just look at me." Kneeling on the edge of the bed now, I grabbed the waistband of his jeans and pulled him back to me. His eyes were bright in the moonlight—and damp, I realized. My mind scrambled frantically to process that information, to figure out what was wrong, what I'd said to upset him so. I came up totally blank.

"Don't go," I said. "You can feed later, okay? Once I fall asleep. Just . . . stay with me for now." I tilted my face up toward his, guiding his lips toward mine with one hand.

I kissed him—softly at first and then more urgently.

He tore his lips from mine. "Don't you see, Violet?" he asked, sounding frantic—desperate, even. "I don't know what to do. I can't decide—"

"You don't have to decide anything now," I interrupted, trying to placate him. "We're here for a week, a break from reality.

Please don't ruin it," I added, my voice quavering now.

He drew back as if I'd slapped him.

And all I could think of was how much I loved him. I felt—what was the word he'd used?—*consumed* by it. In an instant, I let down the wall around my thoughts.

Read my mind, I urged telepathically.

For a split second, he looked confused. And then something shifted in his features—comprehension lit his eyes as all my feelings for him poured out of my mind like a sheer, overwhelming tidal wave.

"God, Violet," he said with a strangled cry, and then gathered me tightly in his arms.

Somehow, we were back on the bed, our bodies tangled together. His lips were everywhere—my mouth, my chin, my throat. I struggled to pull his shirt over his head; he did the same with my tank top. Once they'd both been tossed carelessly to the floor, his lips found mine, nothing but bare skin between our pounding hearts now.

It all happened so quickly—just a matter of seconds, really. There was no time to think, to plan, to do anything but gasp in recognition when he drew away and gazed down at me in an eerily familiar pose—incisors elongated, his eyes rimmed in red and filled with desire, with bloodlust.

I must have cried out when his head dipped down toward my

neck. I felt his teeth scrape against my skin as I tried desperately to roll out from beneath him.

There was a sudden rush of air as he slammed himself against the door, a look of pure horror on his face as I scrambled back against the headboard, cowering with the covers gathered over my half-naked body.

"Tell me now—did I hurt you?" he asked, his voice strangely calm.

I reached a hand up to my neck. It was fine—not even a scratch. "No," I said. "It's okay. Why don't you . . . you know, go take your walk or something."

He just stood there silently, the muscles in his jaw working feverishly as he struggled for control.

"I'm fine. Go on," I urged. "We can talk in the morning. You'll be okay after you feed."

"No. That was too close." He shook his head. "I can't do this anymore, Violet. I tried . . . I really did."

"What are you saying?" I asked, my voice trembling.

His gaze met mine, and all the air left my lungs with a *whoosh*. Pain, guilt, revulsion, self-loathing—they all battled for dominance there in his features.

"I'm sorry," he said.

And then, just like that, he was gone.

* * *

Two full days passed before Aidan's return. My friends tried their best to entertain me, but I mostly kept to myself, not wanting to ruin their vacation. "Don't worry. He'll be back," I told them with forced cheerfulness, but I wasn't sure I believed it myself.

I'd moved my things to the master suite, a shock of familiarity startling me the moment I'd stepped inside the room that had been his mother's.

I recognized the plush carpeting beneath my feet—robin's-egg blue with a dark brown pattern of scripty curlicues and little birds. I recognized the view outside the window too—it was green, as far as the eye could see. Rolling hills, a willow tree.

I knew this room. I'd seen it before, in a vision.

I tried to convince myself that if I stayed right there, he'd have to come back. After all, I'd seen it. Us, together. There. Apparently, we had unfinished business.

More than anything, I wished that Matthew had been there to help me through it all. But he wasn't, and whenever I tried to call his cell, I got his voice mail—each and every time.

Apparently they'd *both* abandoned me.

Still, I was surprised when I woke up on that third lonely morning and found Aidan there, sitting in a chair by the window, his blond hair turned gold by the sun.

"You're back," I said, sitting up and rubbing my eyes. "God, what time is it?"

"It's nearly noon," he said, his expression guarded, entirely unreadable.

My stomach growled noisily. "I guess I missed breakfast. Did you happen to notice if they've gotten lunch yet?"

He shook his head. "I've sent them all away for lunch, to a restaurant in the village. They won't be back for a couple of hours."

That was weird. "Okay," I said with a frown. "Are you planning on telling me where you've been? I was worried out of my mind."

"I had some business to attend to. Affairs to settle," he said cryptically.

He was being purposely obtuse, I realized. "Why don't you tell me what's going on here," I demanded, annoyed now.

Looking almost grim, he reached over to the round, piecrust table beside the chair and retrieved a leather case.

"What's that?" I asked, eyeing it curiously as he opened it, revealing what looked like an enormous hypodermic needle and a single glass vial.

"It's my cure," he said simply.

"Your cure?" I asked, my voice rising. "What? How?"

"Dr. Byrne gave it to me before we left New York."

"*That's* what he wanted to talk to you about?"

Aidan nodded. "He feels certain he's perfected it. No way to know for sure, of course, but it worked with my blood and tissue samples, right down to the cellular level. With the samples we took from the vampire in Atlanta too. At least, that's what he tells me."

I glanced down at the humungous needle and then back up at him again. "So . . . now what?"

"Why don't you get up and get dressed. I'll go to the kitchen and find you something to eat, and I'll bring it right up with some coffee, okay?"

I didn't like this, not one bit. He was acting strange, oddly formal and aloof. "Fine," I said. "Just give me fifteen minutes; I want to jump in the shower first."

I'd never showered so quickly in my life. It was chilly, so I threw on a pair of jeans with a tank top and a hoodie and quickly ran a brush through my hair.

When I stepped out of the bathroom, he was back with a tray that held two slices of thick toast, a jar of jam, and a mug of steaming coffee. "This was all I could rustle up," he said. "I think I got the coffee right, though—lots of sugar and cream."

"Perfect. Okay, you talk while I eat." I reached for a piece of toast and took a bite, settling myself into the chair opposite him.

"This is going to sound much worse than it is," he warned.

I washed down the toast with my coffee, waiting for him to continue.

"It's simple, really. I fill the syringe with the correct amount of serum. He's marked it here." He lifted it from the case, showing me the little dash made in black Sharpie. "And then I'm going to need you to inject it for me."

"Like in your arm or something?" I asked. "Why can't you inject it yourself?"

"This part sounds complicated, but it really isn't, not if you think about it," he said, then took a deep breath before continuing. "You have to inject the serum directly into my heart."

"What?" I shrieked, setting down my mug so hard that coffee sloshed all over the tray. "Are you crazy? I can't do that."

"Yes, you can. Look, it's a heavy-gauge needle, nice and thick and just the right length. You hold the syringe here"—he grabbed it firmly in the middle, demonstrating—"just like you would your stake. Make sure you use plenty of force. Don't worry, the needle won't break.

"But you've got to inject it into the right spot, okay? You know how to hit a vampire's heart; you've done it plenty of times before. Once it's in, press the plunger all the way down with your thumb. And that's it, Violet."

"That's what Matthew said I should do?" I asked, too stunned to say much else.

"Those were his specific instructions. "

"I don't understand. This sounds crazy. I mean, what if I miss? What'll that do to you? And what if I *don't* miss? We have no guarantee that it'll work, that it won't just kill you on the spot. Besides, why now? We're supposed to be having fun. We *were* having fun," I insisted, feeling panicked now. "This can wait."

"You saw what happened the other night." He shook his head, looking grimly determined. "I'm not risking that again. Don't you see? I want you, Vi. I'm not going to stop wanting you. And to have you, I have to bite you. I can't *help* but bite you. And God only knows what'll happen when I do."

"Well," I floundered, "what about Mrs. Girard? You're supposed to be . . . I don't know, doing stuff with the Tribunal or something."

"I won't continue to be her pawn."

"You're not her pawn," I argued, desperate to convince him not to do this—not now. "You're the *Dauphin*; you're their king. She answers to you, not the other way around."

He rose from his chair, moving around the table to kneel before me, taking both of my hands in his. "But that's not what *I* want. Don't you see? I don't want to be their king. I want to be a boy—a mortal boy. Someone stole my life from me a century ago, and I want it back. Not next month, not next year or the year you finish university. I want it now.

"And if it doesn't work—or worse, if it kills me, well . . . what better place than here, where I was born? All your friends are here, Vi. If I don't make it, they'll take care of you, comfort you. And that business I had to see to—my assets, my belongings, I've left them to you. The apartment in Paris, everything. You'll be fine. We've got to do this. Today. Right now."

I reached a trembling hand up to my temple. My head was pounding, a dull, throbbing ache. "I can't," I said, tears gathering in my eyes.

"You can," he insisted. "I have faith that you can, that you love me enough to set me free."

Downstairs in the grand hall, the clock chimed the hour with a single booming note. Aidan stood, reaching for the syringe and vial.

I watched wordlessly as he uncapped the glass vial, inserting the needle in and pulling up the plunger to fill the syringe with the serum. "We don't have much time—I expect them back within the hour." He pulled me to my feet, holding the syringe out to me. My hand trembling, I took it.

I started to cry then, deep, gulping sobs that racked my entire body. "I can't do it," I choked out.

"You *have* to do it, Vi," Aidan pleaded.

"No." I shook my head, the tears blurring my vision as I backed toward the bed.

"Please, I beg of you. It has to go into my heart. You can do it; I've taught you how. Don't let me down, not now."

"No," I blubbered, wanting it to stop. "Please, no. Don't make me, Aidan. I can't."

"Yes, love. You can. Right here." He tapped his chest. "There's no time to waste—you must do it now. Now," he repeated, his tone urgent.

"Why me?" I asked miserably.

"Because I love you with all my heart. It has to be you—don't you see?"

Taking a deep, ragged breath, I raised my gaze to his.

This is for us, he said in my head. *It's the only way. The only chance we've got.*

I knew then that he was right. That he loved me enough to risk it, that I loved him enough to try.

"Okay," I said at last.

"Thank you," Aidan answered.

"Now?"

He nodded. "Now, love."

I could do this—I had to. I took a deep, calming breath, finding my center. Once, twice, three times. When my mind was clear and focused, I raised my arm, my fingers clutched tightly around the syringe's smooth barrel. I took one step back and then lunged forward, my arm swinging in an arc that led directly to Aidan's heart.

A scream escaped my lips as the needle pierced his flesh. Aidan's eyes widened, his mouth forming an O of surprise. Quickly, I pressed the plunger all the way down with my thumb before releasing my grip on the syringe.

And then I watched in horror as Aidan crumpled to the floor, the needle still protruding from his chest. His blue-gray eyes were open wide, staring unseeing at the ceiling—all hint of life gone from them, just like that.

"No!" I shrieked, my voice echoing around the room, bouncing off the walls. Frantic now, I dropped to my hands and knees beside his body and laid an ear against his chest, desperately hoping to hear or feel something, anything.

Oh my God. Oh my God. There was nothing. Not a sound, not a heartbeat, not a single movement. A jagged sob tore from my throat, and I clapped a hand over my mouth, silencing it, swallowing back the bile that had risen in my throat.

The cure hadn't worked. It hadn't worked! He'd said that it would, but it didn't. It hadn't. I'd killed him—destroyed him, just like the rest of them, with a single strike to the heart!

What have I done?

I knelt over him, my hands shaking as I touched his face, my fingers skimming lightly from his cheek to his jaw, his lips. His skin was so soft, as pale and perfect as always. If it weren't for his eyes, he could be sleeping. But he wasn't—I knew that he wasn't.

I'd killed him.

Entirely numb now, I somehow managed to pull the needle from his chest and toss it aside. I raised a trembling hand to my mouth and kissed my fingers, then pressed them to his lips. "Please forgive me," I whispered, unwilling to say those other, far more permanent words. And then I reached up and closed his eyes.

This was what he'd wanted—to be set free. He'd wanted the monster inside him gone, no matter the cost. He'd been willing to take that risk, but what about me? Was I supposed to be happy for him? Happy that he'd won?

How could I be happy when it felt as if my own heart had stopped beating along with his? How could I go on, knowing that he was permanently erased from my future now?

With nothing left to do, I laid my head against his chest and cried, my tears soaking his shirt as I clutched his lifeless body to mine.

I have no idea how much time passed before I felt it—a subtle movement beneath my cheek. A pulse, a twitch. Something.

I imagined it. I had to have imagined it. But . . . there it was again. I held my breath, straining to listen more closely now.

And then I heard it—a faint but distinct *thump.*

I let out my breath with a gasp and then held it again. Listening, waiting. Hoping, praying. *Please, God. Please, please . . .*

Thump.

Followed by silence. Maybe I *had* imagined it—or just heard my own heartbeat echoing in my ears.

But then there it was again, loud and strong against my ear: *Thump.*

Please! Oh, please, oh, please, oh, please.

Thump . . . thump . . . thump.

Thump-thump . . . thump-thump . . . thump-thump . . . thump-thump.

It was rhythmic now, continuing on uninterrupted. *Holy hell and God in heaven!*

"Aidan!" I scrambled to my knees, my gaze snapping up to his face . . .

. . . just as his blue-gray eyes opened.

"Violet?" he asked dazedly, struggling to sit.

I threw my arms around his neck, laughing and crying all at once as relief washed over me in coursing waves.

"You okay?" he asked me.

"Are you kidding? Am *I* okay? Oh my God, Aidan! You were dead; I swear you were. And then—"

I stopped short, my breath hitching in my chest. "Matthew!" I cried out. There was a searing pain in my head, almost like a part of my brain were being ripped away. And then . . . emptiness. That space that Matthew normally filled—that connection we shared—it was gone. *Gone.*

I doubled over in pain—pure physical agony. What was happening?

The door banged open and Cece ran in, the rest of them following behind. "What's going on? Are you guys okay?"

I was vaguely aware of conversation, of voices speaking all at once. My friends' worried faces surrounded me. But I couldn't make out what they were saying—the pain was too sharp, too intense.

"Matthew!" I finally managed to shout above the din. "Someone . . . find my cell," I gasped. "I have to call him. Now. Now!"

Several seconds passed, and then someone pressed my phone

into my hand. The pain was blinding me now, making white spots dance before my eyes. "Someone dial. Please!"

"Here," came Cece's calming voice. "I'm dialing. Just hang on, Violet. Okay, it's ringing now."

I raised it to my ear. Two rings. Three. And then someone picked up. Oh my God, someone picked up.

"Violet?" But it wasn't Matthew's voice on the other end. It was someone else's. A woman's. I recognized it—Charlie.

"Where's Matthew?" I asked her, my voice shaking. "Is he okay? Charlie, tell me he's okay. Please!"

I heard her take a deep, rattling breath on the other end of the line. And then I knew the truth—knew it right down to the marrow in my bones.

"He's gone," she said, her voice laced with panic. "He just collapsed, and . . . Oh my God! He's gone. Gone! I called 911, but . . . it's too late." She was sobbing now. "It happened just like he said it would." I could hear a siren now, growing louder, drowning out her sobs.

"No," I whispered. "No." The phone fell from my hand, tumbling to the carpet beside me. My mind struggled to comprehend it all, to reconcile everything that had happened in a matter of minutes.

Things seemed to move in slow motion then, like a hazy

dream—a nightmare. Someone picked up my phone and pressed it to their ear. Someone else reached for me, an arm behind my back, cradling me. I saw mouths moving but couldn't hear the words. There was nothing but a loud ringing in my ears, drowning out everything but the sound of my own heartbeat, which grew louder and faster. Too fast, making me breathless.

And then I blacked out.

Epilogue ~ A British Ex-Vampire in Paris

Four months later, Paris

"Be careful with that thing!" I called out from my seat on the terrace. I had a heavy textbook open in my lap, a notebook balanced on one knee as I scribbled notes, studying for an upcoming exam.

"Hey, are you doubting my dagger-throwing skills, Vi? Because I could hit that target with my eyes closed."

I couldn't help but roll my eyes. "Yeah, that explains the nicks in the plaster beside the target board. And anyway, it's a baselard," I added. "Learn the lingo."

"Semantics," Aidan said with a shrug, stepping out onto the terrace to join me as he returned the weapon in question to the sheath strapped beneath his left shoulder. "I'm starving. How 'bout you?"

I laughed.

"What's so funny?"

"You, starving. That's still so weird to hear."

His mouth curved into a grin. "It's such a bloody inconvenience, all this needing to eat."

"Hey, you're the one who wanted to be mortal again," I said with a shrug.

He leaned against the stone railing, the noon sun glinting off the Eiffel Tower behind him. I still couldn't believe his physical transformation. His once-pale skin was bronzed now, thanks to lazy afternoons spent lounging shirtless in the Tuileries. His hair had grown longer, the golden waves nearly to his shoulders now—shoulders that were much broader, more muscled than before. He looked vibrant, healthy. Alive.

And mind-bogglingly hot. It was all I could do not to jump his bones every time he walked into a room—or out onto the terrace, as was the current case.

"Did you ever hear from Jenna?" he asked, mercifully oblivious to my current train of thought.

I shook my head, glad for the distraction. "Nope, and I don't expect to. She's got too much pride. She teased me once about being your pet, about how you kept me on a short leash. Well, who's the pet now?" I had to laugh, thinking of Jenna's current situation.

She was in Paris, too. Working as a model—high fashion, runway, and print. But there was a catch. She was living in a Tribunal safe house, under vampire protection. It was the only way she could remain safe from her vengeful pack, now that she'd graduated from Winterhaven. I didn't know the details, but apparently she and Mrs. Girard had struck some sort of deal. She was working for them—the good vampires. Which was pretty funny, actually. Jenna and I, on the same team now.

And speaking of Mrs. Girard . . . she hadn't gotten her *Dauphin* after all. But she *did* get an even more powerful weapon, instead—the cure. That helped a lot, in terms of her forgiving us. Instead of imprisonment and torture, the Tribunal now simply sentenced dangerous, uncooperative vampires to be cured. And once cured, a vampire couldn't be turned back. In those first few months, several had tried—and several had died. For realsies, this time around.

"What about Trevors?" I asked. "How's he doing these days?"

"He's good, back in London now. Enjoying every day he has left, he says." Because Trevors had chosen to take the cure. Aidan had been pleased for him—happy that Trevors had been able to decide his own future. It turns out Aidan had been paying him generously all these years, and Trevors would be able to live out his final days in style and comfort. He deserved that.

I picked up my cell, checking the time, smiling wistfully when I saw the photo that served as my wallpaper—the group picture from the prom. It had been only five months ago, but it felt like a lifetime. I set it aside with a sigh, glancing back down at my notes.

"I should probably be studying, too," Aidan said. "You're making me feel like a slacker." He folded his arms across his chest, causing his newly cut biceps to bulge. My attention was drawn to his new tattoo—the medieval-looking dagger with the scripted *M* atop it. *M* for *Megvéd*.

M for *Matthew*.

Tears sprang to my eyes. I took a deep breath, forcing them to remain at bay. I'd already shed an ocean of tears over Matthew.

"Do you think he made the right decision?" I asked, probably for the millionth time. "Matthew, I mean."

"I think it was the only decision he *could* make," Aidan answered, same as always. "More than anything else, he wanted you to be happy."

I nodded, swallowing the painful lump in my throat. I'd thought Kate's death had been difficult, but it was nothing like the agony I'd felt when I'd been told of Matthew's. Even now, it felt like a limb had been torn from my body.

It turns out my *Sâbbat* blood was in the cure—its most vital element. Matthew hadn't told anyone except Charlie. Once he'd figured it out, he'd kept the formula a secret from the rest of us, locked away in a password-protected file. We'd been completely oblivious to the risk when I'd injected it into Aidan. But the moment my blood had entered Aidan's bloodstream, Matthew's heart had stopped beating. Just like that.

Looking back, I'm pretty sure that he'd expected it. Prepared for it, even. And yet he'd given the cure to Aidan anyway, insisting that he try it, certain that it would work. And it had.

But at what cost?

I'd asked myself "what if" over and over again, driving myself crazy. What if we'd known my blood was in the serum? What if we'd realized the risk? Would we have done it anyway? Matthew had made sure that we never had to make that choice. He'd made it for us.

"He loved you, Violet," Aidan said softly. "We'll never forget him or what he did for us."

"Never." Not as long as I lived.

My cell pealed a lengthy text tone—the *Batman* theme—startling me. I picked it up with a scowl.

"Not again," Aidan said. "Second time this week."

"Afraid so." I quickly scanned the message. "A situation to be neutralized in Montparnasse—that's weird, in the middle of the afternoon? Must be Wampiri. We're supposed to meet at the Trib in an hour. Just great." I let out a heavy sigh. "I'll text Amelie and see if she wants to do backup. I think Sasha has some family in town this week or something."

"That's okay. Sasha scares me."

I set aside my textbook, rising to join Aidan by the balcony's railing. "Yeah, she kind of scares me, too."

Amelie and Sasha—my two *Sâbbat* sisters. It hadn't taken us long to find each other. Turns out we were drawn to one another once we'd all reached our eighteenth birthdays—go figure.

Amelie was from Switzerland, a tiny, angelic-looking blonde who seemed so sweet and gentle—right up until you saw her in action with her stake. Sasha was from the Ukraine, and she looked much more the part. Spiky blue-black hair, tattoos everywhere.

Both bore the same mark as me on the inside wrists of their dominant hands, and both had a *Megvéd* counterpart. We were a happy little family of six. And then there were the *Krsnik*, Slovenian vampire slayers who morphed into animal form at night to hunt their prey, who'd recently come to Paris, eager to join our cause. My *Sâbbat* sisters and I had welcomed them, glad for their assistance.

My new slayer friends didn't fill the hole in my heart left by the absence of my Winterhaven friends, but still . . . they were good people. I liked them. Eventually, I might come to love them.

"You think we'll get back in time for class this afternoon?" I asked idly. "I really don't want to miss art history."

"We probably will." Aidan wrapped an arm around my shoulders, drawing me closer. "I was thinking I'd take you out to dinner tonight. Someplace special, to celebrate our anniversary."

I still remembered the first day we'd met—exactly two years ago today—like it was yesterday. I'd dropped my schedule like a total klutz, and he'd picked it up and handed it to me with the most brilliant smile. But it had been his eyes that had gotten to me—that *still* got to me. Well, that and the British accent.

I love you madly, he said inside my head.

I turned to grin at him. *I know.*

It still surprised me that we'd retained the ability to speak telepathically. We hadn't expected to, once he became mortal again. But then, he was my *Megvéd* now—at least, my substitute one—and a *Sâbbat* and her protector were supposed to be psychically connected. Maybe the injection of my blood into his veins aided that connection, strengthened it somehow. Who knows, maybe he was always meant to take Matthew's place. Fate was weird that way. We tried not to question it too much.

Just then, a butterfly—its vividly colored wings a mix of black, violet, and indigo blue—fluttered down toward us. Instinctively, I held out my arm, wrist up, and it came to rest directly on my mark. For several seconds it sat there, its wings slowly moving up and down, as if it were studying the image of the stake inked onto my skin. I could feel the air stirred by its wings, the tickle of its legs.

I held my breath, keeping as still as possible, wanting to make the moment last. It reminded me of Matthew, made me think that he was there with us in spirit. After all, I'd been with him in his office when I'd first envisioned my tattoo—I'd pictured the stake with a butterfly resting on it. I'd later realized that the butterfly wasn't meant to be part of the mark, and yet here it was . . . just as I'd seen it.

And then the beautiful insect took flight again, its tiny wings beating furiously as it rose and fluttered away.

"Good-bye," I whispered, watching until it became a tiny speck against the Parisian skyline and then disappeared.

Aidan released me and took a step back toward the open French doors. "You ready to go slay some vampires, *Sâbbat*?" he asked.

I nodded. "How 'bout you, my *Megvéd*?"

"Together?" He reached for my hand.

I took it, clasping it firmly in mine. "Always."

ACKNOWLEDGMENTS

As this series comes to a close, I owe an enormous debt of gratitude to the following people:

My agent, Marcy Posner, who believed in a book featuring a vampire in a time when "no one was buying vampire books." Thank you for always working tirelessly on my behalf—for an entire decade now!

Brilliant editor Jennifer Klonsky, who began this series with me, and equally brilliant editor Nicole Ellul, who stepped in and helped me see it through to the end. Thank you both for your amazing insight, support, and guidance along the way.

Amalie Howard, for helping me get this book done, chapter by chapter. Seriously, I couldn't have done it without you. Your friendship, encouragement, plotting genius, and always-insightful comments kept me going—and kept me sane. *Tres leches!*

Cindy Thomas, for always being there to work out plot tangles, listen to me whine about my characters, and to deliver the stink-eye when needed. Thank you for being such an awesome friend. Much love!

The HB&K Society, for all the fun, food, and conversation.

Here's to many more Berkshire writing retreats. Sit-n-dance!

The readers and bloggers who got behind this series from the get-go, for sharing the love and spreading the word. You have my heartfelt thanks and gratitude!

My brilliant daughters, Vivian and Ella, who read my chapters without complaint and don't mind talking endlessly about imaginary people and what they should or shouldn't do. Thank you for helping me plot and for coming up with really awesome ideas. Love you both!

And lastly, my husband, Dan—for everything.